shades of grey.

SHADES OF GREY.

ALAN COOKE.

© Alan Cooke 1991.

ALL RIGHTS RESERVED.
No part of this manuscript may be reproduced, stored in or introduced into a retrieval system or transmitted in any form by any means (electronic, mechanical, photocopying, recording or otherwise) without the prior written permisson of the copy-right owner.

SHADES OF GREY

CHAPTER 1.

JESS.

'Men are fools. The way they bawl after you in the street, like you're a dog or a chicken. Then cuss you when you don't respond the way they want you to. On the trains they use the crowd as a excuse to rub up against you. They're disgusting, pitiful. I admire the girls who know how to use and manipulate them, because that's what they deserve. They're all the same, bollocks for brains. You don't believe me? Well it' true, a man will do whatever his dick tells him to. Lie, cheat, leave his kids..... It doesn't matter whether he's a handsome, intelligent, and considerate charmer, or a nasty lazy ignorant good for nothing, the dick's in charge, remember that. Yeah I've heard there's a few with some ambition, a shred of honesty... a couple who know how to treat a girl. Well if you're lucky, (or stupid) enough to think your man fits that description, just keep your fingers crossed and hope he doesn't change into a slob.

'When I met Ziggy I thought he was charming, intelligent and all those other things you want them to be... but now... I'm bored, I'm fed up and I'm miserable, and it's all because of him.'

ZIGGY.

'Women is just pure pressure man. They don't understand, everyone has got it in for the black man. They say we're lazy, irresponsible, aggressive.... the list goes on. But this is a racist society and it's us, the black man who the white man is attacking, the black woman doesn't hold the same threat to them as does the black man, in fact if they can sell their white ·supremacy ting to our women what greater insult can they pay us? If our women think they are superior to us then where do we go from there? Tell me, where do we go? Their white supremacy ting bwoy! that's the roots of racism man, their need to perpetuate the myth. They'll do everyting they can to put us down. So as well as all the propaganda, there's no jobs, so no money. Everyting stems from that man, I don't care what you

5

SHADES OF GREY

say. Money can't buy love? Well show me a lonely rich man! You feel small, it's demoralizing. White people hate you and our own women think we're scum.'

 JESS.

'Why couldn't he be more like his twin brother Dexter? Intelligent, ambitious, smart. Ziggy can't even hold a job down for more than a couple of weeks. He was caught handling stolen goods about a month back, the case comes up soon, if he get's fined it's me who's really going to be paying. Why should I work to support him? I can't afford anything but the cheapest cloths, shoes, perfume. I want to be able to eat out once or twice a week, go to the theatre, the pictures. Have someone buy me flowers now and again. Other girls do.- We never go out.'

ZIGGY.

'What is wrong with her man!? I can't have no friends, I can't put a few shillings on a horse or smoke a lickle someting or drink a lickle drink? What is this prison!?'

JESS.

'His dirty stinking friends. If he's not out with them they're in with us, smoking their dope and playing cards. One night when they were all stoned out of their minds, one of them, Derek I think his name was, he made a pass at me! I couldn't believe it! Ziggy was only a matter of feet away. I could have told him, but it would have only caused a fight, he'd probably have blamed me anyway.'

ZIGGY.

'Why do women love to argue so much? I wouldn't mind but they're not even good at it, there's no logic to them, it's just quantity and to hell with quality. After a while I can't take no more I go to the pub, or if I ain't got no money I find myself a quiet place to just sit and be alone. She thinks I'm sulking, maybe I am, but I can't argue round and round in circles getting nowhere the way that she can.'

JESS.

'Life's getting ugly, especially when he's drunk. I just stay out of his way. Even when he's sober, I make a harmless comment and he's ready to jump down my throat. He's never actually hit me but it's been pretty close a few times. All he seems interested

SHADES OF GREY

in was getting high and getting drunk. Everyday I come in from work and there he is, slumped out in front of the telly, drinking or smoking herbs. Some days that's all he does, from dawn till dusk. If he doesn't go out to the bookies or to the pub, that's it. Now he's stopped washing and he's getting fat, and I thought it was the women who were supposed to let themselves go once settled in a relationship. When he comes to me, pawing me like soppy labrador, it makes me sick, and I can't bare him to touch me.'

ZIGGY.

'I swear she's got a man. She must have, 'cause nowadays she don't want me to touch her. Probably some fucking white fucker from her office.'

JESS.

'I feel numb, emotionally. I don't know if I still care about him or not. It's got to the point where I wished he'd have an affair, or something, at least that might evoke some emotion in me other than this mundane boredom. Yeah, that's my life in a nutshell mundane and boring. He says I'm at a funny age, he says the decline for women begins at twenty four, he jokes about trading me in for a new model. I wish. I wonder what age the decline begins for men.'

ZIGGY.

'I know I should do better, but it takes time, that's what she won't accept. You can't just get up one day when the whole world is against you and turn your losing into winning. It takes time. I need time to get my shit together, but she won't accept that, and that's not helping me. You know, they say men can't handle successful women, but I think it's the women who can't handle unsuccessful men, and it's like a vicious circle, if the one closest to you is pushing you down you ain't never getting up.'

JESS.

'I'd tried to discuss things with him, but he just wasn't interested. It got so I felt that I couldn't go on with things the way they were much longer, I would have to make him listen or go crazy. But he didn't seem to have any notion that anything might be wrong. God! The chore of smashing his idyllic perception of our monotonous existence, then having to deal with resolving

SHADES OF GREY

differences he wasn't even aware existed was just too steep a mountain to climb. I couldn't face it, in the end it seemed easier to let it go for another day. So that's what I did, day after day, time and time again.'

ZIGGY.

'I'm thirty now man, and I think it's about time I started a family. I thought to talk about it loads of times, but the time was never right. I wonder if she'd prefer to get married first. I see myself the father of four kids eventually, three boys and a girl, the girl being the youngest. That way her brothers can look out for her and relieve me of the burden you know. These will be be my first children, I ain't had no other kids man. I have refrained from sprinkling my seed around. She appreciates that man. It's kinda rare to find a mature man without a herd of children scattered around the borough. That makes me one of the most eligible bachelors around yeah? Jess is a beautiful girl, she could have any guy she wanted you know, but she chose me.'

Her beauty and his eligibility somehow made them, not just deserving of each other, but.... worthy. Their union felt sacred somehow, like the union of Joseph and the virgin Mary. Yes, it felt that right. He had put Jess up there on a pedestal with the virgin Mary.

He remembered that Jess had mentioned something about wanting to talk about their lives together. Maybe she was feeling insecure he thought, women needed security, marriage, children a home of their own,

"after all she is twenty six now."

JESS.

'I couldn't take it anymore, so one day I just left. Just like that. It was so simple, I packed my bags and went home to mum. But you know what? I didn't last a day. I missed him so much. Funny that. Anyway I decided to go back, and what did I find? Him in bed with another girl. He begged me to forgive him, promised me things would change. No, that's it I said.... but did I leave him? Did I hell. I don't know why I stayed, I don't love him. But where would I go?- A thousand places truth be told. I could go anywhere I wanted to if I had the courage. Maybe that's what it

SHADES OF GREY

is, just fear. I don't know. I couldn't make the break, but I told myself it wasn't going to be as it had been before. I'd made up my mind, from now on I was going to live my life to the full.'

*

It was a warm summers night in August. Jess had gotten home from clubbing at around 3am. She had had more to drink than usual owing to the fact that a group of louts had naturally taken a fancy to herself and her friends, and had insisted on buying the drinks. The girls had managed to dupe these guys for three bottles of champagne, all for a few fake phone numbers and empty promises of dates to come.

Ziggy was waiting up for her, he had decided that tonight was to be the turning point in their relationship. As he heard her key turning in the lock Ziggy rushed to their front door. The last thing Jess expected to see was Ziggy on his feet. But when she pushed the door open there he was, beaming from ear to ear. 'Why was he not sitting in his favourite chair?' she thought. She found the sight of him at 3am irritating, she thought the sight of him at any time irritating, everything he did nowadays she found irritating. 'Maybe I should tell him it's all over' she thought through her drunken stupor.

He took her hand and led her into the living room and sat her down in his favourite chair. Still holding her hand be began stroking it gently with his other as he went down on one knee. Whatever it was he was doing she hoped it wouldn't take too long. She thought of a funny incident that had occurred that evening, it made her want to laugh, but she didn't want to share the jovial moment with Ziggy, so she didn't.

"Jess, I've been thinking about us..." he began.

'The girls had really had a good time' she thought, 'maybe they would take those guys for another three bottles next week, no, that would be pushing it' she decided.

"I want us to be together always....." Ziggy went on.

'I don't know though' she mused, 'the guy that was interested in me wasn't too bad, maybe I should have given him my real number.'

"and I want to settle down with you, have children in our own home...."

9

SHADES OF GREY

The words children, and a home jolted Jess's preoccupation away from her nights adventure. She began piecing together some of the words he'd said earlier from her subconscious. Jess slowly became aware of what Ziggy was talking about, he now had her full, if startled attention. 'I hope he's not saying what I think he's saying.'

"I love you Jess, I love you, and I want you to be my wife."

'Fat chance' she thought. She felt her stomach knot, and a lump rise up in her throat. He looked her in the eye.

"Will you marry me?"

She felt dizzy. Her body tingled from head to foot. Her vision blurred and tears were rolling down her cheeks. 'He wants to marry me,' she weeped 'he's proposing to me..... Why not, she thought drying her eyes what else have I got to do next week, the rest of my life?'

"Okay," she heard herself say. He threw his arms around her and began to cry.

So within a month they were married. As soon as she'd said 'I do' she knew it was a mistake. She thought it might have been before, after all she was drunk when she accepted. But Ziggy's proposal was the most exciting thing he'd said to her in the three boring years she'd known him. Had she over reacted? Well she'd rung her parents at 3.15 that morning to tell them the good news. She then called all her friends, by 5am that morning everyone she knew had had an invitation. In the cold light and sobriety of the next day it did indeed seem as if she'd over reacted. But what now could she do? Ring everybody up and say it was all a joke? They'd think her a fool. Maybe it was just nerves she'd thought, she'd heard it wasn't unusual for the bride to want to pull out, right up to the very last moment, but then it would be alright for the rest of their lives. She *thought* she might be making a mistake right the way up the alter, but as soon as she'd taken her vows and said those two words, 'I do'- she was *sure.*

And so it was, she'd done it, got married to a man she couldn't stand, and he hadn't a penny to his name. 'Things could be worse' she thought, 'at least he wasn't a short.' She hated short men.

SHADES OF GREY

If anything Ziggy was more boring after marriage than he was before, she remembered that unfortunate night in August, at least he had managed to get to his feet then. Ziggy was sprawled out like a sack of potatoes in front of the TV. They'd only been married three months.

"He used to be a lap dog now he'd become a vegetable, you wouldn't think it possible."

Yesterday she'd heard him mumbling something about wanting to become a father. Jess took fortitude from the fact that no matter how drunk she was, she couldn't get pregnant while she was on the pill.

CHAPTER 2.

Day 1. Wednesday 4th December 1991.

"Girl, you're lying! You trying to tell me you ain't even a little curious?!" Roslin inquired with a shrill exclamation.

"Not even a little." Jess replied boringly.

"Not even a tinsy winsy bit.... hm?"

Sharon and Maxine simultaneously shifted their eager backsides forward in anticipation. Jess through them a sedate look, then cross her legs as she yawned at the tedium. She began mouthing the words 'I wanna sex you up' to a remix cut of the track as her eyes wandered aimlessly about the dance floor. Couples, dowsed in a dim seductive blue light gently dispersed by tinselled rays of red and green, wedged their hips tightly together, head to head, rolling, dipping and gently rocking to the groove. Jess caught the gaze of the Dj, a squat thick dumpy fellow resembling one of the 'Fat boys'. He had been mouthing the same phrase at her and winked as their eyes met. She cut him disdainfully.

She knew that the girls were still watching her, awaiting a smutty scandalous reply to Roslin's last question. But alas she would disappoint them. Jess continued the song gently swaying with the rhythm. Her eyes slowly shifting to each girl in turn a look of indifference. Her antics however did not deter Roslin, a

11

SHADES OF GREY

short yellow skinned fresh faced girl who did nothing by halves.

"Whass his name, Dexter? I bet you and him already...." Roslin was interrupted by a sweaty 'boy-face' who had just finished 'rubbing up', offering her his dripping palm.

"D'you wanna dance babe?"

Roslin screwed up her nose as if to a bad smell and waved him away. The 'boy-face' froze awkwardly.

'Bitch!' he thought to himself, 'I knew I should have asked her friend, up close she looks the better of the two anyway, and I did check the way she was watching me earlier, she was up for it for sure. So what do I do? I come ask this faisty old cow battyface.' He looked round at Sharon, 'Yeah man, or I could have check she. Damn! But she ain't go wanna come now, after her friend turn me down.' He humbly wound his sweaty palm in, slow and discreet. 'What am I gonna do now man!? All the nice gyul dem tek up and the guys are watching me man, shit!'

"You mus' tink you nice eh?" He said looking down his nose at her.

"That's right," Roslin said without looking at him. The 'boy-face' gave her a look to kill but backed off slowly rather than take any more shame.

"Roslin you're wicked you know," Sharon said.

"You tink I come 'ere dress up and smelling sweet fi some renk lickle bwoy to fling up 'im dorty self pun me?"

"He had a nice body though."

"Yeah, but I ain't go start looking fi no toy bwoy till ah reach fifty at least."

The girls sat in the basement bar of Pinkies nightclub surrounding a glass table on which shone a fibre optics refractor. Fitted to the under-side of the table a pulsating light display reflected a hypnotic glow through the four glasses, a bottle of wine, and annoyingly into the girls hyper active pupils. A hubbub of exhilarated chatter hovered just below the music. Each of the girls was made up to the nines, each had squeezed her curves into a black short tight micro mini and dowsed herself in her favourite perfume. Of the four Jess was easily the most stunning. She was a slim, long legged, shapely brown skinned wide eyed girl of 26, who stood five elegant feet seven inches from the

SHADES OF GREY

ground. Her skin was smooth and un-blemished. Her eyes were a stunning and unusual kind of greeny beige. Her nose as with the rest of her was perfection itself. Why then she had to temp as a secretary to make ends meet seemed a travesty of justice to her. At the very least a girl like her deserved a rich man, able to keep her in luxury and a style more becoming of a queen while she waited to be discovered. But Jess had a preference for black men, and nigger's with cash were hard to find.

Roslin sat opposite Jess and between Sharon, a curvy braided haired buxom dark skinned beauty, and Maxine, her younger sister by a year, though you would never have thought so to look at her. Maxine's hair was close cropped, her face was a picture of innocence and her body had the slim athletic leanness of a long distance runner. The two girls listened intently as Roslin probed.

"I know if I'd just discovered that my sexy boyfriend had a twin brother I'd be wondering all kinds of things."

Roslin slithers and wiggles provocatively as she speaks. She accentuates certain syllables almost to the point of song, sensually, suggestively but all with tongue in cheek.

"Imagine, there's this guy you think you know, inside and out, men-tal-ly, phy-sic-ally, in-tim-ately, and it's like, wow! Then up come this other guy who looks exactly the same! Eyes, nose, mouth, bone structure, voice. Oh baby! Now a girl can't help but wonder where the similarities end, now can she?"

Meanwhile, Willis, a lanky gangling oaf stood nervously among the revellers, roasting in a heavy tweed suite and white polo neck. He was trying his damnedest (all be it discreetly) to emulate some of the wicked movers around him. This was clearly beyond his capability. The sight of Roslin winding up her backside on the chair catches his eye.

"I'm sure we'll all get to know him in good time..." Jess began.

"Yeah sure, but some of us better than others right?" Roslin cut in as she winks to Sharon and Maxine.

"Are you suggesting.... look I have Ziggy, I'm not interested in his brother."

"Huh, that's what she says now. But we all know don't we

SHADES OF GREY

girls, the unattainable is always the most desirable."

There was then a long pause, like the 'time out' at a basketball game, 'I wanna sex you up' merged smoothly with Omar's 'There's nothing like this,' then just as you might have thought the subject had been dropped or forgotten, Roslin broke the silence.

"Is he like his brother in the sack is what we're asking?"

"Huh hm! the sixty four zillion dollar question. Maxine chipped in."

Willis begins moazing over like a giraffe with two left feet towards their table.

"Boy, I'd like to line them up naked, side by side and compare," Roslin said blatantly.

"Too see if their feet were the same size? Sharon asked with a mock naivety. Willis now hovers, fidgeting awkwardly over their conversation, un-assertively waiting for his opportunity to speak. Roslin though aware of Willis's sweltering mass towering above them continues un-perturbed.

"Hey, now I've tried that shit and it don't work, you wanna know how well a man is hung, you gotta look at his dick!"

The girls break out in a chorus of laughter.

"Ros! You're outrageous!" Sharon said.

"Just kidding Jess, you know that don't you, just kidding..." Then without a break looking directly at Willis she says, "Can I help you?"

As he blurts through a wet buck toothed grin he showers the girls in a light saliva spray which falls like multi-coloured flakes of snow through the disco lighting. With his eyeballs magnified two fold by the bi-focal lenses of his thick glasses, his face took on a frog like proportion.

"Hello, my name is Willis. I was wondering if you might like to dance?"

As Roslin looked Willis up and down, she felt like she wanted to laugh and cry at the same time.

"No," she said mischievously, "but why don't you have a seat next to Jess here and we can talk."

"Okay," he said gormlessly and moved to the seat next to Jess. They watched as a clumsy Willis fought a battle to get his

SHADES OF GREY

long bandy legs under the table, which he almost topples several times before he settles.

"Do you come here often?" he asked genuinely. The girls choked a while on their stifled sniggers before Sharon answered in her best bimbo voice with as straight a face as she could manage.

"No this is our first time," she fluttered her eyelashes, the girls burst out laughing. After a few puzzled seconds Willis joined them though he didn't know why.

"I haven't been here before," he said pointlessly.

"I bet you can tell what star signs we all are just by looking at us." Roslin teased. Willis smiled as if he'd finally caught on to the send up, but then splashing with every syllable said,

"I'm a physiologist, which means that though I try to remain as objective as possible, I tend to have a more scientific approach to these superstitions and such like. And while I acknowledge the moons affect on the oceans of the world, and our bodies being 75% water, the reasonable supposition that it affects us in some way too, as yet I remain un-convinced that man can interpret these effects, or that our birth date has any baring on the matter whatsoever, in fact......"

"It's hot, isn't it?" Roslin interrupted, "Don't you think it's hot? Aren't you hot in that thick woolly sweater?

"Oh, a... well... maybe a little. I... Oh, may I get you ladies a drink?"

"Wouldn't that be sweet," Roslin jumped in blatantly. A gin and tonic, two dry white wines and a rum and black." Then with a plastic smile she sent Willis dutifully up to the bar.

The girls gave each other a look of dismay. Their look to Roslin begged the question, 'why did you ask him to sit with us'. Roslin's expression was an apologetic 'sorry girls, okay I boobed alright?'

"He sounded like a constipated parrot who'd just eaten a tape recorder sideways." Maxine groaned.

"I've met some doe doe's in my time but this guy takes the bake. The guy has no sense of humour at all!" Sharon said. Roslin wasted even fewer words.

"The guy has no sense full stop!"

15

SHADES OF GREY

"Why don't we slip away while we can?" Maxine suggested.

"We can't just walk out and make the guy look a fool," Jess said.

"We can, we didn't make him, and he already does," Maxine jived.

"Relax. Let's just have a drink, then we go right? No big ting," Roslin said cooly. Sharon elbowed Roslin in the ribs uttering discreetly from the corner of her mouth,

"It's alright, we'll go. We can see that you two want to be alone."

"God can you imagine? I'd go crazy."

Maxine's gaze was drawn to two cool looking guys across the other side of the dance floor.

"Look at those guys. Now why couldn't they have come over?"

From a dark secluded corner of the club, surrounded by smoochers swaying to the groove of 'Southern California,' the tall slender figure of Toby emerges. His face drawn from not having slept in three days looks a decade older than his nineteen years. He wears three earrings in his left earlobe, a peanut like negro nose, the up turned top lip of a babies mouth, and a chin that showed no evidence of ever having seen a razor, but his eyes, bagged and veined had an intense haunting deepness which told you he was no joker.

Having just coked up with Redd and Zapp and charged with a 'dutch arrogance' they swaggered stylishly, confidently about, each in punjab zoot trousers, short waiter jackets, hats and FX specs. They especially drew the attention of the straight laced middle aged squares, who stood at the bar spending money looking for excitement, but were too old fat and frumpy to join in the real fun.

The music abruptly exploded with a mighty thunder of 'Her' by 'Guy.' The crowd effuse a loud ebullient cheer. The dance floor becomes a romping stomping orgy of gyrating limbs and torso's. Spinning, twisting and twirling like a herd of groovy cyclonic acrobats and ballerina's.

Toby pirouettes onto the dance floor, followed keenly by Zapp and Redd. They 'lindy-hopped' into the 'running man' then

SHADES OF GREY

leaped simultaneously into the air landing a perfect split. The trio elegantly exit the dance floor leaving others to 'follow that if they can.' Roslin, Maxine and Sharon eyeballed the three-some. After a little squabbling they had decided that Redd was Roslin's, Toby was Maxine's and Zapp was Sharon's. Sharon switches her attention to a group of guys in cycling sorts ripped tee shirts and cod pieces.

"His head on his body, and that's my man."

"Nah, he looks too cheeky and his legs too skinny. Now his face on his bum with his legs, now that's my man," Maxine countered.

"Bwoy!" Roslin exclaimed, "I feel sorry for you, but even sorrier for him! Just a face stuck on an ass and two legs? no neck no arms...." They laugh.

When the girls got together they eventually got around to talking about men. What they should do, what they shouldn't, what they were doing and what they weren't. They had a good time doing it too. The girls usually started out complaining, but it wasn't long before they got round to the nitty gritty. From the way a man looked, walked, talked, right down to any distasteful habits he might have or his lack of enthusiasm for personal hygiene. They took him apart, sometimes literally.

"If we were to get all the nice guys, take all the good bit's and stick them together, throw all the bad bits away, the world would be full of perfect men," Sharon said.

"I don't know about you but most of the guys I know are big headed enough as it is, you make them all perfect we're gonna have to widen all the door frames to get them into the bedroom.

"You girls are obsessed with sex," Maxine said as selfrighteously and scolding as a frustrated matron.

"Oh, listen to the whore house virgin. We heard about you and Daniel, in the kitchen, on the freezer," Roslin jived her. Maxine was at first shocked, but then just stuck her nose in the air contemptuously, raising her eyebrows in ridicule, as if she'd just heard a rumour that the queen had posed for Penthouse.

"I don't know what you heard, but it's all just malicious gossip," Maxine said defensively.

"Okay then, let's hear your version," Sharon said. Maxine

SHADES OF GREY

took a moment to quell her indignation.

"I don't know anything about no freezer," she said, delicately. She paused again, as if fighting back the tears for her injured reputation. She sat hands clasped resting on her thighs, her knees press tightly together like a decorous Sunday school teacher.

"I paid Daniel a social call.... he invited me it for a coffee.... we had it in the kitchen...." Her pitiful facial expression suddenly began a saucy grin, she slapped a celebration with her fingers as she cried, "on the washing machine!" The girls explode into a raucous fit.

Each of these girl claimed to be a bedroom bombshell, and each of them was, except for Jess. Each would give a blow by blow account of her previous nights sexual encounter in much the same way that a guy might, the difference being she usually told the truth. When they got together they revealed the intimacies of their love lives to the finest detail, excluding nothing. Except for Jess. Jess had always given good audience to the stories of their erogenous escapades, but she'd never disclosed any details of her own. If pressed she would lie un-convincingly of her conservative bedroom antics, just as she lied about her many other sexual liaisons, for in truth she had known only one man.

Jess's reserved manner served only to fire curiosity and rouse suspicion from the other girls, who would secretly speculate about Jess and Ziggy's wild, uninhibited, unadulterated, passionate love making sessions. But as often is the case when the imagination is left free to roam without constraint or guide, the conclusions are invariably subject to wild exaggeration. This was most certainly the case with regard to Jess, for it was not the nightly animal ravaging's that the other girls delighted in she craved. Though she would never have admitted it to them, as far as sex was concerned, she couldn't really see what all the fuss was about. Yes she was curious about Dexter, and yes she had made numerous comparisons between the brothers and wondered how it might be if she were not with Ziggy. But it was not Dexter's bedroom athleticism that was the subject of her wonderment, but his capacity for love and

SHADES OF GREY

affection, his thoughtfulness and sensitivity, for it was in these ways that Ziggy was inadequate. Every time Ziggy rolled off her body and began snoring without so much as a kind word or caring touch, each time, after he had taken but not given, leaving her feeling empty angry and frustrated she wondered about his brother.

Willis returned with a tray full of drinks. The girls each take one then walk towards the dance floor near to where Toby Redd and Zapp are grooving. Willis is left not knowing whether to follow or sit and wait for their return.

Toby is suddenly hit by a bout of dizziness which makes him stagger.

"You all right man?" Redd asked him.

"Yeah fine," Toby replies blinking clear his vision.

"You looked fucked."

Toby just smiles.

"This place is dry man!" Redd complained.

"I know," Toby concedes, but it's a good place to score a blow right."

"And some of de gyul dem look fit man," Zapp added eyes roving.

"Yeah but it's time to chip." Redd insisted.

"Chill out a while bro, I got ma eye on this chick," Zapp said.

"What chick?" Redd asks, then finds the answer to his question at the end of Zapp's bold coke bolstered gaze, a shapely angelic looking sister wrapped in the arms of a burly herculean. Toby and Redd exchange a look then laugh.

"You must want to die," Toby said. But Zapp, un-deterred and buzzing louder than a bee in a honey jar walked directly to the girl, grabbed her up and kissed her full in the mouth before she or anyone else knew anything about it.

Now it wasn't obvious from his face just how mad 'Hercules' was. But you could tell from the venom he put into every vicious punch that he wasn't pleased. Zapp's face exploded with the first blow, his flesh parted and blood spurted out like it was trying to get away from the beating. Toby and Redd jumped on to 'Hercules' but were effortlessly shaken off and then set upon by two 'herculetts' who seemed to come from nowhere. Zapp was

SHADES OF GREY

being hit again and again, his face ballooned under the merciless pounding to resemble the un-cooked dough of a jam filled ginger bread man in the moon. After the brutal pasting had rendered him un-recognisable he was lethargically thrown to the wall like a rag doll. Toby and Zapp were then allowed to take his remains out into the street.

"That's too bad," Roslin said indifferently, "they were cute guys."

Toby and Redd were fuming and wanted to go back, but they knew in their heart of hearts that if they did they were in for more of the same, and anyway Zapp was in a sad way, he needed help, bad. The club was still kicking as if nothing out of the ordinary had gone down, nothing had. A few ravers stepped out to breath a little sympathy for the beaten trio, others who didn't want to be around were going home before the anticipated arrival of the police. Toby ran to a telephone box and called the hospital, while Redd stayed with Zapp.

The sirens of ambulance and the police arrived almost together. Zapp was placed on a stretcher. Toby and Redd wanted to go with him but were told they couldn't unless they were family. As the ambulance sped off both began the long slow treck to the hospital on foot. Two policemen addressed the crowd.

"Did anyone see what happened here?" one said. The policeman's repeated appeal for witnesses was greeted with a stony silence from the crowd. All the ravers were concerned with was keeping it rocking till dawn.

"They're not going to speak to a couple of white cops, this is a job for Benjamin." The other cop nodded agreement.

Detective sergeant Winston Benjamin was a black cop with a reputation for being mean and tough. Hated by many but respected by everyone.

*

Toby and Redd had been sitting in the casualty ward waiting room for almost an hour. Redd was fuming.

"Man, the next time I see that big guy I'm gonna kick his butt. They got me mad now. I'm gonna go down there- if you wanna come you can- and throw pure licks in his ass, and as for his

20

SHADES OF GREY

friends if they want theirs they can have it. I used to do jujitsu you know. I have to hold back normally 'cause if I loose my temper... man!... I'm a killer you know that? I can..." Toby suddenly rises to his feet.

"Let's go."

"Where?" Zapp asked him.

"Let's go get him."

"What!? Don't be silly man you see the size of the guy!?"

"I know where we can get a gun."

"Gun!? Gun!? Are you crazy!? Gun!? You must think you're dirty Harry or somebody...."

"Are you coming or not?"

"Look, sit down Tobe's man, lets talk this thing out..."

"You're full of shit?" Toby said cooly and walked out into the street.

Toby caught a bus from the top of sixth avenue in Manor park to Stratford broadway. A Pakistani bus conductor wearing a maroon coloured turban was singing 'Maybe it's because I'm a Londoner' in a broad cockney accent much to the amusement of his passengers.

TOBY.

'The world's full of jokers man, and their all full of shit. They think I'm playing, but they're gonna find out man, I don't play. I left school with nothing, not even a GCSE. They didn't give a fuck, so I didn't give a fuck. I was hardly ever there anyhow. When I did turn up for a lesson they wouldn't even know who I was. And my dad, huh! Their lot came over to the 'mother country to walk on street paved with gold. They bought the hype man, all that crap, they bought it! He's got so much respect for the white mans way, their education, their law and order, they're so wrapped up in the fucking colonial thing man... One time, I came home and told him a teacher had hit me, I was only twelve, I had these big bruises on my hand. You know what he did? He hit me again. He wasn't even interested in my side of things, I must have been bad he said for the teacher to hit me. Another time I was fifteen, the police picked me up for being drunk, dad had to come and get me from the station. He slapped me around the head and kept shouting about how I'd shamed him. He was

21

SHADES OF GREY

shouting it loud for them, and when he slapped me it was for them too, but they were laughing, and not just at me. My dad loves to suck up to them but they know better than to fuck with me man 'cause like I said, I don't play. Anybody fuck with me and I'll fuck with them and I don't care man, I don't give a monkeys. But then who does? That's why I get high. When I buzzing I'm a better man, I see shit more clearly man, I don't hesitate, I know when people be trying to fuck with my head man, and I does just deal with it man. When you're buzzing man, you see things the way they should be. Colours, music and lights, the good and the bad guys, just like a movie.'

The singing bus conductor approaches Toby.

"....that I love London town. Fares please."

Toby just gives him a mean look, the conductor sees trouble, he doesn't want it, he goes on to another passenger without taking Toby's money. Toby sits stern faced and resolute with only one thing on his mind, revenge.

A short walk down the Romford road then Water lane brought him to the haunted look of a derelict house. He climbed over a wall to the back of the house and entered through a back door. In the pitch darkness he uncovers a black kit bag from it's hiding place under a floor board. Inside the bag there are two guns. With the black bag slung over his shoulder Toby made his way back to Pinkies.

His adrenalin was pumping as he re-lived the fight in his mind, that's why he was carrying the guns he told himself. But somehow, the fight seemed un-important, it was about something else now. Was he really going to shoot a man? He wasn't sure. He'd told Redd he was, he'd told himself that too and went all the way home for the guns. But... the thing was he really didn't want to. To kill a man... you kill a man and you take away everything, and not just from him, you take him from everybody else, his mother, his kids... Maybe if the guy begged him, begged for his life in front of everybody, and said he was sorry about Zapp he'd let him go. That would be the ideal...

"No, the bastard has got to pay. When it comes down to it Zapp has a mother too right? And we don't take shit from nobody."

Toby stood outside the club shifting from one foot to the other in the cold. At around 3.30 am Toby saw 'Hercules' leaving with the girl that Zapp had kissed clinging to his arm, and the 'Herculetts' in tow. Toby stepped out into their path, they didn't even seem to recognise him.

"This is for Zapp," he said and shot 'Hercules' through the heart. He was dead before he hit the ground.

CHAPTER 3.

'My name is Benjamin, dat's dee name my father gave my mother when he married her. She christened me Winston, so you can call me dat if you want, but Winston Benjamin is my name. Now if you want to use my full title you have to call me Detective sergeant Winston Benjamin dee first. Yeah, I was one of dee very first black policemen in this country. I joined dee force back in 1967 amidst much opposition from within what was, and still is a very racist institution. My fellow police officers were outraged dat I had been allowed to become a British Bobby, their greatest fear was dat dee force would become inundated with negro's. Of course dat never happen. In those days white people would stop in dee street and stare at me in me uniform as if I was an alien from space. Many of me friends dem did look pun me wid a whole 'eap a suspicion, some a dem say dem regarded me as dee enemy from within. As a young black copper of 27 I did often wondered if dey was right, now almost 25 years on, wid all dee tings I have seen, you know I still don't know dee answer. But jus' because I is a police man don't tink I sell out you know. Though I have been content to work within dee system over dee years, I have never accepted dee honorary white status some of my more liberal colleagues have tried to bestow on me. No sah! True, I does put on a London accent for dem, but only because dem cyan't understand me when I speak broad, you know?

Bwoy! I make sure dey know where I stand so If it ever come down to an out an out war, black against white, dey know what

SHADES OF GREY

side of dee line to find me. I tell dem, I is no better or worse dan any of dee blacks locked up in dem jails, and I tell dem I would probably have done exactly as dey had, given dee same circumstances. I've jus' been lucky dat's all. Luck and dee grace ah God has helped me chroo all dee shit dey have shovelled pun me over dee years. Some guys had to deal wid bigger shovels and couldn't make it, dee truth is I doubt if I could have done any better. Now I know dis attitude don't sit well with dee powers dat be, in fact it pissed dem off no end. But dats dee way it is pa pa.

Dee ting is I is a damn good copper, or dem would a find some way of either chrowing me out or locking me up already. A whole 'eap a time is me get dem outta trouble, and dem know it!

I is on first name terms wid most of dee black yout dem in dee neighbourhood chroo me visit to schools an' yout club in dee area. In many a delicate situation, I have been dee one dey had to rely on to find a peaceful solution. One time dem kick up a disturbance in dee grove, jus' prior to dee riots of 84. A group of about eight young racist British Bobby fools had tried to arrest a black guy in a bar on dee Ladbroke grove. Dem claim dat he fitted dee description of a mugger who had 'stolen a lickle ol' ladies hand bag. Truth was dee guy had been in dee bar all evening surrounded by an army of 'im friends, and as it turned out there had been no mugging anyway. It was just a show of strength dat was to go horribly wrong..... for dem. One of dee rookies was killed and dee others were being held hostage at knife point in a stalemate situation lasting almost chree days! Now short of bringing down dee mother of every guy in dee bar to plead with her son to give himself up, dee police had not a clue on how to settle dee matter without further bloodshed. It was I, Benjamin who had to bring dee situation under control 'cause no one else could have. Certainly no one in dee force, plainly I had prevented a volatile situation from exploding into a riot. Dem know I is indispensable, or as I say already, dem would a fling me out from time. Even dee most right winged fascist of dee division, a guy call Nash, even he have to admit, I know what I'm doing.'

Benjamin dozes in the drivers seat of an old Ford Cortina

SHADES OF GREY

mark II on the Graham road in Hackney. A plump round faced dark skinned man of medium stature, he was a divorcee with two kids, Natasha, and Louise. He had a passion for West Indian food and a love for seventies reggae music. Occasionally he throws an eye on the door of an ordinary looking house across the street, from which the faint monotonous thud of bass and drums murmuring through the concrete, can be felt like the rumble of a simmering earthquake. It is 3.30am. Benjamin gapes a yawn the size of a lions roar, then un-screws the top to a vacuum flask, pouring out a coffee into the lid. He watches the arrival of a group of five skimpily dressed girls, shivering as they loitered in the street outside. They are apparently contemplating whether or not to go into the blues. None of the girls looked to be over the age of consent. As the father of two young girls himself, Benjamin is outraged, anyone of these blooming vestal flowers could be one of his daughters in say, five years time. 'Where were their parents?' he thought. He felt like hauling their skinny asses in for soliciting or something, just to teach them all a lesson. He wound down his window ready to deliver a fatherly lecture.

"Excuse me... girls," he called to them authoritatively. An hour glass figure with the sweet innocent face of an pretty fourteen year old turned towards Benjamin's Cortina.

"But wait!" she said coarsely "look pun dis crofty ol' hard back pervert wan check we!"

Benjamin choked on a mouthful of coffee and tipped half a cup down his front. He was as mad as hell and more than a little embarrassed. He reached into his breast pocket for his badge and thrust it through the open car window.

"Police!" he bellowed conspicuously. "I'm gonna close my eyes and count to three, if any of you pip squeaks ain't on your way to bed by the time I open up, your mothers will be collecting you from a cell in the morning. Now pick up your little butts and get out of here. One.. Two...Three..."

Benjamin opens his eyes in time to see the girls scurrying off down the road like a flock of frightened penguins.

"Damn kids, now I smell like a fist full of brazillian beans."

Benjamin hated 'stake outs', if there were two in the car at

25

SHADES OF GREY

least you could take it in turns to sleep, but in this case it wouldn't matter, nobody could sleep through the noise coming from the 'party house'.

The boom of the thudding bass is cut by the singing treble of hi hat as the front door of the 'party house' cracks open. A suave looking guy with a skinny dreadlocks woman on his arm emerges from the blues. She throws an innocuous glance to the Cortina, Benjamin takes his cue. He gets out of the car and follows. They turn the corner into Clarence road. Just as they pass under the amber of the lamppost, the dreadlocks woman takes what looks to Benjamin like a small white packet from the guy. 'Was that it?' Benjamin thought 'that could have been it, looked like cocaine to me. Come on Spikey, give me a sign.' The dreadlocks woman makes a subtle wave behind her back to Benjamin with her palm. Benjamin is confused.

"What's that!? Is that a come on, or is that a stay back?"

The couple began to laugh and joke, her hand is waving, but more vigorously now. 'This must be it,' Benjamin thought. He ran up behind them, grabbed the guy and pushed his face up against the wall.

"Police! Legs apart! Hands up! You have the right to remain silent...."

"What's going on man!" the guy protested.

"...but anything you do say may be used as evidence against you."

"I ain't done nothing man! What's the charge?"

"Possession of narcotics for starters, well done Spikey." Spikey is looking fed up, she slowly removes the dreadlocks wig. She is a young pretty ton boy of about 25 new to CID. When she was first paired off with Benjamin he was apprehensive to say the least. But she had proved herself many times in the field as it were, particularly when it came to going under cover. She'd saved his ass several times too. She was loud, vibrant, hip and eager, just as Benjamin had been when first he joined CID some twelve years previous.

"We don't like cocaine pushers around here." Benjamin said as he snatches a small white piece of paper from Spikey.

"What cocaine!?" The guy protested.

26

SHADES OF GREY

"This coc... cocai... where's the cocaine he gave you?" Benjamin asked Spikey.

"He didn't give me any cocaine."

"But I saw him give you..."

"His phone number," Spikey cut in. She was pissed off. Benjamin looked at the piece of paper. On it he sees a phone number. He is stumped. He releases the guys arm.

"So you're a cop eh?" The guy said to Spikey. Spikey just shrugged her shoulders disappointedly.

"I'm sorry fella," Benjamin began "I thought you were..."

"You'll be hearing from my solicitor first thing in the morning man. Wrongful arrest racial harassment..." the guy is looking Benjamin straight in the eye, he makes a wry smile. "...and you a nigger too! Huh, yeah a nigger with a badge, working so hard for the white man to keep the black man down, that's why we ain't never gonna get nowhere. You fucking coconut, you should be ashamed."

"Watch your language boy I could arrest you for that." The guy offered his wrist to Benjamin for handcuffing.

"I'm sure you could.... *boy.*" For a moment neither he nor Benjamin move, the guy then throws Spikey a dirty look before walking off down the street. Benjamin breaths a heavy sigh.

"Why didn't I become a taxi driver.- So what was that, a pick up? I thought we were here for a bust."

"The joint was clean, I thought I may as well enjoy myself, and I was doing okay until you showed up."

"I thought you were in trouble."

"Trouble? Why would I be in trouble? Did it look like I was in trouble?"

"Well... yes it did. You were waving like you were in trouble. Come and get me quick, I need your help, please."

"No I wasn't. I was waving, there's no one in there, I'm going off with this groovy guy, so go take a hike, see you in the morning. So what do you do? Thanks daddy, thanks."

"You should thank me, I just saved you from making a big mistake."

"Oh yeah?"

"Yeah. That guy was a jerk!"

27

SHADES OF GREY

"He was no such thing."

"Does he have a job, a place to live?"

"I don't believe this!"

"I doubt very much that his intentions were honourable."

"Honourable!? Get real daddy I...."

Just then they hear a call on the radio. "Grey watch to Panther, grey watch to Panther, proceed to Pinkies Nightclub, suspected homicide."

Benjamin jumps in the passenger seat, Spikey in the drivers. They speed off.

SPIKEY.

'Doing this job you hardly ever get to meet nice guys, nice guys that aren't cops that is. And when I do, the minute they find out I'm a police woman they go funny on me. I don't know, maybe all the guys I meet are murderers thieves and drug dealers, I mean why else would they be so frightened of me? But I really like this job. I've always wanted to to something different. At school while the other girls were playing rounders and stuff, I'd find myself thinking how easy it would be to break into the science lab. I worked it out with my brother Kelvin. Up the side of the building and through the roof! Piece of cake. I thought I was destined to be a cat burglar or something. I'd thought about the army, I mean I wasn't too sure about the politics of it, you know, just a nameless cog in a massive engine, with no voice. I mean me, a black woman, I couldn't deal with that. What if this country decided to attack Trinidad or something?

When I was seventeen my brother died. He was only a year younger than me. He started hanging out with a wrong type of crowd you know, got in trouble with the police a few times, but I never knew he did drugs. They say he brought on a heart attack with a cocaine speedball. A heart attack, I mean he was only sixteen! Mum went to pieces. I never really knew my dad, he was killed in a motor accident mum said, when I was about three. It's just the two of us now. Anyway after Kelvin died I started thinking of how to stop people from trying to get into the science lab, thought about ways of telling people that drugs were for losers. I think that's why they took me into the force, and then into CID. They could see how passionately anti-drugs I was, and

SHADES OF GREY

with me being young and looking like a black punk rocker, I suppose they thought I'd be able to talk to the kids. Spikey's not my real name, but I got stuck with it after I started wearing my plaits out so that my head looked like a gladiators mace or something, freaks guys out so they daren't bother me too much... not even the one's I want to. Anyway, they team'd me up with Benjamin, daddy I call him, You don't have to ask why. I think we make a really good team though he won't admit it. We compliment each other, things he can do I can't and stuff I'm good at he might be weak on. He has me drive this car in emergencies for instance, and could you see him in this wig?'

CHAPTER 4.

Day 1. Night.

When the ambulance arrived to attend to Zapp lying bruised and beaten on the cold pavement, Jess and the girls were having a good time getting down. But they had already left by the time Toby had returned, and so knew nothing of the shooting. By the time Benjamin and Spikey had arrived the girls were riding the short mini cab journey home.

They were in a boisterous mood, so much so the mini cab driver thought about trying his luck with one of them... anyone of them. They sounded drunk to him and were probably dying for a screw. He figured that was worth taking the night off for. But when the girls ignored his tired chat up lines he decided he'd best concentrate on making some money. He also decided that he was going to charge them an extra two pounds, just for spite. As usual Jess was the quietest of the four, she had something on her mind she dare not share with the others, for while they happily chatted about 'boy face' and 'Hercules' and the fight and cod pieces and Willis, Jess found herself wondering what Dexter was doing.

Jess had been seeing Ziggy for a year before she'd met Dexter. She didn't even know that Ziggy had a brother let alone a twin, Ziggy never mentioned it. The reason why, (he had later

SHADES OF GREY

tried to explain) may have had something to do with being identified as one half of a single entity as kids.

"Adults do that," he said. "As kids we were always referred to as 'the twins', not Ziggy and Dexter. I grew up not being sure of my own name, or that me and him were really two totally separate and whole people. Plus the fact that we don't really get on."

Jess had to admit to herself that she was guilty of that adult sin. Once she'd met Dexter she saw him and Ziggy as two halves of the same person. She knew only one half. She and Ziggy had been together nearly three years now. She remembered being pestered by a short fat hairy man in a club, and Ziggy had come to her rescue by pretending to be her boyfriend. She was instantly attracted to him. He had those tall rugged good looks she liked. She detested short men more than anything else she could imagine. The thought of going to bed with anyone under five foot seven inches tall sent shivers down her spine. She'd once dreamt, and had since often imagined looking down at the top of his scalp peeping from the bed cloths as he buried his head in her breasts, at the same time his toes reaching down only far enough to stub the bone of her shins. Yuk! No short men for her. He could be stinking rich and as generous as a grey cloud in a down pour, she didn't care. She'd rather an ugly son of a bitch any day.

Ziggy had spun her a line about being a record producer and needing a singer for a band he was working with. That was all it took. In truth Jess really couldn't sing a note, Ziggy had flirted with the music business, but wasn't particularly gifted. The two of them made an ugly noise together. With the help of a couple of cheap microphones and a tape machine, they were asking for trouble. Thankfully they eventually abandoned their ambitions of becoming stars after a series of rebukes from.... everyone really, managers, A&R departments, family, friends and several neighbourhood tom cats who might have improved their recording substantially, had they been employed as backing vocalists. Ziggy had subsequently decided that his future lay within the realms of a steady day job. But Jess's daily fraternization with her mirror had instilled a belief in her that a

SHADES OF GREY

beautiful girl such as she was destined for the big time..... some time. Preferably while she was still young and beautiful. The fear that her looks might fade before the world had had a chance to enjoy them had fuelled her paranoia. Her flirtatious engagements with her reflection now included a regular period of surveillance, where she scrutinized her face for the faintest sign of a crows foot. That would signal the start of a downward spiral to old age. She was only twenty six she kept reassurring herself, but couldn't stop thinking about how Ziggy had teased her that a woman began her decline from the age of twenty four. She had laughed it off of course, but as silly as it was, his statement had sown the seeds of an insecurity that was now in bloom.

The first time she met Dexter, it was like meeting Ziggy again for the first. She saw a hungry desire in his eyes that excited her, the same look that Ziggy had used so successfully to win her at the night club, a look that familiarity had since subdued. She knew Dexter fancied her, most men did.

Dexter.

'There's no love loss between me and my brother, there hasn't been since we were kids. In fact I'm not sure we were ever friends. It's a shame and I don't understand why. People say that it's because we're so much alike, but apart from the fact that we're twins we have nothing in common. He's always been the aggressive one, I was the placid one. We fought a lot as kids, I guess that's natural. But the difference was I hated fighting, he loved it. The only time he was ever interested in me was when he wanted something, like help with his homework. I helped him out in the beginning, but then it got so that it was more than just help he wanted. Soon he had me doing it all. Once after we'd got sent to different schools he even tried to get me to go to his classes for him, of course I refused. After that things just got worse. Everything I had he borrowed, the thing was I never got them back, I resented that and so when I saw Jess...... When I saw Jess, I have to admit I was jealous. She was the first thing of his that I ever wanted, but I didn't go for her, not seriously. Oh I'd kid around and flirt with her but I was careful not to push it any further than that, because I knew I was falling in love with her.

31

SHADES OF GREY

Jess.

Dexter was a charmer, he was always kidding around. Sometimes he'd pretend that he was Ziggy with a suit on, then suggest I take the rest of the day off with him. He'd send me little presents with love notes from 'husband number two'. I liked that. He often talked about me leaving Ziggy and running off with him, it was our running joke, at least I thought it was a joke. Then there were the office to office telephone calls, that got more and more frequent and became the highlight of many a boring day. We started to meet up for lunch and for drinks after work, it got to the point where I was seeing more of Dexter than his brother, my husband. It was almost like having two husbands, just as Dexter had said- or maybe two halves. Throughout the time we spent together Dexter was always the perfect gentleman. It was fun at first. Not just at first, it was always fun, but I began to feel that things were changing for him, like he was taking our relationship seriously. Though he did his best to hide it I could see that he wanted more than just a friendship. He was good to be with and he was fun... but he wasn't Ziggy. So I broke it off, I stopped seeing Dexter completely.

Dexter.

After Jess told me that she didn't think it was a good idea that we see each other anymore I threw myself into my work. If I'd had a girlfriend of my own perhaps it wouldn't have been so tough. But I've always been a shy kind of person, working was the only way I knew how to keep myself going. I avoided Ziggy like the plague, I felt like breaking his face, it was like he'd stolen something from me, the most precious and cherished possession I had, not just borrowed and not returned this time but stolen. I wanted to smash him to the ground and kick him in the face, me the placid one! But the truth was that regardless of how precious she was to me, or how much I cherished her she wasn't my possession, and he hadn't stolen anything from me. I wanted to steal her from him, and that was wrong. She was right to break it off, I wouldn't have, so where would it have all ended up?

CHAPTER 5.

Benjamin an Spikey arrived at Pinkies in less than 5 minutes. When they were in a hurry Benjamin always had Spikey drive. She was as crazy as hell behind the steering wheel and she scared the shit out of him, but she was the fastest thing on *four wheels* he'd ever seen. Not only was she fast, but she was safe too. With all the hair raising near misses she'd had, never once had she so much as wiped the paint on anything. He would never admit to her that he admired her driving though, instead he claimed that putting her in control of the car was all part of her training, he was just giving her some valuable experience that was all.

The police were trying to keep people back from the morbid sight, but it seemed like everybody wanted to have a look at a dead man. You'd have thought Wesley Snipes was in the middle of it all instead of a corpse. Photographers were clicking flashes and reporters were milling among the crowd listening out for anything they might invent a story around. Benjamin and Spikey pushed their way through. The inert mass of Hercules was hunched up under a white bed sheet like a mini snow mountain. Blood was everywhere, literally running down off the pavement into the gutter, just as his life had gone before it. There didn't seem to be any sign of the murder weapon but Benjamin hadn't really expected there to be. He thought it sad to see a young black man senselessly gunned down in the street. He wondered what it all meant, the start of a gangland war? A race riot? A spate of tit for tat killings? He scanned the crowd, there were many young faces there familiar to him, he hoped that maybe one of them had the answers to these questions or at least some clues. He called out to a young guy.

"Hey Jeffery." Jeffery came forward.

"You know him?"

"I ain't never seen 'im before," Jeffery said, "he ain't from

33

SHADES OF GREY

around here."

"What's this all about?" Benjamin asked him.

"I don't know man I swear, there was a fight... but guys are always fighting, ain't no one ever been shot before!"

"The guy he was fighting with...?"

"Strangers man." Jeffery cut in. Benjamin paused for thought. Jeffery was shaken up sure, but he seemed nervous too, Benjamin wasn't sure if it was just the shock of a killing or whether he knew more than he was telling.

"Okay. Go home now, if your memory improves you know where to find me."

"I ain't holding out on you man I swear."

Benjamin approached a young jumpy looking constable.

"Constable."

"Sir?"

"Has there been any reports of a disturbances here tonight?"

"Not to my knowledge sir."

"Check that out and report back to me."

"Yes sir." The constable gets on his radio.

"This is a tough one," Benjamin said to Spikey, "It's gonna take all my skill and experience to crack this case that's for sure. It looks like these guys were from out of town, which could mean we're in the middle of a rival gang war, and who knows what else. Maybe some columbian drugs barons are behind it all or maybe...." Spikey rolled her eyes in disbelief.

"Wait a minute, wait a minute!- What are you talking about?" Benjamin reacts with indignation, as if defending slur on his integrity.

"I don't expect you to understand, but when you've been a cop as long as I have you get so you can smell trouble brewing, and..."

"What you think this is, Miami vice? There ain't no gang wars or Columbian drug barons in Stratford. This is a straight forward revenge ting innit."

"You think so huh?"

"Course. Look, that kid is lying, he knows the guys who were fighting, they're probably friends of his, that's why he won't say. Now most of his friends are gonna fall into the black, male,

SHADES OF GREY

eighteen to thirty five category yeah? I mean that narrows it down some straight away don't it? Piece of cake, find the other guy in the fight and there's your killer."

"You police academy graduates, you're so smug. Wait till you've been on the street a few years, see how much you know then."

"Come on daddy, that's all there is to it and you know it, I bet you a fiver we wrap this up by tomorrow night."

"Your on."

She made it sound so easy, but Benjamin knew that unless they got a lead it was a pains taking process of checking out every person who had been in the club that night. That would take more than a day, it was easy money. Though this was one five pound bet he wouldn't mind losing.

The constable approached with his radio pressed to his ear.

"Sir, we do have a report of an incident tonight. A young man was taken to hospital at just after one O'clock this morning."

"See. Just like I told ya." Spikey said "A piece of cake."

*

The casualty ward waiting room at 4am was full of street alcoholics whose injuries had been sustained by their having fallen over simply because they were too drunk to stand. Redd was still sitting in the waiting room when Benjamin and Spikey arrived. Benjamin flashes his badge and speaks to a nurse at reception.

"Excuse me, my name is Benjamin, I'm from the police department. I understand a young man who had been involved in a fight was brought in tonight."

The nurse flips through her records.

"Yes that's right, a Mr Zapp?"

"That sounds like our man. Can we see him we need to ask him a few questions, it's very important,"

"Well you can see him," the nurse said, "but he wont be answering any questions I'm afraid. He's in a coma." The nurse shows them into an intensive care unit. Zapp lies in an oxygen tent attached to a life support machine.

"Is it that serious?"

"We think he may have suffered some brain damage. Now if

35

SHADES OF GREY

you'll excuse me..."

"You said he may have suffered brain damage?"

"We think so." The nurse said impatiently.

"When do you think.... I mean, will we be able to talk to him?"

"I don't know. He has a fifty fifty chance of pulling through, after that if he's able, he wont be strong enough to talk for a week at least. Now if that's all, I have other patients to attend to."

"Sure," Benjamin said, "you run along."

"Visiting hours are from 10 am to..."

"We'll just be a couple of minutes okay?" The nurse huffs a disgruntled groan, then leaves them in the intensive care unit. 'Damn' Benjamin thought, One step forward two steps back. A week was a long time to wait for a piece of evidence which may not be conclusive. If he wasn't able to tell them anything worthwhile it would be back to square one, only they'd have wasted a week. He was beginning to feel five pounds richer already, but it was no consolation. Benjamin turned to Spikey.

"How do you figure it?"

"There was a fight, Zapp and some other guy get beat. Zapp ends up in a coma the other guy gets a gun goes back, and bang."

"Hm.... So all we have to do is find the guy Zapp was with tonight and that's our man." Benjamin sticks his head out of the door, he calls to the busy looking nurse.

"Oh nurse." The nurse looking stressed and annoyed approaches.

"How did Mr Zapp arrive at casualty?"

"In an ambulance."

"Alone?"

"Yes Mr Benjamin, he was alone." she said irritably.

"I'm sorry to have to persevere I'm sure you're very busy. If anyone calls or makes any enquires with regard to Mr Zapp would you call me? Anyone, anyone at all."

"Have you spoken to his friend, I sure he can be of more assistance than I can."

"Friend? What friend?"

"Why don't you speak to him, I'm very busy..."

"Who? Where does he live?"

SHADES OF GREY

"Why don't you ask him..."

"What do you mean ask him?"

"Jesus! and you call yourself a detective, I mean walk up to him and ask him, what are you asking me for, I look like a mind reader to you!?"

"Wait a minute, you mean he's here?"

"What do you think I mean, he's sitting out there in the waiting room."

Benjamin and Spikey peer round to Redd sitting on a chair with his eyes closed, his legs crossed at the ankles and stretched out front, his arms are folded.

"Well I'll say this for him, he's a cool one. Let get him."

Benjamin and Spikey creep up on Redd's sleeping body like they were trying to catch a canary back in it's cage. Benjamin slaps a pair of handcuffs on him and begins reading him his rights. Redd is too drowsy to realise what is going on. Spikey radio's for backup. Within minutes a bemused Redd is arrested for murder and is taken away in a 'meat wagon'. Benjamin and Spikey look pleased with themselves. Once inside the Cortina Spikey thrusts her open palm under Benjamin's nose.

"Give me five!" Benjamin happily slaps a five pound note into it.

"Home James," Spikey jests in her best lady upper crust voice.

"Yes me lady."

Benjamin starts the car, they drive leisurely away.

"I'm so hungry I could eat a horse," Spikey said rubbing her tummy.

"I swear I don't know where you put it all, you never stop eating but even your bones are looking thinner these days."

"Oh daddy don't say that, I'm trying to put on some weight."

"Look, I know a place where we can get some rice and peas and chicken and...."

"At this time? Where?" They pull up outside an all night west Indian restaurant.

"Here, Bella's ital food restaurant. Why don't you come and get something decent to eat? Put some hair on your chest." Spikey looks at her non existent bust.

37

SHADES OF GREY

"It's not hair I'm after," she says to herself. "We can't eat dinner now, it's almost time for breakfast."

"Well we'll have some breakfast then. I feel like celebrating."

"A champagne breakfast?"

"Why not." Benjamin said. Spikey smiled,

"Thanks but I've got to go home, my mum will be waiting up for me."

"Waiting up? But it's after four in the morning!"

"I know, but she worries, you know how it is.... Oh I'm sorry I forgot, you're wife died."

"Milli? No she's not dead, she just couldn't stand for me to do this job. She said she didn't want to become a widow and have to bring the kids up by herself."

"So are you divorced now or separated or something?"

"Divorced, she found a guy she wanted, and he wanted her too but wasn't so keen on the kids. I said I wouldn't give her a divorce unless she gave me custody, we worked it out."

"Does she come by to see the kids a lot?"

"Never, she and this guy went to the states, she calls sometimes to speak to the kids, but that's about it."

Benjamin was looking pitiful, Spikey could see that talking about Milli had brought up many painful memories. They sit in silence while Benjamin drives slowly through the street like a man in a hurry to go nowhere, a man with nowhere to go.

They pull up outside Spikey's house. The lights are still on, Spikey's mother draws aside the corner of the curtain and peeps out.

"Why don't you come by for breakfast, I've told mum all about you, she's dying to meet you." Benjamin smiles appreciably at the offer.

"Thanks, but it's late, maybe some other time."

"Okay, I'll see you later," Spikey says with concern as she gets out of the car. She stands on the pavement watching as Benjamin pulls slowly away, down the street and out of sight.

38

CHAPTER 6.

Day 2. Morning.

An alarm sang out from a digital clock radio tea maker. At the same time it's frequency selector display lit up and the flat tones of a BBC presenter announced that it was seven am and time for the news.

"A twenty four year old black man was shot dead outside the Pinkies nightclub in Manor Park East London last night. This follows the killing of a black youth in Thamesmead London just eight day ago, but the police say they do not believe that the East London killing was racially motivated. Attacks on blacks an asians is said to have risen by twenty three per cent during the first six months of this year compared to the same period last year, but police today have banned an a anti racist march through the streets of East London because several right wing fascist groups were planning a counter demonstration along the same rout. A spokesman for the Anti racist attack group have protested, saying that the police should have prevented the racist from marching instead of banning a peaceful demonstration. They claim that it shows where the true sympathies of the police lie. The police have declined to comment. A spokesman for the National front said they would not cancel their demonstration just because of the ban, and expected a turnout of around two thousand people.

The government has warned all residence in the Thames area not to drink their tap water as it has been contaminated by a chemical leak. No further details of the leak are available at this point but, John Durban minister for the environment said it was purely a precautionary measure and that there was no need to be alarmed...."

Guss turns off the radio. He rolls over stretching his arm out across Wilma to the other side of the bed, and switches on a twelve inch portable colour television. A voice very much like the

39

SHADES OF GREY

one from the radio continued the report of the water contamination. Guss sat on the side of the bed, yawned and then stretched himself to his feet. He wore a pair of heavy cotton pyjamas with thick blue and white strips. He shuffled his feet into a pair of house slippers and walked out into the bathroom. While pasting his toothbrush he turns on the shower tap. To his surprise the water spurts out a dirty greenish tinge. He calls to Wilma,

"Wilma you see how dee water a come out of dee shower?"

"No, wha' happen?" She enters the bathroom. "Oh! Is dat dey talking 'bout on television?"

"But I want to tek a shower!" He complains.

"Well dem say is alright to wash, but don't drink it, jus' to be on dee safe side."

"But it's green! I cyan't shower in dat, it go bring me out in a rash."

"Well leave it let it run a while." She said calmly on her way out. Guss left the shower to run and went to get the mail. As he came down the stairs he could see his son Toby out cold in the hall way in a mass of dried Vomit. Guss pulls Toby up onto his feet.

"Get up! Get up! Stand up straight you damn stupid junky!" He bawled slapping Toby's face. Wilma appears in her dressing gown at the top of the stairs.

"Guss! Guss don't hit him!"

"Look at how dee bwoy ah just ah chrow up on dee cyarpet like 'im is a sick dog or someting!" Guss exclaimed incredulously. Toby leans up face against the wall, and though he is barely conscious he clenches the strap of the black bag tightly in his hands. Guss takes a hold of Toby by the scruff of the neck.

"I go beat you make you eat back dee sick yer nasty wretch you!" He rages. Guss again slaps Toby around the face. Toby throws up all over his father. Guss explode's into a dialogue of abuse and obscenity as he reaches for a heavy leather belt. He folds it in two and begins lashing Toby wildly. Toby crashes down on all fours under the beating. Too weak to move, licks were falling like rain and he is taking blows from all directions.

SHADES OF GREY

Wilma comes hurriedly from the kitchen with a bucket of hot soap disinfectant water. She wrestles to hold Guss back. Guss has lost control, he pulls Toby up from the floor and repeatedly strikes him about the face with his open palm. Toby's face quickly become swollen and bloody Wilma is bawling at Guss.

"Stop it Guss! Guss! You'll kill him! Oh God! Guss! Guss!"

Guss stops suddenly and lets Toby's body slide limply down the wall to the floor. Wilma stoops down to tend to him. Toby is delirious, he backs away from Wilma in terror. He does not recognise her as his mother, he does not see the tears run down her cheeks from the pools that have welled up in her eyes. He sees instead the blooded eyeballs of a snaky haired Medusa, her forked tongue licking the saliva devilishly from her decaying fangs. His father appears a satanic ghoul, howling a flesh crawling cry from hell, as if craving a taste of live meat. He screams. Now suddenly all is black, he is unconscious. His eyeballs dance wildly in their sockets, as he foams at the mouth. Wilma bawls hysterically.

"Don't you see is sick he sick? How you could beat dee bwoy when 'im sick!?"

"He deserve what he gets." Guss bawls back, "Is he 'imself mek 'imself sick, den he come here and chrow up on me cyarpet. He lucky I don't kill 'im!" he said un-repentant. "Now clean up dis mess before I really lose me temper."

Wilma weeps as she hugs Toby's head in her lap, gently rocking back and forth.

"Is because he went out and took a drink without he had anyting in he stomach, look, he ain't bring up notting solid, is like a baby sick, look. He probably ain't have notting solid to eat since I don't know when. You used to do dat youself. I had to get up all chree and four o'clock in the morning to clean you up, I never once lash you wid belt."

"Is drugs I tell you! I never used to tek drugs! the bwoy's a bloody junky!" Guss marches up the stairs spitting his anger. "I'll chrow 'im out! I'll chrow 'im out on dee streets you tink is joke!? And if you give me any shit I'll chrow you out too!"

Wilma struggles to drag Toby into the front room. She lays him out on the settee. Toby begins having wild violent spasmodic

SHADES OF GREY

fits. Wilma tries to hold him down but is thrown to the floor by a powerful convulsion. Her panic takes her to the kitchen, she returns with basin of cold water and a cloth, she wipes his face. The coolness seems to calms him, soon he is still and breathing normally as if asleep. Wilma runs up stairs to the bathroom where her husband stands half dressed, shaving with an electric razor.

"Guss, dee bwoy sick, we have to tek 'im to a hospital!"

"I don't know 'bout you but I going to work, you wan' tek 'im to hospital call a taxi."

Wilma turns away in disgust, goes to the phone and dials 999.

"Mind dey don't lock 'im up. is against dee law you know."

"Hello... An ambulance... 63 Chesterton terrace plaistow... please hurry.... Is Evans, Toby Evans."

Wilma put down the receiver then ran back down the stairs to her son. She pushed open the door to the front room hoping to find Toby if not better, at least as well as she'd left him. But he was gone.

"Guss! Guss!" She called. "He's gone. Toby's gone."

Guss walked slowly to the top of the staircase and looked down.

"He smart dat's why. 'im jus play up for attention dats all, you fall for it every time. He hear you dialling 999 of course 'im tek off. 'im smart."

CHAPTER 7.

Day 2. Evening.

The metronomic drip from a punctured water main, echoed about the brick walls of an old garages desolate interior. It accumulates to form an oil slicked pool in the craters of the fragmented concrete floor. Six black guys form a circle about twenty feet in diameter, each stood as noble and upright as any knight of the round table. Their shoulders were draped in cloaks of black and each was crowned with a black berry.

Toby was slumped in a corner his mind near delirium looking like shit warmed up.

Toby, Isac, Lennox, Calvin, flick, Digger and Danny were the seven Posse members, who believed themselves to be disciples of the black Panther movement of seventies America. Each in turn had declared allegiance to the 'cause' in a ritualistic ceremony. Danny, was the leader and the oldest of the seven, although only twenty five he looked forty. His eyes were eagle like, piercing and bloodshot. He wore a thick moustache sandwiched between his large nose and a fat top lip. His hair was already going grey at the sides and he was slightly balding at the crown. He had a wearily unhealthy look about him, indicative of alcohol and drug abuse. He calls to the other six.

"The system! We've got to smash this system, or we ain't going nowhere. We've been fucked about by the white man so much most of us don't know who we are. Brain washed into believing that white is good and black is bad. They've made us hate ourselves and turn against each other so that now, we're not just fighting the white establishment, we're having to fight the Black aspirators as well. The Tom niggers who bought the white mans hype and believe that 'white is right' and that we must 'work within the system'. We are imprisoned in a system that is structured to preserve race and class barriers, working within it we only strengthen it and condone the sins it enforces. The system that enslaves us cannot liberate us, it must be smashed

SHADES OF GREY

and restructured along with all those who work to uphold it. White, Tom nigger, women, children, don't matter who they are, your mother, your father, your sister or your brother. We've got to smash the system!" They all cheer.

"What's going on out there huh? What's going on out there!?"

"It's a lie!" They all call out.

"Testify! brothers testify!"

"Today I had to re-address a situation!" Isac bawled out.

"Tell us about it bro," Digger bantered.

"I was standing by the door on the central line tube right, minding my own business right. Just reading some of the racist slogans from those fascist stickers you find on the windows, you know, the usual thing. Now the door opened at Holborn, this white fucker gets up from his seat and walks right across my foot without saying a word! He didn't even turn back and say sorry I mash your toe you black bastard, he just walks on like he didn't give a shit!"

"So how did you re-address the balance bro?" asked Lennox.

"I addressed the situation using my Isac Newton approach, every action deserves an equal an opposite reaction. I got off the train and I kicked his ass!" They all laugh.

"Very diplomatic brother," Digger commended, "well done."

"I did see a fit looking sister," Calvin enthused, "sucking up to this ugly, nasty looking white pig like 'im was a mink coat. Bwoy! I did feel sick man, sick." he added disgustedly.

"How did you re-address the balance bro?" Lennox asked.

"I ain't do it yet, but tonight I'm gonna find myself a serious piece of pork, take her home and wreck her poom poom bwoy!" They laugh again.

"Okay, but make sure she's kicking man, don't hog no dog you here?"

Flick, a slender faced pretty boy of eighteen leaped to his feet. His dark complexion and high cheek bones framed large brown deep set eyes. He wore a pencil thin moustache low on his upper lip and a growth at the point of his chin. His hair was cut low but for a beebop at the front. He wore on one side a set of head phones through which public enemy was pumping loudly from a walkman through his head.

SHADES OF GREY

"This pale face fucker was out to make himself a hero, I swear! I run in, the place was almost empty. I shout everybody on the floor face down! Everybody gets down on the floor no problem, you know what I mean? Sweet. Right, now I see this old guy yeah? I mean old, must have been about ready to retire. I points the gun in his face and I shout, open the safe! He was so scared man! Anyway he opens it no problem. The money was there waiting, the whole thing's a piece of cake. Then this little guy.... how I hate little guys! This little guy sets off the alarm innit! I sticks the gun right up his nose and I says give me the jewels you bastard or I'll blow your head off. You know the punk just laughed in my face like 'e knew these guns were from the kiddies store, I swear if I'd a had a real gun... I'd a shot the fuckers head off for true man, I swear."

"Why you so full a shit man?" Lennox said and everybody laughed as Flick protested,

"It's true, it's true!" Suddenly Toby screams out.

"I lost my job today!" The laughter subsided. "The foreman man, he had been giving me shit for a long time man, always on my back, for nothing, and I was the scapegoat for everything. Finally I couldn't take it no more, I couldn't. This guy was out to get me man, I know it."

Toby rocked from side to side, his eyes reddened from the painful memory of the persecution he had suffered.

"In situations like that you gotta hit first, ain't no good hitting back, you already out of the game."

Toby's body tensed visibly, anguish turned the clenched fist of his right hand in the palm of his open left as he re-lived the words he spoke.

"I was late right. But it was the first time in a month. I'd been getting in early every day 'cause I know he just was waiting for an excuse to get me. I knew that. I could feel it. Now dem white guys does come in late all the time, they're always late! But the foreman, he ain't saying nothing to 'em right. Now this morning I couldn't help it, the train was late, I knew I was gonna be late and that fucker would be waiting. As soon as I reach through the door he looks at me, I didn't look at him but I could feel him looking at me. Then I heard his footsteps coming, getting closer,

SHADES OF GREY

getting louder and louder. The fucker was coming to fuck with me! He was coming to fuck with me!! So I fucked with him first!!!"

Toby jumps to his feet in a chaotic frenzy, beating the air with his fist and bawling at the top of his voice.

"I hit him! And I hit him! And I hit him! And I told him don't fuck with me! Don't fuck with me!!!"

The other members of the Posse are stunned to silence. They watch and listen in bemusement at his deranged rambling.

"I shoot people you know! For less than that, so don't fuck!... Smash it yeah! Fucked and brain washed man! White's and, Tom nigger and women, and mother, and father and.... and... "

Toby stands motionless as if entranced, he is pouring a sweat, he does not breath, his eyes seemed to protrude their sockets like the humps of two boiled eggs in their cups, an eruption simmers at the pit of his stomach, his heart thunders against his chest. Calvin rested his hand lightly on Toby's shoulders.

"Chill out man, don't let the pressure take you down." Toby seemed to respond to Calvin's reassurance almost instantly, he sits down and is calm, but solemn and withdrawn. Danny steps forward.

"Look man. You need to pull yourself together. This isn't good for you, or the Posse... We feel that it might be best if you resigned."

"Resigned? I founded the Posse man! I am the Posse! If anyone should resign it's you, self appointed leader. Your wet man, with your semi detached house, wife and two kids. You should join the Tory party. And as for you Lennox, you right on and liberal collage graduate forget it! We need fighters man not fucking book worms. Dennis, you're a asshole...."

"We were expecting this sort of outburst," Lennox cut in, "we've already discussed it Toby, and our decision is final. You're out."

Toby is shattered. Calvin exchanges a look with several of the guys as they walk to the other end of the garage, then Calvin too begins a slow retreat leaving Toby alone with himself.

CHAPTER 8.

Jess had had a rough time at work, it was one of those days when her mind wasn't on the job. Typing errors were two a penny which meant she was typing the same documents twice or maybe three times over. She had been in one hell of an irritable mood so now all she wanted was to lie down.

She stepped wearily up the flight of stairs towards her flat on the third floor, she was feeling depressed and the nearer she got to the flat the more her depression grew. As she reached the second floor she could hear that the couple who had just moved in the flat below hers were having a blazing row. She hoped it wouldn't be loud enough to penetrate her floor boards but she suspected it would. She crawled up another flight. She leant against the railing directly outside her front door, too tired to walk another step, she had to rest. She felt as if she'd climbed a mountain. Turning the key in the lock, she was hoping and praying that Ziggy would not be there. In fact she wished he'd put his head in the gas oven or jumped out of the window, that would save her the trouble of killing him that evening, for she was sure that it would come to that if she saw him. Luckily Ziggy was out. She felt a headache coming on, and her backache had begun to bite again. She was right about being able to hear the rowing couple below, it was loud and clear. She rubbed the small of her back as she bent over backwards. She grimaced and ironic blend of relief and agony. She'd heard that the best thing for a bad back was to lie on the floor. She looked down at the lino. It was cracked, discoloured and in several places worn to the black. From her occasional midnight trip to the bathroom she knew it to be the thoroughfare of many a bug, cockroach, louse and mouse.

She picked a half filled coffee cup up from the sideboard, it felt warm, obviously Ziggy had not long been gone. She tipped it's tepid remains down her throat. She then craned her neck round till she was looking over at the bed. It was broken down

SHADES OF GREY

and un-made but it called as sweetly to her as would the cool beer to the thirsty alcoholic. She limped over and fell on it. Eyes shut, she exhaled long and slow. It felt good. It was lumpy soft and soggy. It's springs had long since yielded under the strain of use and abuse over the years. Sharp ends now protruded the surface with avengeance to stab the weary flesh of anyone unfortunate enough to need this contorted infestation claiming to be a mattress. Jess knew all the strategic points where a limb could rests it's weight and feel relatively safe, and her body instinctively assumed a posture which respected the minefield like hazards she endured on her nightly trip to slumber. Occasionally a freshly fractured coil would ping up and pierce her skin with a zinging. She'd lived with that mattress for almost as long as she'd lived with Ziggy, it was probably the cause of her complaint, in part at least. But it spite of everything, right now, it felt good.

The row from below now seemed to have crescendoed to a new ferocity, plates crashing peppered the air with sound waves, as did their screaming swearing and shouting. Then strangely a quiet period. Now the war from below which had till now cluttered the audio spectrum subsided completely, leaving space for a bird high up in a tree to tweet, a radio from the flat adjacent to sing, and a car engine from the street below to roar like an angry lion.

As well as Ziggy and herself, the flat accommodated a dirty thread bare settee and a cheap coffee table, whose veneered finish had long deserted it, leaving exposed an unsightly chipboard surface. The chipboard itself had acquired a multitude of egg, grease, coffee and beer stains, as well as having been used as an ashtray to boot. Eating from the rancid coffee table was an exceedingly unpleasant experience, but it was the only table they had.

She opened her eyes, the ceiling hung like vast polystyrene cloud. Jess hated polystyrene, just a she hated the wood chip paper painted with a dirty pink gloss that covered the walls of the studio flat. She laughed as he recalled the wording of the advertisement and subsequent conversation with the estate agent. It read; A FULLY FURNISHED LUXURY STUDIO FLAT.

"Studio flat!?" Ziggy exclaimed.

SHADES OF GREY

"Eh, yes sir. So called because of it's open plan design". The estate agent said straight faced and without embarrassment.

"Open plan!?"

"Yes sir, we require two references plus a months deposit." Ziggy laughed.

"Fully furnished!?"

"As you can see," the estate agent replied nonchalantly.

In truth it was just one room with the same broken down bed, an ancient gas cooker, a sink, an infested settee and the coffee table.

"Listen 'ere mate." Ziggy said. "A pig wouldn't puke in this hole, a dog wouldn't dodo in this dump, and a cat wouldn't piss in this shit house so up yours fuck face."

Jess's face could not help but crack a wide smile. If it wasn't exactly poetry it had a certain poetic justice about it, anyway it was music to her ears. She remembered thinking that only William Shakespear might have said it better. Ziggy strutted about articulating a few more choice obscenities, then swaggered arrogantly out into the street like a vintage John Wayne having shot the sheriff. But two days later they were eating crow. Jess had to go back and apologise for Ziggy's uncouth behaviour. She was more or less begging for the flea pit. They'd found out just how expensive accommodation was.

Jess raised her head slowly from the pillow just high enough to see two 5 litre can of white vinyl silk emulsion over by the designated kitchen area. Ziggy had promised to paint the place a hundred times if he'd promised once. She gave them a 'so you're still here' look before a twinge of pain told her to lie down again.

Just as she was beginning to settle the phone rang, her outstretched arm lazily lifted the receiver. It was Roslin, she'd rung to hear the latest gossip and complain about her husband.

Within a month of her wedding to Ziggy four of Jess's friend were also married. She couldn't believe it, like a flock of sheep. Now they were married they'd put a stop to their husband going out without them. Their husbands had in turn put a stop to their going out also, and so there it was, a total curfew and the end of girls night out. All they had now were gossipy telephone calls. On hearing that Jess was not too forthcoming with anything

49

SHADES OF GREY

interesting Roslin decided to ring one of the other girls, though she didn't say so in so many words.

"We should get together soon, why don't you and Ziggy stop by for dinner one evening?"

"We will," Jess replied limply.

"See you soon, bye," She hung up. Her voice was replaced by the B.T. buzz. Jess wondered why they called the thing a dialling tone. Tone had always suggested something musical to her, a buzz was just a buzz. 'Dialling buzz?' perhaps not she thought.

She glances over at the cans of paint, then rolls over on her side facing the window. She closed her eyes and was just beginning to doze when came a knock to the door. Jess rolled onto her back where she paused a few seconds, she then raised her head without disturbing her shoulders which were both still squarely at rest. A knock at the door meant that Jess had to get up. Maybe she would have anyway. Maybe she should get up, open a can and start painting those walls- or maybe she should roll over and go to sleep. She allowed her head to fall back to the pillow. If it were a salesman or a jehovah's witness they'd go after two polite knocks and a wait. The second knock came, it bordered on the firm to accretive. The third, suspiciously loud and urgent prompted Jess to quickly re-access her list of possible callers. The forth a resounding pounding made Jess leap up, her concern for any ailment she might be suffering from was replaced with a slight worry.

"Who is it?"

"Open the rass clart door before I kick it down." It was Ziggy and he sounded drunk. Jess opened the door. He pushed passed her and staggered into the room. He swayed unsteadily on the spot with a whiskey bottle in one hand and a cigarette in the other.

"I thought you were on late shift this week?" Jess said.

"Don't ask me no question. Why do you want to know that, so you know what time to bring your man up here? Where is he? He coming or he gone?"

Jess tried to go by him but he helds her firm, he takes a swing from the bottle and breaths the stench of liqueur over her

SHADES OF GREY

as he speaks.

"You better tell him not to come again because I ain't working nights anymore. In fact I ain't working at all."

"You've lost your job again." she said.

"How you know I lost it? How you know dem racist fuckers ain't take it from me unfairly huh? You always so quick to condemn me in favour of these white fuckers."

Ziggy grabs Jess by her hair, his cigarette begins to singe it. Jess is in pain.

"You're burning my hair!" she cries.

He takes another swing from the whiskey bottle.

"How you know dem white fuckers ain't plant gunja in my locker, so they could have an excuse to sack me eh?" Ziggy is pulling and pushing Jess by her hair, Jess is in tears.

"Ziggy you're hurting me! You're burning my hair!"

"You love dem white fuckers innit?!"

Jess takes hold of Ziggy's wrist and sinks her teeth into his hand. He screams out in pain. He lets her go.

"You bitch!"

"You were hurting me!" Ziggy slaps her to the ground. He hovers menacingly over her for a moment cussing and sucking whisky noisily from the bottle. Jess was expecting him to kick or stamp on her, but instead he turns away and leaves. As soon as he was gone Jess picked herself from the floor and began packing her things. She was leaving Ziggy, but this time she swore she wasn't coming back. It was home to mother and a shoulder to cry on. Tea and sympathy, and someone to fuss over her. After all that's what mothers were for wasn't it?

*

As it turned out mother was anything but sympathetic which surprised Jess as Ziggy had never been her idea of an ideal son in law. But it seemed now they were married mum felt her daughter had an obligation to make it work. Divorce was taboo.

"Bored? What you mean you bored? Jessica, a man that too exciting will not stay around," mama preached in a kind of posh West Indian accent. She wanted so much to sound like her majesty it seemed, but every now and then some broad 'back a yard J.A.' would creep in.

51

SHADES OF GREY

"He will always have girls chasing him, and men are weak, they can't deal wid dat," she stressed. "You young girls are all dee same, always want what you can't get, and when you get it, you don't want it."

"What are you talking about!?" Jess said defiantly.

"You know what I talking 'bout. You chase an exciting man, when you catch him, you try change him! Dat make sense to you!? Why you don't just take an ordinary man and be satisfied?"

Basically aim low and you wont be disappointed was the message, and so it went on... and on.... and on. Finally Jess decided that she couldn't take any more of her mothers rambling. Nobody could live with her mother once she'd got going, least of all her father. He had always been a weak man as far as his wife was concerned. When she spoke he shut up, it had always been that way, as far back as Jess could remember, mother had always been in charge. Father had let her down on several occasions, the first time she remembered was when she was just eight. The whole of her class were going on a school trip. Dad had given her the fare. She was all packed and ready for the road, but then mum had said she couldn't go, all because she had torn her dress while climbing over the park fence with the boys, instead of using the gate as she'd been told to do on several occasions. She remembered vividly the moment her father took the money back with a pathetic apology. From that day her standing with her school friends had diminished beyond recovery. That's what mum and dad wouldn't have understood, it wasn't just about going on a school trip, it was about being there with your chums, or not being there. She wasn't there. So now she was an outcast. It was to affect the rest of her junior school life. A similar incident occurred when she was thirteen, mum had forbidden her to go to the youth club dance. Jess had appealed to her father but again he submitted to his wife without a fight. So it was her secondary school life was similarly affected, she just couldn't bounce back, and was to instead retreat into a shell she had been unable to shed until she left school and went to college. Those she saw as the two most crucial points of her life. Up until now her father had let her down both times, but if he

SHADES OF GREY

were ever looking for an opportunity to redeem himself in his daughters eyes this was it. Jess looked to dad for some kind of support during the torrid heat of a verbal onslaught from mum. It was a vicious and relentless pounding, a miss match on a par with Godzilla meet Mickey mouse or sledge hammer versus an oily dollop of putty. Fathers little girl was being orally bludgeoned mercilessly to submission. Surly no loving father with any backbone or even a single fibre of paternal concern could bare to sit by while his daughter suffered so. He would spring to her defence wouldn't he? That's what fathers were supposed to do wasn't it? Not this one, he buried his head in a news paper in order to avert the gaze of both wife and daughter. Now it seemed he was even afraid of Jess. She took her bag and walked out of her parents house.

CHAPTER 9.

Jess found herself in a pub off the Upton lane. Inside everything about it was old. Leaded stain glass windows, huge gothic stone archways and pillars, intricate hard wood carvings and dim lighting. It was like the inside of a church with a huge bar. Distorted jazz emanated from a broken down hi fi. Jess sat at a table with a glass of white wine and a pint of lager. The wine she sipped, the lager stood as if waiting to be drunk by some burly male she waited for. There was no one of course, but guys thought twice about sitting at her table in case a sixteen stone wrestler were to come in and throw them off his seat. It did mean of course that as it got later she might have to do a little 'oh where is he' acting, it was also a waste of a pint, unless you were a lager drinker. Jess wasn't. But she had decided that she would drink it anyway, such was her depression. 'If you're going to drown you're sorrows what does it matter what you do it with' she thought.

She'd noticed Toby the moment he walked in the pub. It wasn't long after that he'd noticed her. Their eyes even met for a

53

SHADES OF GREY

moment across a crowded smoke filled room, just like in the movies. Toby paused at the door, he looked around as if for someone in particular, then went to the bar. He ordered a port and brandy, sunk it it one, then ordered another. Jess's table was directly behind him. She watched as he threw his head back and then slammed the glass down on the counter. Where had he been all her life she thought. As if to answer her he turned and looked directly into her face. He paused a while, his eyes went to her glass of wine, the pint of lager then back to her. He picked up his glass from the counter and walked over.

"Mind if I join you?" he said as if he didn't care whether she'd say yes or no. 'What about the lager ploy' she thought. He either didn't care whether she was meeting someone or he'd seen it all before, either way it was okay with her, she liked his couldn't give a damn attitude. She shrugged her shoulders, as if to say he could if he wanted but she really didn't give a damn either. Toby sat down, he was looking rougher than Humphry Bogart with a hang over.

"What's your name?" he asked her bluntly as he lit a cigarette.

"Jess," she said flatly trying to match his cool. He offered her a cigarette which she took, she pushed it sensually between her lips, he flicked a flame from an expensive looking lighter igniting first his then hers. She took in a huge draw exhaling a long thin dense cloud of smoke. It was her first cigarette in almost nine months. As soon as her body had tasted the nicotine she realised how much she'd missed and needed that cigarette. From her deep smoke screened sigh, Toby could tell that this was a woman with something on her mind, but so what, he had things to think about too. Still, she did looked interesting.

"What you doing tonight?" he asked directly. 'Wow' she though, 'he doesn't hang about. Straight to the point no messing.' She liked that, she wanted to say 'anything you're doing' but that wasn't the way she was playing it.

"Why?" she said.

"We can hang out together if you want," he said.

"Where?"

"I know places," he said cooly. 'I bet you do' she thought.

54

SHADES OF GREY

"Okay," she said.

Toby, his face baring the faintest of smiles, gave Jess a slight nod of his head. Jess wanted to ask Toby where he'd gotten his jacket from, she wanted to ask where he'd bought his shoes too but thought it sounded too corny. Toby didn't seem bothered about making conversation, she wanted him to, badly. Jess thought briefly about what her mother had said about wanting what she couldn't have but then shut it out. Toby got up and sank the remainder of his drink.

"I just have to make a phone call then we're out of this place okay?" Jess smiled in agreement.

Toby asked the barman for the phone. The barman told him that their's was out of order but he could make a call in a phone box around the corner. Toby showed Jess his open palm which indicated he'd be five minutes, he then left the bar. Jess wanted to go with him but again she was playing it cool.

Five minutes later Jess hadn't moved, she was still sitting in the same chair, watching a diminishing number of bubbles rise through the lager to the top of the glass and dispel into the atmosphere. Ten minutes later she had taken to clock watching, literally counting the seconds with the second hand, and the minutes with the minute hand of a antique looking clock that hung over the bar. Fifteen minutes later she was anxiously looking out through the window for any sign of Toby. There was none. Fully thirty minutes later she had drunk the lager and was on her way to the phone box. She hoped to find him there, and if she did she would want to give him a piece of her mind for keeping her waiting. But again she would bite her lip and play it cool, as if she had been just passing and really didn't care that he'd not come back after five minutes as he'd said. Though she knew that if she really didn't care she would have gone home after five minutes and not given Toby a second thought.

*

Toby picked up the receiver in the call box and dialled a number from memory.

"Conrad? Hi man, it's Toby. Hey look I need some stuff..... whatever you got man, but listen, I need it now Yeah?... I'm by the Mac on the one way system..... Okay I'll wait here for ya."

55

SHADES OF GREY

Conrad lay on the sofa sipping a can of beer in front of the television. A black leather cap sat over his dirty looking tightly natted hair. He wore tee-shirt, a pair of baseball trousers and a pair of house slippers. His fair skin and small slitty eyes gave rise to speculation of his being in part of oriental extraction, and had led to him being referred to as 'chinky'- but only behind his back. A large nose and thick lips however left no doubt that he was predominantly of negro blood. The skin about his eyes and forehead wore an oily shine while his beard was patchy and untidy. He was a big man. Muscular but fat too, due to a life style that combined gym workouts and junk food. Depending on his mood you'd either find him in the gym pumping iron, a hamburger joint stuffing his face or in a betting shop losing his money. Workouts and food were a drug for him, as was any form of gambling.

He was pissed off with himself. He had just lost all his cash. Three hundred and twenty eight pounds. He had been on a losing streak right from the start but decided to stay with it. Bad news. Bad luck had been with him all day, but instead of running from it he had embraced it as a friend, like a fool.

"Days like this, the best thing you can do stay in bed," he told himself. He'd told himself that before, but it made no difference, this time had been the same as the last time, and would probably be the same as the next.

With the benefit of hindsight he was a wiser man, he cursed and lectured himself for being so stupid, but that's what money did to Conrad, made him stupid. Today was a loss, he'd sell Toby some E and maybe make a hundred but he would still be down two. But what the hell.

*

Toby was thinking about what had happened to him earlier. His mother and father and appeared like two monsters from a Simbad movie. If he'd have had a knife or something he might have killed one of them, or both of them. But there he was ready to take the same shit again. But it was just a bad trip, he told himself, a one off. Truth was he needed a fix, and when he was in need he had a way of justifying his habit to himself,

SHADES OF GREY

regardless.

Toby walked up and down the street, window shopping for what seemed like an hour, in fact it had only been a matter of minutes. All he thought of was shooting up, Jess was far from his thoughts. Twice a police car had stopped to check him out. The two incidents were so similar it was almost comical. Each time the two policemen had got out from their pander car and approached him with;

"What's your name? Where do you live, and don't say up a tree. What are you doing here nigger?" Then it was, "Turn out your pockets sunshine." They would then look for something they could call an offensive weapon. But Toby was clean.

"You got any identification?" Toby had his driving licence. He let them see it both times. Both times they radioed through his details and a police description of him and waited for an excuse to nick him, both times they were unlucky. Both time they left looking disappointed that Toby hadn't risen to the bait. The condescending way they spoke to him and the racial taunts hadn't made him retaliate with some verbal of his own, thereby committing that crime of 'abusing a police officer.' That was worth one night in a stinking cell at least, sometimes with a free beating thrown in, and if you were really lucky you'd get an appearance in court and a fine! It may not even stop there, if they manage to trump up the charge significantly.... who knows. The second pair had resorted to some old familiar lines Toby now knew by heart.

"We had to come and get a closer look because in the dark you fitted the description of a suspect."

"I understand officer, we all look alike in the dark don't we." Toby said sarcastically. The policeman smiled knowingly. That had told them that Toby was not the hot headed sensitive type who could easily be goaded into trouble. 'But that was okay,' the cop thought, 'your day will come.'

Two minutes later and the un-dipped headlight from Conrad's black BMW flooded the shop windows casting Toby's shadow to the wall like an emblem for a Batman movie.

"Dim your lights man! What you tink this is, an evening kick off at Upton Park?"

"Chill out bro', everyting cool." Conrad grinned.

SHADES OF GREY

"Cool? The whole place is swarming wid babylon man. Dem already check me twice!"

"Yeah!? Tyoops! Dem rass clart babylon ain' 'ave nottin better fi do? Char!- Is alright, me no deal here anyway. Hop in sah, take a ride to paradise."

"Just take me to the squat man, I'm beat." Toby said. Conrad agreed.

For a while they drove in silence. Toby kept an eye out for police cars, Conrad seemed unconcerned.

"Hey where you get your stuff man?" Toby asked.

"Why, wha' wrong wid it?" Conrad said defensively.

"I don't know, it feels funny man. The shit knock me out last night."

"It's good shit dat's why. Strong. probably dee stuff you used to bin cut wid crap, mek it weak. But this is pure, you na see it?"

"Okay," Toby said as he was getting out of the car. "take it easy bro"

With the stuff safely in his pocket, he disappeared round the back of the squat.

*

By the time Jess got to the phone box Toby and Conrad had gone. She was half drunk, fed up and pissed off. If she had seen Toby then, she would have given him a tongue lashing worthy of her mother and to hell with being cool.

Jess kicked the paving of the Romford road, she then took a moment to settle her temper. She looked east down towards Green street and thought about going back to her parents, then she turned west towards town and thought about going back home, pretend as if nothing had happened as she'd done before. At least it was a place to stay. She turned west again then back east. East or west she asked herself, which way shall I go. The high road or the low road? Suddenly an idea came to her. She'd take neither. She hailed a taxi and went north up the 'grange' heading for Wanstead.

*

After dropping Toby off Conrad got back in his car and drove up through Dalston, past Islington to Kings cross and a flat on the King cross estate where Sonny, his little boy lived with his

SHADES OF GREY

mother. Conrad had four children, three boys and a girl each by a different woman. He was proud that he, a single man had 'bred' four women. It made him feel like a super stud.

Conrad ran up the stairs to the fifth floor flat. He did not consider calling the lift for although the stairs were littered, dirty, dark and stank of urine, he knew that the elevator was likely to be worse. He rang the bell of number 25. He could hear Sonny crying inside as he waited for the door to be answered. Sonny's mother Marie appeared. She was a tall strong dark skinned fit looking woman with long eyes, high cheekbones and full lips. She walked with the stylish elegance of a catwalk model.

"What's he crying for?" Conrad demanded at the same time taking in the classy air that emanated from Marie.

"Nothing," Marie replied reluctantly, turning away and walking back to the kitchen. She pushed to one side the wooden beaded curtain at the kitchen entrance. Conrad followed her. The kitchen was tiny, just enough room for a sink, cooker and a single wall unit. The plaster on the walls and ceiling was cracked and flaking but numerous plants, pictures, charms and ornaments gave the kitchen an organic feel. Marie was mixing some custard powder.

"What do you mean nothing. What the matter Sonny?" The healthy looking two year old toddler stopped crying, slowly looking alternately from his mother to his father in silence.

"What's the matter a?" Conrad repeated his arms outstretched inviting Sonny to come to him. Sonny looked confused. Marie looked on amused.

"He doesn't know who you are," she smirked.

"Come to daddy" Conrad coaxed "Come on, come to daddy."

Finally, Sonny walks to Conrad who picks him up.

"Have you fed this child yet?" Marie looks at Conrad with daggers in her eyes. She flies off in a rage.

"Look you come to see this child whenever you feel like, which isn't very often. You don't even bring him a sweet much less some money to help support him. Left to you the child would starve to death! Every stitch of clothing on his back I bought for him with no help from you, so don't come here demanding to know if and when I feed my son!"

Sonny starts to cry. Marie takes him from Conrad and

SHADES OF GREY

comforts him.

"It's alright Sonny, it's alright". She wipes his tears and cleans his nose with a tissue, kisses him lovingly on the cheek and hugs him. Sonny collapses into her bosom and caress her face with his little hand. Mother and baby at one. During all this Conrad stands by feeling quite redundant and useless.

"I was gonna bring some money for him but the big end went on my car. In fact I was gonna ask you if you could lend me a few quid."

At that Marie shoots Conrad a dirty look. Conrad wanders off into the living room, tail between his legs. The living room walls were painted a matt cream to which various pictures of black celebrities mostly un-familiar to Conrad hung. A bookcase full of books was decorated with African and West indian ornaments and craft work. The furniture, a settee, a wooden dinner table with four chairs and a leather foot rest complimented each other favourably. A colour television and stereo completed the set up. The whole flat was immaculately clean. Conrad searched for money about the books in the bookshelf.

"I've gotta hand it to you Marie," he called out, "the place looks nice, better than mine any day."

"You've got yourself a place now then?" she inquired from the kitchen. Conrad looks in a large vase, then inside an open envelope.

"No." he countered quickly.

"I'm still at a friend."

"Where?" She continued. He checks behind the clock on the mantle finding sixty pounds. He tucks the money in his back pocket.

"Oh, here and there." He answered secretively. Marie smiled to herself. It amused her that Conrad thought himself to be in such demand, that he felt it necessary to keep his address a secret. Conrad walks into the kitchen. Marie is stirring the custard, Sonny is now asleep on his mothers shoulder.

"I'm gonna shoot off now, things to do."

"Okay." She replies simply and unconcerned.

"I'll pass by next week yeah?" But Marie did not answer, she was now totally preoccupied with Sonny.

Conrad skipped down the stairs to his waiting BMW. A moment later he was gone.

*

Toby bopped and jerked while miming to a cassette recording of Bel Biv Devoe's 'Poison'. He was as high as a mid day sun and feeling just as hot. Earlier he had banged himself in the arm with a 'Speedball' of whatever it was he'd got from Conrad. A flame charred spoon and a hypodermic needle sat idly on the kitchen stove still burning. Toby dressed himself in his black posse outfit. He zipped up the black kit bag and slung it over his shoulder. In the broadway there was a pool hall the guys had been raving about, tonight he would check it out.

CHAPTER 10.

Dexter sat at the computer in his study, an upstairs room of his two bedroom flat. Jacket sashed over the chair back, his black tie hung loosely from the open neck of his white shirt, his sleeves rolled up to his elbows. It was the classic man at work look. Smoke from a smouldering cigarette butt discarded to a white porcelain ash tray floated up slowly towards a shadeless light bulb, forming a stagnant cloud above his head. A cold half cup of black coffee stood neglected as he studied the illuminated computer screen. His concentration was broken by a faint knock to the downstairs street door. Dexter walked to the door intercom, pressed the talk button and enquired as to who was calling. It was Jess. 'Jess?' he thought, 'wow!' Of course he wasn't expecting her. His first thoughts were that something was wrong. He pressed the button to let her in and told her to come up. He could hear the feminised clatter of high heel on steps that would bring Jess to him in a matter of seconds. What was she doing here? Where was Ziggy? Maybe they'd had a fight about something and she'd come to him. The short staircase and her quick pace allowed him only a few moments for conjecture, before her exuberant face was at his. She threw her arms

SHADES OF GREY

rapturously around his neck and kissed him deep and hard. He could taste that she'd been drinking. Was that why she was here? Should he be responsible and not take advantage? She was his brothers wife he reminded himself. But she felt good, damn good. After a few seconds Dexter was able to break off the kiss just long enough to ask if anything was wrong. But Jess resumed her passionate embrace without bothering to answer. Common sense and her high spirited behaviour told him that there couldn't be too much to worry about, at least Jess didn't seem to think so. He allowed himself a little lustrous indulgence before curiosity begged him to break away and ask his question again, this he did a little more firmly. She simply smiled at him.

"I just wanted to see you," was all she said. Then with all the provocative gusto of a night club stripper she leant back against the wall, casually flicked off her shoes and allowed her coat to fall to the floor in a lazy undress. He ogled her greedily, with the rampant sexual urges of a randy virgin schoolboy playing havoc with his libido. She floated sensuously towards him, 'like an angel on a cloud,' he thought. He breathed deeply, inhaling her scent, savouring her aroma like a love sick wine taster. Her face hovered inches from his, she tantalized his mouth with the slightest brush of her lips then withdrew playfully, only to return with a hot wet lick of her tongue. They kiss, suddenly she pushes him down into his seat and stands astride him, winding her pelvis suggestively in front of his face, purring like a sultry tigeress.

"Do you want me?" she whispered passionately through her pouting peachy lips. Her hair flowed like a silky water fall about her face, through which her eyes shone like pools of desire. Dexter expelled a hot nervous sweat as he stuttered and stammered the flustered gibberish of a blithering idiot. He loosened his collar.

"I... I don't know..."

"You don't know!" she echoed amused, as she undid the buttons of his shirt and drew her finger nails across his chest. They kissed again, it was hungry and frantic. His hands cup her breasts, again she breaks away, teasingly.

"I hope I didn't disturb you" she said coyly, walking around as if looking for another girl.

SHADES OF GREY

Dexter, now ready hot and bothered, took a while to collect the facilities that would enable him to respond. Once composed he dropped smoothly into the banter that was synonymous of their playful relationship.

"t's alright she's gone, and I've had a cancellation, so I might be able to fit you in."

"Might!" She said. Dexter shrugged his shoulders if to say 'Maybe'.

"If you play your cards right". He added. They laugh. Jess looks at the glowing computer screen.

"All work and no play?!"

"We can play a little" he quips.

"Good." She approaches.

"Later." he said jovially ducking out of her arms and sitting in his work chair with the same movement. 'What am I doing?' he thought. What was she doing, here, with him? Were they really going to do it, after all these months of teasing? Would she? Should he?' He needed time to think.

"I.... I've... I've got a lot to do," he stammered and began typing, aimlessly sifting through papers for no reason other than to demonstrate the point.

"Okay." she said faking misery. She sat resolutely in a chair directly opposite him innocently tapping her fingers gently on her knees. Then she crossed her legs in such a way that it exposed all her thigh and part of her panties. 'She's wearing black french frilly panties' he thought. Now he'd seen her panties, he imagined she'd have on the bra to match. Now he saw her only in her underwear. He felt himself reluctantly growing a hard on. He tried to check it with thoughts of cold showers, he bit his lip and squeezed his eyes shut. A second, then he peeped out discreetly through his eyelashes. 'She's still there,' he thought, 'in just her black french underwear. So sexy and sultry....' He imagined her to be a 'clinging crier.' She'd hug him like a baby and hardly speak but to call his name in a kind of whispering moan of ecstasy. 'Yeah', he thought, he could do with some of that right now. He was gone and going further, happily musing away on a wild fantasy. But he had work to do! He told himself resolutely. He shifted his eyes from her posterior, he was going

SHADES OF GREY

to look her in the face and tell her to go, he was busy, and they shouldn't be doing this. He looked up, she pursed her lips to the sexy pout she knew would drive him crazy. Dexter stared back down at a page fighting hard to keep his concentration. He reached for the cup and took a large gulp of the now stone cold coffee. Then he looked up at her, and for a while they looked at each other. Him weak and longing, her cocksure and provocative.

"God I love you." He gasped.

Dexter's eyebrows rose high up his forehead. His face wore the pathetic whimpish expression of an infatuated Rudolf Valentino. 'What a twit' she thought, 'why are men such fools? A look, a touch, a bit of flesh and he loves me. Why doesn't he just say he wants me? At least that would be honest.'

Jess knew she'd only be able to put up with Dexter for a few days, by then the novelty would have worn off. Already she began to feel the grey mood of boredom creeping upon her.

CHAPTER 11.

Day 2. Night.

Toby walked into the pool hall with the kit bag on his shoulder. He held up a crisp new fifty pound note between his middle and index fingers. A dude who had stepped out from among a group of five beautiful girls, stood directly in front of Toby eye-ing him up and down. The dude nodded and gave Toby a condescending smile. He was about the same height as Toby. A handsome, fair skinned, slick looking black dude in a blood red suit and jewellery. He was around thirty five.

"Okay lets shoot it," He smirked, then called to the barman.

"Bob give me whisky." The dude gestured cooly to Toby with a raise of his eyebrows, which Toby understood as an offer of a drink.

"Just water," Toby replied.

"You're old enough to drink I hope." the dude said sarcastically.

SHADES OF GREY

"Sure. But I never touch it while I'm working." Toby cracked. The dude smiled,

"And a glass of water" he told the barman.

Toby broke off, the cue ball smashed into the triangled formation of crystalite coloured sphere's, scattering them in all directions. Several fall into pockets. Toby smiled. When he was buzzing he shot great pool, and right now he was as high as a kite. He swaggered arrogantly round the table posing ceremoniously to view his next shot. His focus danced about the multi hue'd clusters on the lush green felt top. He chalked his cue tentatively while he considered the options. The longer he took, the more he posed an pondered, the more expert he appeared to onlookers. His huge arsenal of shot variation coupled to his vast vision of the game gave him endless permutation of play strategy, which in turn warranted serious consideration; or at least that's what he thought. He circled the table again bridging for one shot, then another. Just as the pro players did on television, so did arrogant club players, when they were high on cocaine, and winning. Finally he sinks another ball with a high speed long shot. The small audience wow and whistle in amazement. Toby shoots a look over to his opponent who stands stone faced, his folded arms hold his cue across his chest as if it were his sweetheart. He raises his eyebrows to acknowledge the shot. The dude had thought Toby too young to be a pool hall hustler, so when Toby walked in and threw open a fifty pound challenge it seemed like taking money from a baby. Now the dude seemed to be taking the lesson of his life, in more ways than one. Just then a shapely blond black girl passes on the way to the bar, Toby slaps her backside without taking his eyes from the table.

"You can have it, but it'll cost you twenty." She said playfully. But she wasn't joking.

"Win the game, you can have her twice!" Somebody called out. A few laughed. Toby smiled though never shifting his attention from the game in hand. He bends down for another shot, a delicate cut into the middle. He went straight to the next, he was a tuned engine now in top gear, on cruise control. Toby leaves the cue ball awkwardly under the cushion with no obvious

SHADES OF GREY

pot, he saunters over to the group of five girls leaving his opponent to ponder.

"Hi girls, I'm Toby Q. He holds up his cue.- Get it?"

The dude plays without potting a ball.

"Ah, gotta go." Toby excuses himself.

Back at the table he is sinking balls with ease. As the final ball rolls down into the pocket, he pointed his outstretched open palm at his opponent, who promptly slapped fifty pounds onto it. Their eyes meet expressing a new found mutual respect. Toby goes to the bar and orders a port and brandy, pays for it and knocks it back in one. The blond comes up, sits two seats away. She orders the same drink. Toby looks at her for the first time.

"Nice drink," he says. She looks at him pleasantly enough but doesn't answer. When her drink arrives Toby pays for it. The blond sips the drink without saying a word. Toby moves to the seat next to hers.

"Hi, I'm Toby."

She ignores him, takes out a small mirror, and begins to touch up her makeup. Toby struggles to strike up a conversation.

"I haven't seen you around..... I don't come here much..... I play pool you know.... Now and again.... You wanna...."

"I'm working." She cut in abruptly. "You want to do business it'll cost you twenty at your place, thirty five at mine." Toby orders two more drinks.

*

The blond leads Toby down the street, round the back and to a dark alley. So far she hasn't said a word. Suddenly she stops.

"How old are you." she asked.

"Old enough." Toby replied.

"You sure you don't wanna run home to your mama?"

"You're soon gonna be crying for yours babe" he quipped. The blond gave Toby a tired disbelieving smirk, then she kind of sighed and laughed at the same time.

"Where'd you learn that one? Never mind," she cut in quickly and led off down the alley. Toby followed. The alley, lined with a row of dustbins either side was dark damp and long. Toby could hear the music from the pool hall they'd just left.

"You must live at the back of the pool hall" he said. She

SHADES OF GREY

turned to him, her mood changed dramatically. She place her arms on his shoulders.

"You're kinda cute you know that?" She draws him to her and kisses him tenderly. A blow to the head sends Toby crumbling against the wall.

"Did you have to hit him so hard!" she scorned.

The dude dropped a brick to the floor.

"Don't you worry about it babe. You did good, you did real good."

The dude begins searching for the money he'd lost in the game. Toby begins to stir. He suddenly pushes the dude from him. The dude falls to the ground, Toby staggers to his feet. Their eyes meet.

"Now I'm gonna have to take care of you for good." the dude said. Toby catches the glittering reflection of a shiny blade. The dude walks forward slowly. "When I'm through with you your mother wont know you. You is dog meat sonny, food for worms."

Suddenly the raucous blast of gun fire ricocheted through the alley. The dudes face is a frozen surprise, he drops dead to the ground. The blonds screams are silenced by two more shots. Toby runs out down the street. He ran and ran until he thought he'd reached a safe distance and it was less conspicuous to walk. He'd killed again, but it was self defence he'd told himself, but what about the girl? Why did he kill her. It was easier to kill her than not to was the answer. If she hadn't screamed maybe she would still be alive.

SHADES OF GREY

CHAPTER 12.

Jess lay next to Dexter's Sleeping lumber, nonchalantly puffing another cigarette and pondering idle thoughts. She'd done it. She came, she saw, she conquered. She'd had him, ate him up and spat him out. She didn't even have to work too hard, didn't have to buy him anything, or take him out, it was all so easy. He was out, but she was raring to go. 'How dare they call us the weaker sex,' she thought. She was a new woman, and she felt that no one man would ever be enough for her again. Jess concluded that when it came to 'a roll in the sack' Dexter and Ziggy were remarkably similar. It was almost like some trade union work to rule. Neither said a word throughout, foreplay lasted about ten minutes, full intercourse, about five, then they'd want to know if she'd come. She'd lie. Then they'd want to know how many times she'd come. She'd lie again. Then they would fall asleep. It wasn't like that in the movies.

According to all her friends, naughty sex, sex with someone you shouldn't, or where you may be discovered, was the best of all. 'Well I know I shouldn't really have done it with Dexter, but it didn't make it any better' she thought.

Jess lay on her back staring at the ceiling, she was now an adulteress and proud of the fact. One thing bothered her though, she'd now had two men, but they'd been so similar they might as well have been the same. 'Not very adventurous' she thought. Only two men in her whole life from a world of millions, and she couldn't find two who looked different?! She felt like laughing, but didn't.

Jess was not in the least bit sleepy or even tired, but she was thirsty. An ice bucket with a bottle of champagne by the bedside was what she wanted, but she decided she would settle for anything cold. She lifted the quilt cover from herself and tried to slip off the bed without disturbing Dexter. She gathered her clothing from the floor and crept quietly across the thick piled bedroom carpet to the door. She glanced over her shoulder to

SHADES OF GREY

the bed and the humped impression that was Dexter, he was still. Carefully she began rotating the bedroom door knob, but no matter how slowly she turned, the mechanics of the lock clunked and clanged with every degree. She decided to go hell for leather and just turn the knob. Dexter did not even stir. The door creaked long and airy, like when opening a old dungeon gate in a fifties horror picture. She tiptoed down the stairs. The kitchen was a mess. Thankfully Jess found some apple juice in the refrigerator. 'Kitchens... boring' she thought, 'whoever it was invented them should be shot.' She kicked the refrigerator as hard as she'd dare in her bare feet.

"People should kill and eat their food there and then, while it's still warm, raw and fresh. Pull their veggy's out of the ground an just bite into them."

She opened the door of the micro wave, slamming it shut with a dismissive flick of her fingers. She briefly tapped a simple rhythm on the electric can opener with a teaspoon, then lifted the lid from the food blender. She flicked the switch on then off looking unimpressed at it's beating action.

"A real man wouldn't need this crap, he would bite open the cans and squeeze the juice from the fruit with his bare hands. They just don't make them like they used to. If I had a time machine I'd go back a few million years and get myself a real hunk. Tall, dark, handsome and muscular. So what if he's got no money. Then I'd send for the girls one by one starting with Beverly.

Dear Bev, here is your time machine ticket. There are so many young handsome free and single guys here, I'm stepping over them in the street so don't bother bringing that skinny no good leech you've been keeping. Love Jess."

Jess took the carton of juice and began to climb the stairs, she could see the bedroom light shining through the gap beneath the door. Dexter had sat up and was waiting for her.

"Apple juice?" she offered.

"Who were you talking to down there?"

"Just myself. Could you hear me?"

"You're crazy."

Dexter held the carton of juice as Jess climbed into bed.

SHADES OF GREY

"I was pretending it was champagne," she said.

"You like champagne?" He asked her.

"I love champagne."

"I have champagne in here." Dexter pointed to a small fridge by his bed side. Her face lit up, a moment later they were drinking champagne in bed. Jess sits in silence with a sullen look on her face. Dexter nudges her gently, she turns to him, he smiles, but she just turns away.

"What's wrong," he asked her, "I thought Bubbly was supposed to make you... bubbly!" He chuckles at his little joke. Jess remains cold and aloof.

"Aren't you going to ask me why I'm came here?" she said abruptly. Her voice had a confronting edge that made Dexter pause and take stock.

"Why did you come here?"

"Because I was bored!" she said angrily, then resumes her moody pathos.

"Are you bored now?" his ego asked her.

"Yes I am!" Jess said irritably.

"Oh," Dexter said dejectedly, his self esteem now lower than a mole in a hole.

"I'm sorry," Jess said, "I didn't mean that.- Ziggy and I had a fight, he hit me, I.... I don't know... I don't know what I'm doing anymore. I suppose I just needed a friendly face, a break, a...."

"Are you going back to him?"

"I don't know, now I've taken a break, I'm thinking why don't I make it permanent, it's probably what we both need."

"You could always stay with me." Dexter said hopefully. Jess squeezed his hand and smiled at him.

"Thanks, but no. How could I? you're his twin brother."

"We're not brothers, we were just born together of the same mother."

"That makes you brothers."

"But you know what I mean, there's no bond between us, there's no cord linking our minds, hearts, and belly buttons. We're totally different. Two totally different people with nothing in common. Just because it didn't work with him, it doesn't mean it wont work with me."

SHADES OF GREY

"It's not just you, or even him, it me too. I'm looking for something, I don't know what it is, but until I find out I'll probably be the same with whoever I'm with... bored!"

"Look, I don't expect you to rush into anything right now, just say you'll think about it.... please?"

"Okay," Jess conceded. Dexter was determined to lift the mood.

"More champagne madam?"

"Thankyou kind sir," As the night went on and the bottle went down they both became a little tipsy. He cracked open another half magnum showering them both in the eruption. He dimmed the lights and put on some soft music, the atmosphere was light and relaxed. To her surprise, Dexter produced a bowl of strawberries and cream, from nowhere. They sat down by the fridge and fed them to each other as if playing a scene from the movie nine and a half weeks. Dexter drooled for her and she allowed herself to be taken. This time the routine seemed different. She was consumed by his passion, a passion so great it devoured her, mind body and spirit, yet she matched it with her own, such was the intensity of their love making. Had he asked her, she would have told him in truth that she had reached orgasm many times. But he did not need to ask. She did not need to say.

SHADES OF GREY

CHAPTER 13.

When Gilbert was asked to come down to London, to a morgue of all places, he prayed to God they had made a mistake. He was praying right up to the moment they uncovered her head, he choked. He held his breath. He touched her face, it was cold. It was Marsha, It was her, but it wasn't real, it couldn't be. 'Marsh, dead? No. No.' She was a cold and lifeless corpse before him, but in his heart and mind he clung to her desperately, and though he could feel her slipping away, for now at least she was still very much with him, still alive. He remembered vividly how he used to pull her nose while she slept when they were both kids, she'd wake up mad, crying sometimes. He used to share his sweets with her, his worms and his coloured crayons, and no one dared bully her because she was his sister. Her first school disco, she was so excited, even though he'd had to bring her home by 9.30. Sports day, and crying on his shoulder because she'd come last in the long jump, he'd started to laugh, then she did, because it really didn't matter. She was so smart, she'd been helping him with his O level studies, his little sister! But she never told a soul. When her exams came it was a breeze, nine O's then three A's. She was destined for great things. So to London and university. Then nothing. He hadn't heard from her in a long time. Now this. Marsha, little Marsha..... slipping away....

"Marsha?" he whispered. Slipping further and further.

"Oh Marsha!" he weeped. Further and further away until he could no longer feel her, no longer hold her.- She was gone, she was dead, it was true. He caressed her nose gently with the back of his index finger, kissed her ice cold forehead and left. He felt a strange and empty kind of deadness inside. He was in shock, mentally and physically. He knew they wanted to see him at the police station so that's where he was going, but he was so numb you could have led him over a cliff.

The policeman he saw was not in the least bit sympathetic,

SHADES OF GREY

he acted like it was nothing. Gilbert wasn't sure if it was because he thought she'd deserved it, or if he had a 'one less nigger attitude'. When detective sergeant Nash asked Gilbert if he knew how long his sister had been a prostitute Gilbert blew up. They had to pry his hands loose from Nash's throat.

Nash was a cold fish. A thin lipped, puffy eyed, stubble chined closet alcoholic, who always looked like he'd spent the night with the homeless in cardboard city. Nash was 35 but looked 50, and he was only five feet six inches tall. Despite his downtrodden appearance he appeared to have quite an extensive wardrobe of well made if miss treated suits. Today he wore a gutter mangled grey.

After Gilbert's outburst they had to get someone else to deal with him, a plain clothed guy from vice. He tried to be a little more diplomatic but the message was the same. Gilbert couldn't believe it, as far as they were concerned Marsha was just another junky hooker who went too far, reached too high for the ultimate trip, then got what was coming to her. 'But Marsha? A junky!? A hooker!? No.... She'd never even had a boyfriend!' After the detective had left him he sat alone a with his thoughts, it was mental torture.

Nash was still nursing a bruised throat when Benjamin walked in.

"What's up with you Nash?"

"I'll tell you what's up with me, one of your jungle brothers tried to kill me that's what's up with me."

Benjamin looked towards Gilbert slumped down and distressed.

"What you do to him?"

"Wasn't me, somebody bumped off his junky hooker of a sister. Now you better get your people to toe the line Benjamin, or I'm gonna stamp on 'em, hard."

"What are you talking about?"

"You know what I'm talking about, you want me to spell it out for you? Blacks are trouble, a race of murdering, thieving, rapeing, granny muggers....."

Benjamin took a hold of Nash by the scruff of his coat collar and slammed him up against the wall, he was a mad as a bull

73

SHADES OF GREY

with a matador on his back.

"Go ahead, hit me. I'd see you bummed out of here so fast you wouldn't have time to wipe your ass."

"One of these day Nash, one of these days." Benjamin pushes him aside.

Nash was one bitter man, he hated black people, but you couldn't simply call him a racist, Nash was the meanest son of a mother there ever was. Rumour had it he was a married man though no one had ever seen his wife. Benjamin had speculated that she must have divorced him, got custody of the kids denying him access, and was now living with her lover (the man his kids now referred to as daddy), in the house he was still paying the mortgage on. There had to be some reason why this guy was so mean. He hated everyone, including himself.

Nash was always goading Benjamin looking for a fight, sometimes Benjamin would ignore him sometimes he wouldn't, it all depended on whether he himself needed to blow off some steam. Today he felt like killing him, but decided not to take the bait. But Nash hadn't given up yet, he was looking for trouble. He walked round the back of Benjamin and whispered in his ear in mock discretion.

"I hear you fucked up a stake out last night, what happened, you fall asleep? Let him get away huh? How big a sleeping pill did he give you, twenty quid?" Benjamin throws him a dirty look.

"fifty? A hundred?" Nash persisted.

"Look if you want to accuse me of taking a bribe why don't you make an offical complain to the captain."

"Me!? Would I do a thing like that? But hey, that big drugs haul you pulled in from Bayswater the night before, Five hundred kilo's of coke, not bad, not bad."

That's why Benjamin was so tired, he hadn't slept in two days. He'd been up the previous night because of drug raid he and his team had been planning for months. It was successful, they had uncovered a drugs ring which had connections throughout the world, they had smashed a vital pivot to the drug barons trafficking operations. A job well done, they'd saved the lives of a lot of kids that night, of that he was sure. The thought that some day one of his kids might be prey to some drug

SHADES OF GREY

pushing vulture drove him crazy.

"But the way I see it, your dog shits in the street, it's up to you to pick it up right? Tell me, were they 'Yardies' or 'Rastas', I never could tell the difference."

"They were Mexicans" Benjamin countered.

"Same thing, you're all foreigners."

Benjamin gave Nash a disbelieving frown, shaking his head pitifully as he walked away. Nash was laughing mischievously as he walked out of the station.

Franklin the duty officer was taking a statement from old lunatic who regularly confessed to crimes he hadn't committed. If the station was busy the old guy would be shoved aside, but things were slack, so Franklin was going along with the lonely old guy who really just wanted some attention. Franklin winked at Benjamin who stopped to listen.

".....the little runt was out to make himself a hero, I swear if I'd a had any bullets in this gun I'd a shot his head off. I ran in, the place was almost empty. I shout, everybody on the floor face down! Everybody get's down on the floor no problem. I see this old guy, I mean old, must have been about ready to retire. I point the gun in his face, I say open the safe, he opens it no problem. The jewels were there waiting, the whole thing's a piece of cake. Then this little guy.... how I hate little guys! This little guy sets off the alarm! I puts the gun up his nose, I says give me the cash. You know the punk just laughed in my face like he new these guns were from the kiddies store, I swear if I had a real gun..."

Benjamin looked over at Gilbert, still seated, deep in remorse, weeping head in hands.

"Why is that guy wearing hancuffs?"

"Gilbert? His sister was blown away over by the pool hall, we only wanted him to make an ID and a statement but Nash wants to charge him with assaulting a police officer."

"Shit, Nash is a... Let him go, if Nash asks, tell him I said so."

"Right. Oh before I forget, forensic sent this down for you." Franklin hands Benjamin a note. Benjamin's eyes widen in disbelief as he reads. Just then Spikey strolled in chewing on a hamburger.

"What that you reading?" she asked. Benjamin sighs

SHADES OF GREY

thoughtfully but does not answer. Instead he counters with,

"What's that you eating?"

"Junk food." She replied.

"As usual," he said.

"As usual," she affirmed unconcerned.

"What's in the box?" He enquired.

"A doenut" She responded in monotone. Benjamin opened the box, inside there were four large sticky jam doenuts. He licked his lips then resolutely shut the lid and backed away, as if the box were an armed gunman.

"How can you eat that shit and stay the skinny beanpole that you are? All I have to do is look at a bakery and my cholesterol's start breeding." Spikey looks to the note still in Benjamins hand.

"What's happening daddy?"

"This is from the lab, it's to do with a girl who was shot over by the 'Pot it' pool hall in Stratford broadway, I think maybe we should go down and take a look."

Benjamin picked up the phone to call Bella's Ital food Reataurant.

"Hello Bella? Is Winston.... yeah.... I might be a bit late tonight, but ah coming, so put some rice and peas, a little coldslaw.... yeah dee usual, and a big big piece a chicken breast aside for me..... Yeah dat sound nice.... You have any carrot juice?.... Yeah, stout and carrot juice with spices, yeah cinnamon and..... bwoy ah hungry you see!... Yeah I know... see you later... bye."

*

They arrived at the 'Pot it', and with only a torch light to guide them stepped carefully along the dark and narrow alleyway where the dude and the blond were shot.

"This is one nasty place to die. Let's go in and talk to some of the patrons."

Inside they found Nash leaning against the bar with a beer in his hand pretending not to see them.

"What you doing here?" Benjamin demanded suspiciously.

"I come here all the time," Nash said smugly. "You come about ol' Dude and Marsha?"

"You talk like you knew them?" Spikey said.

SHADES OF GREY

"Everybody knew Dude and Marsha... especially Marsha, you know what I mean?" he said with a wink and a dirty grin. "Well, the pimp and his whore got what they had coming to them," he went on carelessly." Spikey through him an icy glare.

"Poor girl" he added insincerely.

Benjamin turned to a group of guys watching a game of snooker. He held his badge up, the snooker players stopped, he had their full attention.

"Anybody know anything about the shooting?" There was a stoney silence. "Can anybody remember anybody having an arguiment?" There is no response. "Anybody notice any strangers in the bar recently?" There is no response. "Anybody know the two who died?" There is nothing. Benjamin looks at the crowd of empty dumb faces, he turns to Nash. "I thought you said everybody knew her?" Benjamin again addresses the crowd. "Does anybody here know their own name." Nobody said a word. "Come on let's get out of here."

As they turn to leave the bar springs back into life with laughing, chating, drinking and the sound of snooker balls cracking against one another. Benjamin stood on the pavement outside the 'Pot it' and gave a worried scratch to his head.

"What's the matter?" Spikey asked.

"I don't get it. That's three murders in two days. And the word so far from the lab is that these two look to have been shot by a similar calibre gun to the one used to shoot the guy outside Pinkies.- But we got that murderer locked up in a cell, haven't we?" Benjamin looks to Spikey who just shrugs her shoulders. He wipes the stubble on his cheek with his palm.

"I don't get it, and what's more I don't like it neither." he said.

Their slow drive home was a quiet one, Benjamin was worried about the apparent link between the two shootings. He was thinking about it so hard that he forgot to drop Spikey off and drove straight to Bella's Ital Food Restaurant.

"Daddy!?"

"Oh I sorry Spikey, I was thinking so hard... Let me just tell her I'm.... Why don't you come in and meet Bella, she's nice you'll like her."

"Hm... Okay, but you know I can't stay long, I called my mum

SHADES OF GREY

and told her I was on my way, if I'm not home soon she's gonna worry."

"Don't worry, we'll only be a second," Benjamin assured her. The two of them waddle into Bella's.

Bella is a short round jolly mother, dressed in a white overall and white hair wrap. The place is meticulously clean, the food looks and smells delicious. Spikey's eyes light up brighter than the fog lamps on an XR2.

"Bella I want you to meet my partner...."

"A A! So you is a police woman? A pretty little ting like you? I thought she was you daughter!"

"Don't be fooled by dee pretty face," Benjamin said, "She's as hard as nails, and smart too." he added proudly.

Spikey looked at Benjamin in amazment, Benjamin took his attention to a plate of fried dumplin so as avoid Spikey's stare. This was praise indeed, he had never even so much as bestowed a well done on her before. She was elated, and slightly embarrassed.

"Is true?" Bella said grinning broadly at Spikey. "So what you having?" Bella asked her.

"Oh I can't stay I..."

"You can't come to Bella's and not eat anyting, dat is unheard of. No one has ever done dat before, you don't want to be dee first do you?" Bella said sounding slightly offended.

"Surly your mum wont mind you stopping off for something to eat," Benjamin said, "I'll square it with her, don't worry, come on."

"Okay," Spikey said.

They sat down. The meal was wonderful. Bella watched in astonishment at the amount of food Spikey put away. Spikey had a sweet too. When she'd finished Benjamin half expected her to explode, but she looked just as twigified as always and infact was eyeballing the pork chops like she could have gone again!

*

In the car on the way home, Benjamin was driving his usual twenty two miles an hour, Spikey was looking worried.

"Now don't worry if mum shouts at you, her bark is worse than her bite."

SHADES OF GREY

"Shout at me? Why should she shout at me?"

"Well you said you'd handle it, she's gonna blame you anyway. But like I said she's harmless."

As they pull up outside they see the edge of the window curtain anxiously draw back.

"Now remember, be firm, mum likes the stronge silent type." They enter the gate and walk nerviously up the drive. Spikey turns the key in the lock and pushes the door open. Benjamin was instantly struck by how sweet smelling and homely the place appeared. It reminded him of the way his own place looked when he was married.

"Mum," Spikey called out.

"I'm in here," came a reply.

Spikey led a nervous Benjamin into the living room. Benjamin froze at the sight of Spikey's mother. She was tall, dark and full figured, not skinny like her daughter. Her eyes were mezmerizing, her cheeks looked ripe enough to eat and when she moved her lips to speak Benjamin felt all strength leave his legs.

"You're late," Mother said. Benjamin took a step forward.

"I.. I can explain... you see, we... I mean I... I mean, what I trying to say is...."

"Mr Benjamin, please ensure that my daughter arrives home at an appropriate time in fucture," she said sternly.

Benjamin wanted to laugh, 'what's an appropriate time?' he thought. He wanted to say 'don't be ridiculous, she's a police officer for Christ sake!' But when mother fixed him with her stare all he heard himself say was;

"Yes mam."

"Good night Mr Benjamin."

"Yes mam."

"I'll see you out," Spikey said. Out in the hall way Spikey whispered,

"I think she likes you." Benjamin seemed delighted at that thought, but Benjamin did not seem himself, he looked as if still enchanted by Spikey's mother.

"What's her name?" he asked Spikey.

"Mum? Her names Jeraldine, but people she likes, she has

SHADES OF GREY

call her Jerry.

"Jerry," Benjamin repeated dreamily.

CHAPTER 14.

Day 3.

As Jess began rousing from a deep sleep, her first thoughts were of Ziggy. She remembered the hazy vision of his face draw on to hers, kissing her, then whispering that he loved her. She dismissed it as a dream and tried to recollect events of the night before. She couldn't. Next she posed herself several question, none of which she could readily answer. What day was it? What time was it? She wondered if she might be late for work. Drowsy and eyes still closed she searched the bedside table top for her alarm clock. It was not there. In it's place a new object, it's shape un-recognisable to her touch. She was for a moment confusion, but tiredness made her reluctant to open her eyes. Instead she waited the few seconds her disorientated brain would need to shake off that early morning stupor, and fathom which of her few possessions she held in her hand. A moment passed, still she was none the wiser. She cranked opened an eyelid, and peered through lashes ladened heavy with sleep. Her fingers held a plastic teak effect clock radio, the likes of which she had never seen before. She looked about her, slowly it begun to dawn, it had not been a dream, neither had it been Ziggy whose lips had tasted hers and uttered those words that morning. She was in Dexter's flat, she was in Dexter's bed.

Dexter had gone off to work leaving her asleep. She sat up and looked about the bedroom as if for the first time, she peered beneath the quilt at her nakedness and at the two champagne bottles on the floor. Had she really seduced him like that? Were her amorous memories of rip roaring bedroom frolics true? Her body ached as if still in shock from last nights sex. She was still on a high. 'So men are good for something after all,' she thought. As she fell back on the bed her hair sprayed against the milk

80

SHADES OF GREY

white pillow, she cupped her breast in her palms, her face was an expression of unbridled passion, a picturesque pose of the un-repentant madonna who had fallen from grace.

"I never thought it could be like this," she jested, then laughed aloud at the cliched phrase.

Jess walked into the bathroom. It was a pale pink with mahogany hardwood around the bath. The towel rail was mahogany too as was the cabinet, toothbrush holder, toilet seat and toilet roll holder. All metal fittings were in brass. Shaving cream, disposable razors, aftershave and other male toiletries littered about the sink. Jess had mentally set aside space for her own things.

She used Dexter's toothbrush, took a shower, then washed and conditioned her hair. Wrapped in his dressing gown she went back to the bedroom where she creamed her skin from head to foot. She lay back on the bed, bathing her bronze naked body in the bright early morning sun that shone through the window. For a few minutes she rolled above the bed cloths as if on a sanded beach in the West Indies. Next she sat in front the dress mirror, manicuring her nails while sipping a cold fizzy drink from the bedroom refrigerator. She thought the flat was immaculate. The kitchen wonderful, fully fitted with matching units. The cupboards, fridge, cooker and sink units were all white. She marvelled at the mod cons she'd chastised only the night before. The microwave, the blender, the toasted sandwich maker, and even the electric can opener. The lounge had everything, TV, stereo, video... What at first glance looked to be books on shelves she later realised was a video library. There were about thirty in all, mostly black and white gangster movies from the fifties. There were also two marked 'pleasure zone X' on a shiny silver label, she assumed them to be blue movies. 'A girl could get comfortable in a place like this' she though.

"But wait a minute, what am I thinking of? The poison of home comforts. This isn't what I want, a week in this place and I'd be a vegetable going crazy, I'd want to jump in the blender and get crushed up for carrot juice." Just then Jess thought she heard a knock. She peeped out into the hall peering down the stairs to the front door. She saw the dark impression of a large

SHADES OF GREY

man through the autumn leaf glass pane. Half a dozen or so letters falling to the doormat told her it was the postman. Her first instinct was to run down to collect her mail. 'Her mail?' she questioned herself. Of course none of them would be for her, she didn't live there, she didn't belong there. Why had she come? Was it to get back at Ziggy?- Ziggy. He was back in her head, and although she tried to get him out he stayed. She found herself making comparisons between her old place and this. There was no comparison. She had been living in squalor with a pig. It was no wonder she was always depressed, Ziggy would be perfectly happy just sitting in their bug ridden hovel doing nothing for the rest of his days. But whether in Ziggy's hovel or Dexter's luxury pad she knew that neither was for her.

"I've got to get out of here."

The telephone, a banana in a boat, began an easy jangle that was novel and made Jess smile. It was Dexter.

"I just called to make sure you were alright."

"I'm fine, how are you?"

"Fine," he said. There was an awkward silence, as both searched for something to say, then both tried to speak at once.

"Sorry," he said "go ahead."

"No you first," she offered.

"I've been thinking about last night, and us.... look my boss is going to be running in our local byelection, It may be good for me if I can get my... I mean my salary could double and we could move away from Zig.... to.... what I'm trying to say is...."

"Dexter, I've been thinking about last night too and..."

"You don't regret it do you?" he interrupted anxiously.

"No," she said, it was nice, but...."

"Okay. Okay, just promise me you wont go anywhere till I get back, then we can talk."

"Dexter, I..."

"Please?" Dexter implored her.

"Okay," she agreed."

"Okay, see you later."

SHADES OF GREY

CHAPTER 15.

An angry young black man marches ahead of a long procession of militant protesters, the atmosphere is charged and dangerous, the mood among these young and hot blooded vigilante's is vicious and ugly. Many of them wear black berry's and black leather gloves synonymous of the black power movement of yesteryear. Toby is among them. He holds a banner high above his head on which the words, WAR ON RACIST! is graffitied in thick black with blood red paint running down each letter. Behind Toby a sea of blacks carry other banners, some baring pictures of MALCOLM X and slogans like BROTHERS GET RADICAL! and REVOLUTION IS THE ONLY WAY! They chanted;

"Black attack back! Black attack back!" monotonously, relentlessly with a hypnotic determination of frightening intensity. They march towards a large man in ceremonial robes, up on a makeshift pulpit in the road outside Pinkies where 'Hercules' had been gunned down. He is surrounded by a vibrant crowd of liberal and for the much part older blacks. He holds a megaphone and preaches to the gathering.

"Brothers and sisters!" he called fervidly, arms outstretched, his body trembling as he bawls up into the clouds. His speech is punctuated at strategic points throughout as individual cry 'Tell it!'- 'Is so!' and such like in affirmation. Their call and response builds to climax with applause and a resounding cry of approval from the crowd.

"Brothers and sisters! Come, take to the streets, let me hear you, let me hear your voices! Take off these chains! Tear off these shackles! Shake off these inhibitions instilled in you over centuries of white oppression. We as black people have the right to speak, it is our God given right, a basic democratic right denied our mothers, our fathers, and our brother and sisters around the world for too long!"

"TOO LONG!" the congregation cry.

SHADES OF GREY

"The devilish white slave masters stole our land, our wealth, took away our names, our history, and forced upon us his religion of white Gods. Gods that teach us to equate white with good and black with evil! Teaches us how to endure and accept the injustices, the pain and suffering that the devilish white man has inflicted on us with prayer, song, and the hope of a better deal in the after life of tomorrows heaven. While he, the devilish white man enjoys his heaven on earth today, at our expense! I say no more!"

"NO MORE!" cry the congregation. At this point the vigilante procession has joined them. They jostled their way to the front.

"All this you see around you and more was built off the backs of the black man, from the sweat of the black mans brow, foundations laid with our stolen wealth and black slave labour! The devilish white man has used the spoils from the rapeing of our land, our precious metals, minerals, oil, to build his empire, then used that stolen wealth to oppress you still further. But I say no more!"

"NO MORE!" cry the congregation.

"I say no more! We will not accept the devilish white mans teachings, that tell us that we, as an inferior race must turn the other cheek."

"NO MORE!" cry the congregation.

"I say no more! We will not accept that the murder of one of our children, ignored by the racist institutions of this society, such as the police, and the media, is any less an abomination as the murder of any white child."

"NO MORE!" cry the congregation.

"The devilish white man has pillaged, murdered, raped and exploited every race of man not white for too long!"

"TOO LONG!" cry the congregation.

"For too long we as black people have been deprived of our history, our status, our wealth and our true identity!"

"TOO LONG!" cry the congregation.

"For took long it been the black man planting the roots, now we want to taste some of the fruits!"

"YEAH!" bellow the congregation.

"For too long the devilish white man has been allowed to

84

SHADES OF GREY

poison our children minds with lies of our native Africa. Teaching the lie that it was a barren land, populated only by black savages swinging like monkeys from trees, in order to perpetuate their myth of white supremacy! We're here to tell him that he is....."

"WRONG!" the congregation roar.

They cheer, whistle, and beat their beer cans together in rapturous applause. But Toby does not join in the celebrations, instead he curses the white man venomously, his hatred for him now acutely tuned. An angry fever infuses his mind with a blinding rage. Just then a wave of rocks and bricks are torpedoed into the air by a mob of National Front supporters. Many are wearing union jack tee-shirts and have painted their steel toe capped boots in red white and blue. They shout obscenities in an uncoordinated loutish uproar. Their faces are a contorted grimace of hate. They carry primitive weapons, brandishing banners with mock caricatures of black people baring insulting slogans and derogatory remarks. The sea of missiles rain down on the congregation injuring many individuals. Every black face then turns to face the mob who subsequently run towards the sanctuary of the encroaching police who are in full riot gear. The police crash through the unarmed members of the congregation at the front. The onslaught is brutal and indiscriminate as they weald their batons about innocent skulls like gladiators at war. The vigilante youths led by Toby, surge through the crowd to meet the attack of the police, and force their retreat. The police are chased westward for two hundred yards down the Romford road to the junction of Upton lane and Woodgrange, this was to become the frontier of the imposed No Go Zone. For two hours the vigilantes were the law of Romford road. Two hours, that's how long it took the police to obtain tear gas, rubber bullets and the authorization to use them.

'Operation dispersion' was clinically and expertly executed. Masked policemen raced into vigilante territory as tear gas was simultaneously fired. The police were even more vicious than they had been before. Their victims, choking and gasping for breath were mercilessly beaten then thrown into the back of 'meat wagons' where they faced further bouts of police brutality. Toby is repeatedly struck about his head and torso, he is in

SHADES OF GREY

excruciating pain but manages to escape along with a few others.

CHAPTER 16.

Dexter sat at the desk in his office twiddling a pencil while thinking about Jess. Last night was the happiest of his life, but he was worried. Jess had sounded like she had something on her mind, maybe she was having second thoughts. Having had her for one night the thought of losing her now seemed unbearable. A buzz from the intercom broke his train of thought. His secretary spoke.

"A Mr Clarence Wallace is on the line."

"Clarence who?" Dexter asked.

"He's from the anti racist thing that been going on in East London. It was looking pretty rough down there. I think he wants some legal assistance."

"I'm not taking on any more legal aid cases this month. Tell him we're busy."

"Okay, I'll tell him."

"Wait a minute, you said it was looking rough?"

"It looked pretty bad on the TV...."

"TV! What TV?"

"It was on the mid day news."

"The mid day new......? Put him on." TV meant publicity, and publicity was good for Dexter's career.

Clarence had to scream over a background wall of an angry chaos.

"The police are killing us down here, and protesters are being beaten and arrested on trumped up charges."

"Are the TV camera's still there?"

"Yes, I think so...."

"Okay, I'm on my way."

As soon as he had replaced the receiver Dexter began putting on his over coat in preparation for the journey to East London. Just then Mr Sobers burst in.

86

SHADES OF GREY

"Don't go anywhere Dexter I want to talk to you," Sobers told him.

"I'm was just on my way to the Anti racist rally in East London. It seems the police have allowed the National Front to attack a peaceful demonstration, and are now arresting the black demonstrators," Dexter said.

"The march was banned wasn't it?" Sober said.

"Yes but..."

"So they were engaging in an illegal activity, will they never learn? It's the system, work within it or bare the consequences. They can wait, and so will you, here. I'll call you when I need you."

Sobers marched into his office. It was Friday, Mr Sobers wasn't due back from his carribean holiday until the Tuesday of the next week. But the sudden death of the local MP had forced a byelection. Mr Sobers, as the Conservative party candidate eagerly rushed back from Trinidad with high hopes of causing an upset. A Tory gain from the Labour party. It would require, an 8% swing, but recent opinion polls had put the Tories ahead by 4% and thus had kindled high hopes of yet another black MP in the house.

A few minutes passed before Dexter was summoned to Mr Sobers office amidst rumour that he might be invited to manage Mr Sober campaign- or something. Dexter approached the large oak door inscribed with the name of Mr Alvin J Sobers and his professional qualifications of which there were many. He knocked politely and waited. A few seconds passed before Mr Sober's gave the response that would allow him entry.

"Ah! Mr Sinclair" he said with his acquired etonian accent, welcoming Dexter as if he hadn't seen him in ages. His office walls were of African mahogany on which there were many paintings, mainly European portraits in wooden frames. An elegant wall light complimented each individual picture. A small chandelier decorated the victorian mouldings of an off white ceiling. A few ornaments of African origin posed awkwardly about his papered desk, the floor was carpeted in a pale green.

"Sit down sit down. I'll come straight to the point as you must be a busy man, at least I hope so." He chuckled. Dexter

SHADES OF GREY

chuckled along more from a habitual reflex than amusement.

"With the forthcoming elections looming, as you might appreciate I'm going to be very busy over the next few days. I'm going to be relying on you to keep things ticking over in there, as well as keeping it quiet in here if you get my meaning. To put it plainly Dexter I don't want to be disturbed. Now I'm going to be busy today with members of my campaign team, and while I won't be burdening you with regard to your current work load, I do not want to be pestered by other members of staff or the general public, not even if it's a murder case. I am officially still on holiday understand? Now be warned I may need to utilise more office space, the laser printer and the photocopier- ah I'll need to commandeer the photocopier over the next couple of days to get my flyer's going. Basically my campaign and members of my campaign team must be given priority over all other concerns is that clear?"

"Yes Mr Sobers."

"Good." Mr Sobers reaches for his cigar box, offers Dexter a cigar which he refuses. "Jacob O'brian, I understand you were at university together. They tell me he's gay, is that true?"

"Who told you that?" Dexter asked suspiciously. Sobers chuckles to himself.

"Your Mr O'brian is now the finance officer for Texicom international, I wish to conduct some business with your Mr O'brian, raise some campaign revenue in exchange for.... well.... I have an appointment with him this evening. Your presence would be appreciated."

"But I have a prior engagement."

"Cancel it! Don't worry you won't have to do anything un-ethical or illegal. I just want you to drive me there, then sit in on the meeting. You won't even have to speak if you don't want to."

"You mean you want me to be your chauffeur."

"If you want to put it like that, yes."

"But I'm a lawyer, I went to law school," Dexter protested. "I have people in need, who need me, now." Dexter dare not tell Sobers that his pressing engagement would be under the gaze of millions via television camera's, for he knew that Sobers

88

SHADES OF GREY

armed with that information would be quick to grab the limelight and leave him in the shadows.

"And I need you here!" Sobers said firmly. "I have a campaign to run, it all about loyalty..."

"I'm sorry I have to go."

"If you go out of that door, don't come back." Dexter was stumped he couldn't afford to lose his job, but neither could he afford to miss a career opportunity like this.

"Why don't you take Hopkirk with you, we were all in the same class, he knows O'brian as well as I do."

Hopkirk was a weasely solicitor who would have kissed Sobers boots if he was told to.

"Because I can't stand the Hopkirk! I don't know anyone who can. So the chances are this chap O'brian has had a belly full of him too! Now I won't hear another word on the subject. Be ready to leave in about forty five minutes. Now, that will be all thankyou."

Dexter was sick, there it was, a chance in a life time, up for grabs. National TV coverage, the press, all waiting, ready to catapult him to the forefront of the legal profession.

"And this ass hole wants me to sit there looking pretty, twiddling my thumbs while he pulls one of his dodgy deals."

Lose a job or the chance of a life time, those were the choices. He needed his job badly and yet he couldn't let this opportunity pass him. If only he were able to be in two places at the same time there'd be no problem. But that was impossible... or was it. Dexter called his brother Ziggy. Maybe Ziggy would dep for him, maybe he wouldn't. His ace card was cash. Ziggy needed it and he had it, enough to buy Ziggy for a day. Ziggy's phone only rang twice before he answered it. He was in low spirits, he had found Jess's note. In it she'd said that she didn't think their marriage was working out, and she was going home to mothers's to give them both a chance to think things through.

"Hey man I need a favour."

"So why are you calling me?"

"Come on man, you're the only one who can cut this. I'd do it myself but I got a lot of things to be getting on with." 'Like your wife' Dexter thought to himself. "Look all you've got to do is

SHADES OF GREY

pretend to be me and drive my boss around for an hour or so."

"It'll cost you fifty quid."

"Jesus man! You're supposed to be my brother."

"Oh yeah that right, call it sixty then." Dexter played it like he was desgusted with Ziggy, but it was what he'd expected.

"Okay, just get your ass down here as quick as you can. I'll meet you on the corner, outside the off licence."

CHAPTER 17.

Ziggy turned up wearing a blue casual sport jacket over a yellow stripped tee shirt and a pair of red jeans. His socks and shoes were black as were his dark glasses and the leather cap on his head.

"What's the matter with you? You're supposed to be me you dummy, you ever see me dressed up like that. Red jeans!? You look like a fucking flag!"

"Fuck you man! Now I want the money up front and don't give me any more shit or the price goes up."

"What!? All you've got to do is drive a car man."

"Look if you could get anybody else to do this you would, this is a specialist job man, requires specialist pay. So cough up." Ziggy slaps his hand out for the money, Dexter pays him.

"Now listen, the less said the better, if he asks you any legal question just write them down and say you'll need to look into it right?"

＊

Ziggy walked into the reception area of Dexter's office immediately conscious of the amused and puzzled looks he got from Dexter's secretary.

"Mr Sinclair....!?" she begun in an astonished but very English voice. She wanted to just let rip with, 'is why you ar dress so? You tink you is a ragamuffin!?' But she resisted the temptation. Just then Mr Sobers came onto the intercom.

"Would you tell Dexter I'm ready to see him now?"

"Yes sir," the receptionist said. She looked worriedly at Ziggy.

90

SHADES OF GREY

"Well, you heard him."

Inside with Mr Sobers was the rest of his campaign team Ben Dawson and Mr Raj Patel the campaign manager. Dawson gave Ziggy a look of amazement. Sobers was not amused.

"Is this you're idea of a joke?" Sobers stared him long and hard, but even acting and looking as he did Ziggy was confident that Sober would not suspect, and if he did what the hell.

"Just don't mess up." Sobers warned him.

*

Dexter found himself in the thick of a violent disorder. Youths both black and white stood toe to toe with police in full riot gear lashing and being lashed. Bricks and bottles versus truncheons and tear gas. Dexter searched about him for anyone who looked remotely like reporter. He spotted a TV crew taking shots of some kids hurling bits of paving stone at the police. He made his way to their van and stood right in front of the camera.

"Good evening viewers, my name is Dext...."

"What are you doing?" The camera man said.

"I'm Dexter Sinclair, legal representation for some of the kids you see here."

"Get out of the way."

The camera man began taking shots of a group of kids turning over a car.

"You don't understand," Dexter protested, "I can give you an insight into the young minds of the inner-city youths, the kind of minds that turn over cars and set them on fire."

Dexter follows the camera man around as he films more of the mayhem.

"Deprivation, unemployment, education, poor local services, poor housing..."

"Look, piss off, we're not interested," the camera man said. Just then a lady called to the camera man from inside the van.

"Okay Dave, let's go. I think we've got it."

"Right," the camera man said as he got into the vehicle. Dexter turned to talk to the woman but she had disappeared into the back. The van began to move off.

"Think about it, but remember it was my idea, my name is Sinclair, I'm in the book!" he bawled after them desperately as

91

SHADES OF GREY

they drove away.

*

Every time Ziggy was asked a legal question by either Dawson, Patel or Sobers he wrote it down and told them he would have to look into it, just as Dexter had told him to.

"Okay," Sobers said, "we'd better wrap up this meeting as it almost time to go."

"Do we have time to pass by my office," Dawson asked.

"I know it's in the opposite direction but there's a few things I need to pick up."

"We'd better get going then," Sobers said. He threw Ziggy a set of keys. Ziggy's eyes caught the Bentley emblem on the keyring in mid air as it flew towards him. Bentley's were his favourite car.

*

Ziggy was sitting proudly at the wheel of the black Bentley. Mr Patel, Mr Dawson and Mr Sobers sat at the back. Ziggy was enjoying himself. The ride was so smooth he thought it felt more like flying than driving.

"Take the next left," Dawson told him.

"My office is in Woodgrange road above the jewellers up on the right."

The Romford road was a simmering aftermath. Cars overturned and still smouldering, shop fronts smashed and looted. The maroon of congealed blood stained the tarmac of the road, and the concrete slabs of the paving. As Ziggy turned into 'the grange' he became aware of a ringing sound getting louder and louder, he turned the music down to hear where it was coming from. Thankfully it was not the car, the engine sounded as sweetly to him as did the stomping sounds of Rily. It was not long before the ringing identified itself as a burglar alarm. As he drew nearer to the bellowing they could see somebody cooly stashing gems into a bag from one of display windows of the double bayed shop front.

"It looks like somebody is trying to break into your office." Sobers said."

"And it's either a brother or some white dude who's taken the trouble to black up," Ziggy added amused.

SHADES OF GREY

"What!?... Is so black people is, dem cyan't see you wid notting fah dem wan tek it from you!" Dawson exclaimed forgetting his airs and graces. "Pull over, I go lick down 'im clart fe 'im!"

"What!?" Sobers exclaimed. "This is election year you know Dawson, I can't afford any scandal understand?"

"But dee man a try teef mi ting....!"

"Dawson!" Sobers cut in. Dawson quickly regain his almost military composure.

"Yes sir," he conceded, "but half my life is in that jewellery shop, myself and Mr King, we have put a lot of money in the place..."

"Samual King?" Sobers asked.

"Yes sir."

"Okay, pull up." Sobers demanded. "I'll get to the bottom of this."

Ziggy sped over. Screeching up outside they hardly noticed the fleeting figure of Conrad scarpering down the road with a pocket full of gems. Toby disappeared into the shop. Dawson called out to him,

"Hey you come here," but there was no response.

Dawson walked authoritatively into the shop, Ziggy, Patel and Sobers followed uneasily. Toby, all in black wore a bullet belt sashed across his chest with a holster carrying a 38 calibre revolver, a 45 was tucked in his trousers. He continued to fill the bag with jewels. Sobers took a step back at the sight of the guns. Ziggy's face drew a smile from intrigue. He watched Toby at work with open admiration. The the way this cat stood his ground, stuck to the job and didn't even flinch at the intrusion, Ziggy was proud of him!

Dawson looked on wide eyed and speechless, his jaws gaped open a gasp of amazement, his face a frozen picture of incredulity.

"What you doing boy!?" he exclaimed.

"Need any help?" Ziggy. offered. There was no answer, not even an acknowledgment of their presence. Toby just carried on in oblivion as the burglar alarm sang out at 110 decibels.

"Give me those jewels you dumb ass!" Dawson said lunging

SHADES OF GREY

for the bag. Toby suddenly swung round pointing the barrel of the 45 in Dawson's face. Intensely they stare into each others eyes.

"Maybe we should come back later," Sobers said cowering behind Dawson and Patel.

"What you doing wid gun you stupid..." Dawson was muted in mid sentence by a bullet that singed through the air, exploding into his skull, scattering his brains and splattering the face of Sobers in blood. A terrified Sobers crumbles to the floor, the dead Dawson falls on top of him. Mr Patel looked petrified into the barrel of the gun in time to take a shot right between the eyes. Ziggy knew he was next, his heart began thumping, his pulse rate doubled, he saw the gun barrel swinging round in his direction, it was all like in slow motion. A thousand thoughts crossed his mind the last of which said I don't want to die. He dived for cover like a rat in a sewer and landed behind the counter. A sea of bullets shattered the glass display above his head, splinters showered down on him like rain. Toby drew the 38, now firing ablaze from both hands like a crazy Kid Curry. The walls and ceiling quaked from the onslaught of his gun fire and powdered fragments of dislodged plaster splattered about as bullets pierced their surface.

Toby walked calmly out into the street. Ziggy heard the blast of gunfire smash the other side of the bay window, and the sound of more jewellery being scraped from among the shattering's of broken glass. A moment, then there was silence. Ziggy peeped through the gap of the door ajar. There was no one. He walked out carefully, eyes searching around for his assailant. Amazingly there was still no sign of the police. Then Ziggy heard a faint wimpering, like a child crying. It was coming from behind the Bentley. Ziggy crept round the side of the limousine towards the weeping sound. There to his amazement was Toby, down on his knees in the road crying up against the car. Ziggy pried both the 45 and the 38 revolvers from Toby's fingers and put them in the bag with the jewels. Mr Sobers came an stood beside Ziggy, both looked down at Toby sniffling and pathetic, no longer the gun touting murdering maniac.

Thought the immediate danger had subsided, the situation

SHADES OF GREY

looked grim from Sobers political perspective. Bad enough that a man in his position should get caught up in a situation like this but during the run up to an election it was politically disastrous. His opponents would have a field day. Already he could see the headlined PROSPECTIVE BLACK CONSERVATIVE MP IN JEWELLERY MURDER SCANDAL! That would mean the end of his career regardless of the out come. What should he do. If he played it straight he was finished that's for sure. He might even wind up in jail, stranger things have happened in this racist bigoted country he thought. Then it came out, while he was consciously still looking at his options, something else stepped in, a survival safety mechanism maybe, who can say. Anyway his mouth opened and words came out.

"We've got to get rid of the bodies and get out of here!"

Ziggy picked up a diamond necklace that lay on the floor. He heard the distant sound of police sirens getting closer as he looked down at the jewels in his open palm. Things did not look good from his perspective either. He was standing by the smashed windows of a high street jewellers with two corpses and a handful of gems, him, a black guy with a record. He was on probation for Christ sake! The alarm was going off and the cops were coming. On the plus side there was the Bentley, if you're gonna have a get away car a Bentley had a lot going for it.

"Make up your mind, we get out of here or we stay to face the music." Ziggy hesitated.

"Come on man! You're a lawyer, you know what I'm talking about, we're looking at twenty years to life!"

Ziggy opened the boot, it was deep and wide. Even in a critical situation like this Ziggy could not help but wish the car was his. The two men loaded the dead bodies into the boot. Toby stared transfixed as in a trance staring into nothing.

"What should we do about him?" Ziggy said. Sobers thought about leaving him but then decided against it. If he thought it would end there he would have, but this was armed robbery, in the state Toby was in he'd probably tell them everything. The faint wail of police sirens was getting louder, coming closer. It was now or never. So with Ziggy in the driving seat, Sobers and

95

SHADES OF GREY

Toby in the back, Patel and Dawson in the boot they took off. As they drove up the mile end road the flashing blue lights and howling siren of several police cars sped in the opposite direction. No one would think to stop a Bentley. They were safe at least for the moment.

"Now you can drop me off anywhere along here I'll get a taxi," Sobers said.

"And what about the cargo in the boot!? What about him!?" Ziggy said referring to Toby.

"I want you to dispose of the bodies and find somewhere for him to stay until I can think of the best way to deal with this."

"No way! You ain't gonna dump all this shit on me and walk off smelling of roses." Ziggy protested.

"Look Dexter, if you value your job you'll...."

"You look, I'm not Dexter right, I'm his twin brother Ziggy, so as far as I'm concerned you can shove your threat up your ass!"

"Look this is no time for stupid games...." With that Ziggy erupted, cussing and swearing in his broadest J.A.

"Wha dee rarsss you ar gwan wid!? It look like I playing games to you!? Look just don't fork wid !!!"

Sobers was astonished. Any lingering doubt that he might have had with regard to Ziggy's true identity were immediately dispelled, now he knew he was stumped.

"What if I said I could make it worth your while?...."

"Now you're talking, how much?" Ziggy cut in. Sobers hesitatesd he dabbed his temples and neck with a shiny red handkerchief from his breast pocket.

"How does five hundred pounds sound to you?" Ziggy laughed.

"How does ten grand sound to you?"

"Don't be silly.- Look if we do this right we can both come out unscathed, neither of us can afford to be greedy now can we?"

"That's right, but the way I see it you have a lot more to lose than I have so why should I be taking all the risks."

Sobers dithered awkwardly, his back was against the wall.

"This is blackmail." he protested.

"Call it what you want, the price is still the same, ten grand," Ziggy said flatly.

SHADES OF GREY

"Okay... Two thousand pounds not a penny more."

"Look, is ten grand me want sah! Or I gwan dump dis cyan a red meat in the police parking lot, I assume is registered in you name. Then I marn gwan walk away smelling as sweet as a daisy. Remember. I ain't officially have dis job. There's no record of we ever having met, in fact apart from laughing bwoy 'ere, dee only people who have seen us together are in dee boot, and I wouldn't rely on dem fi backup if I were you."

"All right, ten thousand! Now just drop me off here." Ziggy stops the car, Sobers jumped out, he looks nervously about him.

"I'll be in touch." Ziggy said as he pulled away.

Ziggy's mind was working overtime, this was the chance of his life. But he dare not mess up, if he did he knew he'd grow to a ripe old age in a cell. But things didn't look so bad. Alright he still had a few decisions to make, like what he was going to do with the two dead bodies in the boot? How was he gonna stop a mentally and emotionally unstable delinquent from either killing someone else, or confessing to the cops? Tricky. But ten grand was a lot of money for a days work, and if he played it right who knows how much he could squeeze Sobers for, and he had the gems. He glanced at a subdued Toby though his rear view mirror. What was going on in his head he wondered. He looked down, by the gear stick was a car phone,

"This is a serious motor!"

When Dexter got back to his flat he was feeling low, he hadn't been able to get his face on TV, so as far as his career was concerned it was back to square one. He hadn't prepared himself for failure, he was so certain that it would work out. To the white viewers he represented an acceptable moderate they need fear nothing from. To the blacks he was a black intellectual who would not let the system abuse them. A certain hit he was sure, but now it had all gone wrong. Despondent as he was he had still thought to stop at the florist and buy a large bunch of roses for Jess.

Jess had spent the day thinking things through, re- evaluating but coming to no firm conclusions. When Dexter walked in she could see that all had not gone well.

97

SHADES OF GREY

"What happened?" she asked him.

"I blew it.- Here I bought you some flowers."

"Oh they're wonderful!"

"My one big chance to make something of my life and I blew it."

"Don't worry about it, there's always another day." Dexter turned to Jess, looking her straight in the eye.

"Is there? Or have I blown it with you too?" She breaks eye contact with him, using the flowers as an excuse to walk away.

"Better get these in some water before they..."

"Jess, answer me. Is there a chance?" Jess fills a jug with water and places the flowers.

"I don't know, I don't want to lie to you and then tomorrow you wake up and find me gone. I just don't know."

"Will you know tomorrow?"

"I don't know, maybe. Don't push me on this, I'm trying to be straight with you."

"So what should I do? Tell me?" Jess make an exasperated sigh. She meets his anxious glare with a concerned sincere look.

"I think... I think we should take one day at a time.-Alright?" Dexter nods his head.

"Alright."

SHADES OF GREY

CHAPTER 18.

Day 3. Night.

From the outside it looked to the police like a straight burglary, a simple smash and grab. But inside the story was different, blood everywhere and an arsenal of used bullets lodged in the walls. Another job for CID's detective Winston Benjamin and his side kick Spikey. They found both 45 and 38 calibre shot. Benjamin looked through the debris of shattered glass that was once a jewellery display cabinet. This was a strange one, what started as a straight jewel robbery had escalated to a homicide. But who and how many had been killed? To Benjamin's trained eye the amount of blood indicated more that one fatality. But nobody lived on the premises of S & J King the jewellers, so there shouldn't have been anyone there apart from the crooks at that time of night. Maybe some innocent passerby had got involved and killed. But the way the bullets had been sprayed about the room from two different calibre guns, it would mean the passerby had to be armed also. But why would anyone choose to endanger their life engaging armed robber's? The place had been smashed up good, It looked like a gunfight situation 'but this ain't no Ok Corral' Benjamin thought. Where was the body or bodies? Did this have anything to do with the shooting at Pinkies and the shooting of the pimp and his whore at the pool hall? He didn't think so, or at least he hoped not. Benjamin knew that the jewellers was a black owned business, so there was the added possibility that this was a racist motivated attack, though equally it could just as well have been a black on black assault he admitted to himself. There had been a spate of arson attacks on black businesses by extreme right wing racist organisations recently, but they had always claimed responsibility within a few hours, usually with a phone call to the station. Time would tell. But would they admit to murder? He doubted it. It could be he thought, an internal fight between the gang members, that would explain why they'd take the corpse's

99

SHADES OF GREY

with them. He sighed and scratched the crown of his head. The permutations seemed endless. There always seemed to be more angles to investigate when black people were involved, or maybe he just felt a deeper obligation because he was a black cop.

He'd start by questioning some of the known local offenders he thought capable of this class of crime. Spikey could check out some of her contacts, it would cost, information didn't come cheap and Spikey had a way of going to the most expensive nightspots to get it. But get it she usually did. He'd wait to see what the finger print men and forensic came up with before speculating anymore.

Benjamin's attention was drawn to the silhouette of a figure out in the street, walking towards the shattered shop window front. As he approached the wimpering sniffles of deep distress grew slowly louder. Gradually the person fell into the ambience of the internal light, which then daubed the tear doused contorted features of an anguished man. He stood for a time, framed in the jagged residue of broken glass still set in the hardened putty of the window frame. Benjamin's eyes followed him as he walked towards the door, guessing that it must be Mr King.

"Are you Mr King?" he enquired tactlessly. King nodded affirmation and whispered a faint "yes" through his tears.

"I'm detective sergeant Benjamin of the serious crime squad. I'd like to ask you a few questions if I may." King made no response to Benjamin's request, but instead walked zombified passed him into the middle of the room.

"Everything I had was in this place," he said solemnly. "Freda and me sunk every penny. I'm ruined."

Benjamin swallowed a lump in his throat. For a moment King just stood sorrowfully staring into nothing. He then took a deep breath and exhaled a short dejected sigh. His swollen eyes met the sympathetic gaze of a dumb-struck Benjamin. King smiled, Benjamin reciprocated hesitantly. King walked towards the door, then stopped and turned around. He looked about the place like a father in mourning, as if for the last time.

"Well, that's it." he said philosophically.

"Don't give up Mr King, that's what they want. Hey, I'll have somebody come over to talk about making this place a little more

SHADES OF GREY

secure. With the insurance money you can... "
"Insurance?!" Mr king laughed, painfully. "I ain't got no insurance. Premiums too high. Yes sir, they certainly did a good job this time.- No, I'd say that was about it."

Benjamin's heart went out to King. He needed to ask him a few questions, but they could wait, now was not a good time.

"Are you gonna be in town over the next couple of days?" Benjamin asked.

"I ain't going nowhere. Nowhere to go. Like I said they got everything I own." With that King slowly sauntered away.

Spikey broke the melancholy mood with a slap to Benjamin's back.

"So what do yer think daddy?"

"Think? Huhm, I think the world stinks, that what I think," he said throwing his eyes back to rest thoughtfully at the spot where King stood only seconds before. Benjamin felt a deep sense of emptiness for reasons he wasn't quite sure of. Maybe it was Mr King, another black man trying to get on the road is kicked back into the gutter. Maybe it was one too many murders in a day, or maybe it was just tiredness.

"Who was that?" Spikey asked tracking his gaze.

"A man at the start of a new end," Benjamin said ironically.

"Poetry! Deep! Deep man!" Spikey exclaimed, genuinely impressed. "Wow daddy! and I thought you was just an two dimensioned, tunnel visioned, rigid thinking old cynic." Spikey strolled the shop floor doenut in hand, seeming only slightly disturbed by the evidence of carnage about her.

"Boy, this world is the pits, I gotta get out before I die." Benjamin smiled. Spikey had a way of bringing things into perspective. She was speaking metaphorically of course, Benjamin had come to understand that 'the world' for Spikey was wherever she hung her hat, be it the room she stood in, a situation or even a person. But her use of the global reference seem to dwarf everything, putting even the gravest of situations in the shade. A lot worse was happening in a thousand places around the world at that very moment, this was just a tiny piece of horror he had to deal with. It was strange thinking in those terms but, Benjamin found it made things easier to handle.

101

SHADES OF GREY

Benjamin caught sight of a small plastic packet among the smashed glass under foot. He bent down and picked it up. He put his finger inside to collect some of the residue of a white powder and tasted it.

"Is that what I think it is?" Spikey said .

"Cocaine," Benjamin confirmed.

"We need to find out who's pushing this and to whom. You're gonna have to go down under, find a snake that's willing to rattle." Benjamin said. Spikey was speechless.

*

Back at the station things were as quite as a mouse at a funeral. There had been no more reports of any break-in's, and thankfully no one else had been killed. No right winged fascist organisation had yet rung claiming responsibility for the J&S King jewellery job, but Franklin, the desk sergeant had a message for Benjamin from the captain. He wanted to see Benjamin right away. 'Shit' Benjamin thought, the captain was a bad news man. He'd never yet wanted to see Benjamin when things were going right. When they'd brought in the drugs haul two days ago he never said a dicky. But now, with a murderer on the loose, he was going to be breathing down Benjamin's neck. Benjamin thought he may as well get it over with and so went straight to the captains office. He knocked on the door, a loud voice called a rough cigar coughing

"Yeah?" from inside. Benjamin entered.

"Winston! You're looking well. Congratulations on the Mexican drug haul, slick work."

Benjamin was so surprised at the praise, he relaxed into a false sense of security, so much so that when the captain hit him with what Benjamin had at first expected, it came as quite a shock.

"These murders...." The captain began, looking worried. "The guy's at forensic came up with some interesting facts today..."

"The bullets found in the clubland kid were from the same gun used to murder the pool hall pimp and his prostitute," Benjamin cut in.

"You got it in one," the captain said sternly, "All three with the same gun, "That looks to me like we've got a serial killer on our

102

SHADES OF GREY

hands, and I wanna know what you're doing about it?"

"Well, we're still making enquiries, so..."

"But have you got anything?" the captain cut in.

"Ah, well... we thought we had the killer but..." The captain sighed in dissatisfaction as he stood up and walked a few poignant paces to the window.

"Benjamin, I think you're a good cop, I respect you, and I admire you as a man, believe me I do."

'Here we go' Benjamin thought, 'patronising bastard! Mixing up the crap and the bull...'

"I understand a little of what you've been going through over the years, with people like Nash and also people from your own community... you've been taking a bashing from both sides, I know..." the captain went on. Benjamin sat back and took in some air, he had heard it all before and knew what was coming.

'... put a little sugar in it why don't ya, why don't you just let me have it instead of wrapping it up in all this shit' he thought.

"Now I'm gonna be frank with you Benjamin, you know as well as I do that it doesn't matter what colour the criminal is, the law is the law."

The captain points his finger out of the window.

"Our streets must be a safe place for our women and children. Now there are people upstairs leaning on me, so I've got to lean on you. We can't have black gangs killing each other on our streets...." Benjamin leapt to his feet,

"In case one of you whites gets caught in the crossfire, huh!?"

"I though you might react like this..."

"This case is only two days old and already you're calling for a lynching, and it seems if you can't find a murderers neck to stretch, you'll take mine. You want my badge you can have it, if not stay off my back."

"I'm afraid not, we're going to be watching you on this one, all the way. You see certain allegations have been made, not to me you understand, if they were I'd have dismissed it as nonsense, and it would have gone no further. No these allegation went over my head straight to the top."

"Who?" Benjamin asked.

103

SHADES OF GREY

"I'm afraid that's confidential."

"Nash," Benjamin breathed venomously to himself.

"The story is that you've been taking a cut of the drugs money. That you know where all the big deal are made and with whom, that the few drug hauls that you smash are pre-arranged between you and the drug lords."

"That's a heap a crap and you know it!" Benjamin snapped."

"I'm only telling you what's been said. These recent killings and the jewel robbery are being seen as drug related crime. So you understand, it's in your best interest that this case be cleared up quickly. So I'd keep the badge if I were you."

Benjamin tried to rub the tension from his brow. He was being stitched up, by Nash initially, but the boys up top were only too happy to go along with it. He wasn't too sure about he captain either. One thing was clear though, his neck was on the line.

"And another thing," the captain said, "The kid you arrested is filing charges against you for assault and wrongful arrest. He says the bruises on his face and abdomen were inflicted by you."

"He was in a fight at Pinkies damnit! that's how he got those bruises! There was a fight a Pinkies! Someone got shot, and I think he knows who did it, and when I get out of here I'm gonna make him tell me who that person was!"

"You can't," the captain said flatly.

"Oh, and why is that?"

"We had to let him go."

"What?!" Benjamin exclaimed.

"His family came down and brought their lawyer with them. If you know what's good for you you'll stay away from that kid."

"But he was an eye witness! My one and only eye witness...!"

"We didn't have a leg to stand on, in fact if it wasn't for Nash having a private word with their lawyer this department could have been in a lot of trouble."

"Nash probably made a deal with the lawyer, promising my ass if he cooperated!" Benjamin shook his head in disbelief.

"The kid made a statement, am I right?".

"Yes and it doesn't look good for you."

SHADES OF GREY

"Okay, just tell me this, who extracted the statement from him?"

"Well Nash..." the captain said hesitantly, "...look I can see what you're getting at but...."

"Anyone that want's to can see that this is a fame up. I know it, and you know it too.

"Think what you want," the captain said.

"This place stinks, that's what I think." Benjamin fixed the captain with a stare, then turned to leave.

"One more thing," the captain said handing a sheet of paper to Benjamin, "the report from forensic. They've apparently lifted a nice set of prints, but they've so far been unable to get a match on them. And they confirm that the blood they found was human," he added.

"Really!" Benjamin cut in. "I was sure it was from a gun touting, diamond loving horse with a drug habit and criminal tendencies." he said sarcastically and slammed the door on his way out.

Benjamin was pissed off, he'd been up two nights on the run, busting a gut for the police department and there they were ready to file an assault and a corruption charge on his ass. Maybe the captain was trying to help, but right now he was too tired to care. Forensic had also derived from the blood samples that there had been at least two dead. They would keep Benjamin posted on further developments. Benjamin was mad at the department but mad at himself too. He had figured this all wrong. He had the first murder down as a crime of passion, a revenge killing, tragic but nothing too weird about it. The killing of the pimp and his whore had looked the result of a dissatisfied customer demanding a refund. He'd thought it reasonable that a killing or two might result from the fracas that ensued. Okay. But the jewellery job....? He couldn't figure it. Having killed two people over the price of a screw, what kind of mind goes on to rob a jewellery store and kill two more people in the same night! A junky? He hadn't thought of that. Why hadn't he thought of that?

CHAPTER 19.

Friday 3. Night.

Ziggy picked up the car phone to call his brother. It was now 1.30 in the am, Dexter and Jess were wrapped up and deep in sleep when the phone rang. Dexter began to stir. He sat up drowsily, switched on the bed side lamp and picked up the phone wiping the sleep from his eyes as they fought the irritation of the bright light. Jess was still enjoying a deep slumber.

"Hello," Dexter said in a sleep ladened voice. Ziggy blurted excitedly, sounding like a horse race commentator in the final furlongs of the grand national.

"Hi Dex, I know it's late but I'm in a jam man. Oh boy am I in a jam. You gotta help me."

Dexter coughed the croak from his voice,

"What's wrong?" he said.

"Oh man," Ziggy wined, "I'm driving down the high street and I hear a burglar alarm, and I see this young dude stashing jewels into a bag as cool as you like. I pulls up to find out who this guy is and he pulls a hot rod on me. I hear the cops coming, but the kids holding me there at gun point with a diamond necklace in my hand. Now the cops are on my tail."

Dexter asked his brother how he'd come to be carrying the necklace. Ziggy explained that he'd picked it up to get a closer look. He knew it sounded stupid, but that was the truth.

"The bottom line is, the kid, he looked like he needed help, and the cops were coming so... I picked him up."

"You what?! Dexter exclaimed.

"I know I know, it was stupid but I couldn't just leave him there. The thing is, you know I'm on probation man, soon they are gonna be knocking at my door, this time I go down man! I just don't know what I'm gonna do. I know I shouldn't be sticking my neck out for this kid and I shouldn't be asking you to do the same for me, but I'm desperate man, I need you brother."

Even though they didn't get on, emphasizing the brother link

SHADES OF GREY

was a nice touch, Dexter was a sentimental fool, Ziggy had traded on the brother trip before, it worked every time.

The line was silent for a moment. Dexter was suspicious, picking up jewel thieves wasn't the sort of kind hearted deed his brother was renowned for.

"Where are you now?" Dexter asked him.

"I'm er, in a call box down the street." He lied.

"Where's the kid?"

"He's right here."

"Okay, go home. I'll get over as fast as I can."

"Thanks bro, I owe you." Ziggy hung up. "Sucker" he added with a smile.

*

Ziggy turned into Halley road heading for home. Dexter got there about 2am. Toby it seemed was still in shock. Ziggy had put him to sit out back, out of sight, if the cops saw him that was it. The guy was a schizophrenic, what he would do next was anybodies guess.

"How's things?" Ziggy said just for conversation sake.

"Fine," Dexter replied, though he wanted to add I'm sleeping with your wife, in fact she's at my place now, I love her. But he didn't, they already had a crisis to deal with, he figured one crisis at a time.

Dexter and Ziggy opened a few beer cans tipping the contents down the sink and discarding the empty cans about the table, so as to make it look like they'd been drinking for a while. They dealt out a pack of playing cards like they were in the middle of a game and went over the story they were going to give to the cops, several times. Two hours later the cops had still not arrived.

"Maybe you've over estimated your notoriety." Dexter said tiredly. Dexter and Ziggy spent another hour drinking and playing cards for real before they decided to call it a night. Ziggy gave Dexter the bag of jewels.

"Look after this will you, I'll pick it up later." Dexter hesitated.

"It's alright, it's only...."

"Don't tell me," Dexter cut in, "I don't want to know. Alright but only for tonight."

SHADES OF GREY

Dexter went back home. Ziggy waited up nervously, still expecting the cops to show. He wondered whether he should go dump the bodies, but it was early morning now and would soon be getting light, he would have to wait for the cover of darkness he decided. Toby walked in from the back room.

"Where's my bag?" Toby asked. Ziggy was momentarily surprised, he had seen Toby kill, but as yet he had not heard him speak.

"It's er... I'm... not sure, I could look for it tomorrow..."

"Don't fuck with me!" Toby said forcefully. Ziggy was reminded of Toby as he was in the jewellers, he saw again the killer in his eyes, it was frightening.

"My brother took it, I... I thought it best...."

"I want it back."

"Sure," Ziggy said, "no problem."

*

Jess was still asleep as Dexter climbed into bed. He was wacked. He hadn't done any of the work he'd intended to. Jess, and now Ziggy had seen to that. A glance at his watch told him it was now 5.45am.

*

Sobers had had Ziggy drop him just a few street away from where he lived. Once he'd gotten safely behind his front door he went straight to the drinks cabinet and poured himself a large brandy. He noticed that his cloths were drenched in blood. He undressed and put his cloths into a bin liner.

Two of his associates had been murdered during a jewel robbery in his presence, now he was being blackmailed by the brother of one of his employees. There he was, on the threshold of political office and now this. He couldn't afford to let anything come between him and his political ambitions. But then he couldn't afford to pay Ziggy God knows how many thousand of pounds either, for he knew a single payment would not be the last of it. God alone knews when that would end. He would be at the mercy of a leech for the rest of his days, he a minister of the cabinet in the pocket of a vagabond. No, he would teach that lout not to play out of his league. He would call the police and reported his car stolen, and give them the name of the thief,

108

SHADES OF GREY

Ziggy Sinclair. All they had to do was pick him up and they would find the bodies in the boot and that would be that. He picked up the phone to call, then thought no, he would go down in person and demand that Ziggy be apprehended immediately, after all he was an important man now.

*

Mr Sober pulled up in a cab outside the police station. Although there was a line of people waiting in a cue he marched straight to the counter with such a superior air of authority he arrived unchallenged.

"I'd like to speak to someone from the Serious Crime Squad." He told a young police constable. The constable politely told him there was a cue to which he should go to the end of and wait his turn.

"Do you know who I am?!" Sobers exclaimed indignantly. "I'm the next MP of this constituency and I demand to see a senior officer of the Serious Crime Squad."

The young Pc was not impressed, in fact he found this black man's grand declaration somewhat amusing. But he also thought to be on the safe side he'd better pass the information on, if only to pass the buck should this nigger really be somebody.

"Okay, let me just take down a few details, your name?"

"Alvin Sobers," He replied. The Pc wrote it down.

"Now what seems to be the problem?"

"My car has been stolen."

The Pc asked for a description of the vehicle and it registration number. He wrote it down.

"Now do you have any idea of who might have taken your car Mr Sobers?" the Pc asked routinely.

"I know who took my car. His name is Ziggy Sinclair." The Pc wrote down the name.

"Right sir we have all we need to enable us to trace the car, my advice to you is to go home an wait...."

"I want to see someone in authority," Sobers cut in.

"There really isn't anything more he can add at this point..."

"I want to see someone in authority!" Sobers demanded. A pause as the two are eyeball to eyeball. The Pc relents.

"If you insist," he disappears into the back.

109

SHADES OF GREY

Spikey waltzed into Benjamin's office with her usual vibrant youthful air in sharp contrast to Benjamin geriatric plod.

"Just in chief, we have a lead. The finger print guy's have found a match, and guess who it is?"

"An old friend, known to both you and I with a record as long as the A13 no doubt."

"Got it in one," she confirmed.

"What's his name?" He asked.

"Our old friend Ziggy Sinclair."

Just then the young Pc poked his head through the door.

"Sir I don't know if you want to be bothered with this but it seems that our perspective MP is demanding an audience with the head of crime. He said his name is Sobers. Alvin Sobers."

"Sobers? Ah yes, I'll see him." Benjamin had heard that the new Tory candidate for the local elections was going to be a black man, and he had made up his mind to switch his allegiance from the Labour party for that reason alone. As a parent of young children he had a growing concern for education, the national health and of course law and order.

"Show him in" he told the Pc.

"That's a relief he's wound up tighter than a yoyo."

"What's his problem?" Benjamin asked casually.

"Oh somebody ripped off his car," the Pc said consulting his notes "a Mr Ziggy Sinclair he says." Benjamin and Spikey look at one another.

"I'll see him in the interview room," he told the Pc. The constable picked up on the change of mood but knew better than to pry.

Sobers fought hard to compose himself as he walked into the interview room, he was already feeling like a guilty man.

"Mr Sobers" Benjamin greeted. The two shake hands. "Detective sergeant Benjamin and my assistant Dc Spikey. Do sit down. Now about your car."

It had taken Benjamin just a few minutes to decide that he didn't like Sobers. To a police nose as old as Benjamin's he just didn't smell like an honest man. There was something devious about him. 'Could I entrust the future welfare and education of my children to this man' he thought? The answer was no.

SHADES OF GREY

Benjamin stared at Sobers long and hard while he ranted on about how he'd given this black man a chance, and the ungrateful wretch had turned to bite the hand that had fed him. Benjamin decided right there and then that the Labour party could have his vote again that year. Didn't matter how black Sobers was, Benjamin didn't trust him and that was that. According to Sobers, Ziggy was employed to clean the car and drive him to and from engagements. That morning Ziggy disappeared with the car and had not been seen since. Benjamin tried never to allow his personal dislike of somebody to prejudice his police judgement, but Sobers was making it difficult. Though he had no reason to disbelieve Sobers, he did wonder why he had taken so long to report the theft, but chose not to ask the question. Neither did he choose to mention that the car in question had possibly been involved in an armed robbery at which at least two people had been fatally wounded. First he wanted to hear the other side of the story.

"Ziggy Sinclair is known to us, we'll issue a warrant and have him picked up. In the mean time if you leave us a number where you might be reached, we'll be sure to keep you posted of any developments. He probably just went out for a joy ride, got carried away, and forgot the time. Chances are your car's fine." Benjamin assured him.

"I hope so." Sobers said making his way out. "But he was a vicious violent looking man. I hope no one has come to any harm." Benjamin was quietly curious. He wanted to ask Sobers why he employed violent vicious men to wash his car but resisted the temptation allowing Sobers to leave.

"A violent vicious man. Strange thing to say," Spikey said.

"Very strange," Benjamin replied.

SHADES OF GREY

CHAPTER 20.

Saturday morning.

Natasha was on skip thirty seven and going strong, she'd bet Louise that she could do fifty non stop. This was her third try. Her first attempt was foiled at forty six when Louise deliberately put her foot in the orbit of the skipping rope. In her second attempt Natasha got to only twenty seven because she said she was 'too tired' so soon after her first try, so she was taking another go because she would have done it the first time had Louise not cheated. Natasha stopped on fifty one and immediately challenged Louise to beat it. Louise accepted the challenge and got to forty seven before Natasha's outstretched foot halted her progress. She too would take another go. The floor boards vibrated with every jump, the vibrations travelled along the boards into the next room and up the four wooden legs of what was once the marital double bed of Mr and Mrs Benjamin.

Joe Frazier, Joe Louis, George Foreman and Sugar ray, were all taking it in turn to hit Benjamin on the left side of his face. The four of them were hitting him with all they had. It was a relentless pounding, Benjamin begged them to stop, but instead two new recruits joined in, his wife Milli and her boyfriend Herman. These punches hurt the most of all. Wack!!

"That's for not coming home when you promised to take me to the theatre," Milli screamed.

"But baby, you know how it is in the police force....!" Benjamin pleaded.- Wack!!

"And that's for not coming home when you promised to take me the the pictures."

"Don't hit me baby, I promise I'll take you tomorrow." Benjamin begged her.- Wack!!

"And that's for not being here when I needed you." Then came a mighty Doof!! And the sight of Herman's smirking face.

"And that's for being a sucker!" Herman said. Benjamin went

SHADES OF GREY

crazy.

"You dirty stinking son-of-a-bitch...." he began. As they all twirled away. Benjamin wakes, his pillow does indeed feel like a boxing glove being rammed in his face. The jumping stops with a ecstatic yelp of, "Fifty two!" but the ensuing screams and shouts of the girls arguing arrives at their father irritable eardrums sounding like a thousand chipmunks having their teeth pulled without anesthetic.

"Why is it they can never get up for school on time, but come Saturday they're up and kicking at the crack of dawn." Benjamin bawls out from under the covers.

"Natasha! Louise!" There was first a silent pause followed by the unison of two fearful little girls voices.

"Yes daddy."

"Didn't I tell you that when daddy is sleeping you should whisper and creep around silently on your tiptoes?"

"It wasn't me it was Natasha...

"No it wasn't it was you, I didn't make no noise daddy."

"Get in here!" Benjamin ordered.

As Benjamin uncovers his dozy head he finds the two girls standing by his bed side, but before he can say another word they each plant a kiss on his crusty face.

"Morning daddy."

"Morning Daddy."

"Hm? Yeah eh, morn... now kids, you know...."

"I'm just going to make you a cup of tea daddy," Louise says and is off.

"And I'll make you some toast," Natasha added as she followed.

".... you're daddy is tired..." he said to the empty room. He sat up in the bed, his mind was instantly filled with thoughts of murder, drugs, Nash, the captain and their vendetta against him. He thought about burying his head under the covers again, but he knew that wouldn't be enough, sooner or later the phone would ring and he'd have to go. He wanted to be so far away from the police department they'd need a satellite to reach him. He felt like taking the kids, jumping on a plane and never coming back. But he knew that when in hell, there was only one way to

113

SHADES OF GREY

deal with the devil, face him and fight. It was no good running away because hell is everywhere and the devil is a patient man, it was only a matter of time before they'd meet again. He could have been a bus driver, he remembered walking passed the depot and the poster of a guy in uniform pointing at him. It said 'London transport needs you'. He could have been driving a bus now but for the lure of the boys in blue. Somebody had to make the streets safe for his children to walk. That's what Milli had never understood. 'Dat is for others to do,' she'd say, 'you is a black man, dey don't want you looking after dem children, dey don't even want you around, one day dem going an' chrow it back all in you face.'

"Oh Milli, Milli..... why aren't you here when I need you?"

Most of the time he never even thought of her, he'd managed to block her out, kill the part of him that was her or at least subdue it till it felt like she didn't exist. It was the only way he found that he could deal with them not all being together, a family. The kids were handling it better than he was, they missed her, but because he'd told them she was just working away for a while, they thought that she'd be coming back to them... one day. He of course knew that she wasn't.

He'd get her out of his system, he'd be getting on with his life, a man and his kids, no big thing, just another one parent family. Then just as it seemed life was half way complete and worth living again, she'd phoned up to speak to the kids. Then he'd know... that she was alive and well... and with someone else.

He had to kill her in his heart every time she'd hung up so that he could go on alone again, but every time he did it, it ripped him up inside. Today though was different, she hadn't called, but she was alive and kicking inside him. He felt her presence as vividly as if she were in the room. Had he given her up too easily? He'd asked himself that question a hundred times. Should he have fought for her, if only for the kids sake? Should he have made this Herman guy fight for her, if only for her sake, and his own?

"Ol' Herman, had it so easy, Milli threw herself at him and I just let him take her. I told myself it was an unselfish act, I thought maybe it was just my ego hurting, if she really wanted

SHADES OF GREY

someone else why should I stand in the way of her happiness? But what about my happiness, and the kids? What about our responsibility to the kids, maybe it was my responsibility to make her see that. Shit Milli, that's why I don't wanna talk to you I just get confused. Look at me, I don't know what I'm doing, what I should have done, what I'm gonna do...."

Benjamin stopped at the sight of Natasha and Louise, a cup of tea and a saucer of toast.

"Who were you talking to daddy?" Louise asked. The sight of his daughters reminded him of what it was all for. No matter how bad it all seemed, in spite of everything he still had them, he'd managed to get something right in his life and he'd done it twice.

"I was talking to your mother."

"Without a phone?" Natasha asked.

"Yes without a phone."

"You're not going crazy are you?" Louise asked.

That was a good question, and rather than answer it Benjamin sent the kids out to play. He wasn't going crazy, although sometimes he wished he was. Crazy men take chances in life. Perhaps if he'd been a crazy man he'd have punched Herman in the nose. Perhaps if he were a crazy man he'd be in America now with Milli and the kids. But the only chances he had ever taken in his life were with his life, for the damn police force. In every other aspect of his life he'd played it safe. He'd thought about joining a lonely heart group or dating agency, he'd even filled out an application form and questionnaire, but he never sent them. 'Those things are for desperate people...' other desperate people.

Benjamin began thinking about Spikey's mother Jeraldine. He wondered whether or not she had a man, but then decided that a good looking woman like her probably had many suitors. But then again, he thought, she didn't look the type. She looked like the type of woman who liked to have just one man. The type of woman who liked to dress as he liked, wore the perfume that he'd bought her, because he'd bought it. The type of woman who liked flowers. The type of woman who could cook, and liked to cook for her man. She'd wait up for him when he was late and worry in case something had happened to him, but when he

115

SHADES OF GREY

came home she wouldn't nag, she'd be so happy to see him, and he'd be so happy to see her they'd wanna talk all night. She'd do most anything just to please him, and make it impossible for him to say 'no' to her. Benjamin picked up the phone, he told himself he was gonna ring Spikey and discuss the case with her. But all the time he was wondering how he might find out if her mother had a man. How could he find out without just coming out and asking her. He dialled the number. A mellow seductive voice answered the phone, it was her, Jeraldine. Benjamin was dumbstruck, he heard her velvet vocal chords again.

"Hello?" It was either hang up or speak, but he didn't know what to say, so he hung up. His breathing was heavy and he had even broken a sweat, he felt stupid but he knew that if he'd spoken then he would have blown it. 'She would have heard the croak in my voice and known I had just gotten out of bed,' he thought. He coughed to clear his throat. He would ring back, but what would he say? What could he say without sounding stupid?

"Hello Jerry... Jerry? Better stick to Jeraldine for now. Jeraldine. Hello Jeraldine, can I speak to Spikey. No, that's no good, all she'd do is say hang on and then hand me over."

Benjamin rehearsed and pondered, then rehearsed again but nothing sounded right.

"Come on Benjamin," he told himself,

"take a chance for once in your life, you wanna ask the woman out, ask her out!"

He picked up the phone and dialled the number, Spikey's chirpy shrill unexpectedly jumped from the receiver.

"Hi daddy, what's new?" Benjamin was thrown for the minute, he had decided being flirtatious but assertive was the correct approach and had gotten himself into a cool but deadly mood. Spikey he quickly decided was an annoying nuisance he would not allow to distract him.

"Let me speak to your mother," he said definitely.

"Mum?" Spikey asked suspiciously.

"Correct?" he said forcefully.

"Oh... alright. Muuum!" he heard her call. Jeraldine's sweetly seductive velvet voice came on the line again.

116

SHADES OF GREY

"Hello?"

"Hello, this is Benjamin. I was wondering if you might like to go out with me sometime."

"How sweet," she said "I would love to. When?"

"Eh... Ah..." Benjamin hadn't rehearsed any further than the asking, but he eventually managed to stammer; "H.. H.. How about... eh... tonight?"

"Tonight's fine, about eight?"

"Eh yeah... I'll eh.... pick you up."

"I'll see you tonight then, bye."

"Bye," he said. As he put down the receiver he punched the air triumphantly, he felt twenty again. He still had the 'ol magic touch he told himself, and from now on, no woman was safe. Then suddenly it dawned on him. He was on duty tonight. 'Damn! he thought. I'll just have to ring back and tell her, Damn!' he cussed again. He rehearsed the lines but every way he said it sounded weak, he didn't want to come over as a silly scatter brained wimp, what could he do? He could bluff it he thought, maybe tonight would be a quiet night, in which case no problem, if anything did come up over the radio he'd have to make like it was an emergency and give her 'the police are never off duty shit'. He'd just have to hope. It was crap, but it was the best he could come up with right now. 'Oh but what about Spikey? Put her in the back seat, tell her to shut up and not to peek?' Fat chance, she'd never go for it, and he was too old to be chaperoned anyhow. He could come clean with her but that didn't feel like a good idea either. He was stumped, but he'd just have to leave it at that and hope a better idea came to him.

CHAPTER 21

Saturday afternoon.

Saturday. It was now 1.30 in the pm, and the couple were still in bed their limbs entwined like strings of spaghetti between the sheets. She had been awake for about twenty minutes just studying the lines of his frown, breathing in his early morning aroma and nestling in the arm and legs that enveloped her. She gently plants two kisses, one on each of Dexter's eyelids. Dexter blinked Jess's face into focus and smiled.

"Hi." She said as she kissed his nose. An exhausted Dexter could only manage a groan response. "Wake up sleepy head." She whispered cheerfully. Dexter groaned again. "You look tired," Jess said.

"And I've got so much work to do. I haven't even begun to prepare the case for the riot victims. What time is it?"

"It's about one O'clock."

"What?! I've got to go and talk to them at least."

"Did you get up in the middle of the night?" Jess asked. The question jolted the drowsiness from Dexter's mind and the events of the earlier hour flashed across his eyes still closed.

"Eh yeah. I er... had a belly ach..." he lied.

"You should have woke me!" she cut in giving him a sympathetic hug.

"Let me get you something."

Jess got out of the reproduction antique four poster bed and stepped onto the thick piled carpet. The walls were a soft pink which was easy on the eye and gave the room a sensuous feel they both liked even in the bright midday sun. She was completely nude. Dexter turned over to look at her. He loved to see her naked. His eyes lured down her neck to her firm breast and thick rounded nipples.

"Has anyone ever told you you've got a brilliant pair of tits?"

She giggled, gently swivelled her shoulders giving them a subtle bounce. His eyes lit up, he licked his lips and swallowed

SHADES OF GREY

hard, his manhood rose visibly. She was exciting him and she knew it. She turned and walked towards the wardrobes huge mirrored doors through which they spied each other reflection. She reached up to the top shelf for the aspirin. Dexter breathed deeply and smiled to himself, the wardrobe had been a good buy he thought, he now enjoyed her luscious curves back and front. She could feel the heat from his lecherous eyes burning up her long legs, then roasting down her back.

"Come here." He said.

"I'm getting you some medication," she teased insistently.

"I want to bite your bum," he said, as a matter of fact as he could manage.

"No, you're not well!" she said dropping two solubles into a glass of water. She returned to the bed fighting hard to suppress a grin as she offered Dexter the fizzing drink. They stared into each others eyes stone faced, he gently held her wrist and took the glass laying it to rest on the bedside table, guiding her towards him, onto the bed and under the covers.

Two hour later Jess and Dexter were climbing out of the hot bath they had shared. Both were dripping wet. Dexter wrapped a velvet soft white towel around Jess's shoulders. She shut her eyes as he gently dried her face. He kissed her mouth, then he dried her neck and kissed her there also. He dried her breast, kissed them too, then rubbed them down again pinching her nipples slow and unnecessary. She groaned then giggled, he bent down ceremoniously to kiss her once more but she drew away from him with a stern but playful expression. He gave her his naughty boy look. They both laugh. The moment was interrupted by the sound of the front door buzzer. Dexter went to the intercom and pressed the speak button.

"Hello, who is it?" He inquired.

"It's me, Ziggy" Jess froze a worried wide eyed glare to Dexter.

"Don't worry, I'll keep him down stairs." Dexter assured her. He squeezed her hand, smiled and kissed her lightly on her forehead.

"I'll get rid of him as quickly as I can." Dexter pressed the speak button again, "I'm coming down," he said.

SHADES OF GREY

Dexter went to the front door, opened it and handed Ziggy the bag. He had no intention of letting him in but Toby pushed passed taking the bag and hustling himself into the front room before Dexter had a chance to object.

"This is nice," Toby said. "I need a place to stay." he was looking directly at Ziggy.

"Eh.... You er.... You couldn't put him up for a couple of days could you?"

"Forget it," Dexter said flatly.

"Just for a couple of days." Ziggy pressed him. "Look, I did you a favour that's why I'm in this mess."

"Favour? It cost me sixty quid, that ain't a favour. And I didn't tell you to go picking up jewel thieves either, that was your bright idea. No way," Dexter reiterated bluntly.

"Come on man. You've got that spare room with no one in it." Dexter hesitated.

"Well actually er.... I er..."

"What?" Ziggy said. He was looking directly at Jess's bag on the floor but did not recognise it. "Oh I get it, you've got a girl staying. She won't mind, where is she? I'll sort it out with her." he teased and began walking toward the stairs.

"No!" screamed Dexter and pulled Ziggy back. "I mean.... I er... sure, he can stay."

"Great." Ziggy said relieved, "You're good to me big brother," he gabbled insincerely on his way out.

Ziggy wondered if he should have warned Dexter to keep an eye on Toby as he was responsible for the two dead bodies that were locked away in Mr Sober's Bentley, but then thought the less said the better.

Dexter and Toby looked at one another, each took an instant dislike to the other. Toby dropped the bag of jewels absentmindedly on a persian rug which covered the polished wooden flooring. Toby looked curiously about his new surroundings.

"Nice flat." Toby said cockily, then fell back onto the settee as if he owned the place.

"Make yourself at home why don't you," Dexter seethed through gritted teeth. Toby got to his feet, browsed a moment

120

SHADES OF GREY

about the room then opened the drinks cabinet. A light automatically came on reflecting about it's glass interior and the numerous elaborately labelled liquor bottles. They were all there, whisky, rum, vodka, brandy, gin, a crystal decanter with matching glasses and an ice bucket. A box of fat cigars lay unopened in the corner. Toby poured himself a large vodka, the ice bucket was empty. He showed this to Dexter as if complaining of the service.

"No ice!" he said incredulously.

"Don't push it," Dexter warned sternly. Toby laughed a little at the threat.

"It doesn't matter, I'll drink it warm." He carried the bottle and his half filled glass toward the television, turned it on and stood watching the dead screen. As the picture began fading up he took a few backward steps again slumping heavily into the sofa. He sipped. The vodka made him cough a little and burnt on the way down. He poured himself another knocking it back quickly this time. The effects of the cocaine were wearing off, his body yearned for more. He eyed a small distinguished looking, intricately carved inlaid table, he put his emptied glass on it. He wanted to put his feet on it, but with Dexter regarding his every move disdainfully he thought he'd better not. He took a drink straight from the bottle, then another. He flicked through the channels with the remote and played with the contrast and colour buttons. The picture was sharp, the colours deep, he flicked through again, took another long drink of vodka then let his head rest on the back of the chair. Now the alcohol slid down his numbed throat like water. He shut his eyes, his heads began to spin. He let the vodka bottle fall to the floor and lay back as if asleep. Jess had heard Ziggy leave and decided it was safe to come in.

"What did he want?" she began to ask then she saw Toby, just as he began to stir from his nap. Her first thoughts were 'oh shit it's him, he must be a friend of Dexter's, does he know Ziggy? Oh god, should I hide, or pretend I don't remember him?' For some reason she was working herself up into quite a state, when Toby saw her, he kind of half smiled. 'Oh shit he's seen me' she thought, 'now what am I gonna do? What am I gonna

SHADES OF GREY

say?'

"Hi, we meet again," Toby greeted.

"You two know each other?" Dexter asked.

"We're old friends," Toby said. Dexter seemed to accept that, if anything he seemed relieved.

"I'm gonna be staying with you for a couple of days."

Jess looked to Dexter for an explanation. He ushers her from the living room.

"What would you say to a weekend in Italy, hm? By the time we get back he'll be gone. And it will give us a chance to sort things out. Look, I've got to go now or I'll blow this thing, and I can't afford to do that. Why don't you get ready for a flight some time this evening, hm?" Jess nodded her agreement, he kissed her on the cheek then led her back into the living room.

"Okay, we're going away for a couple of days, on my return I want to find this place just as I left it, but with you gone understand?"

"Sweet," Toby answered. Dexter turns to Jess,

"I'll see you later." He kisses her again then goes. Toby slowly looked her up and down. Jess was dressed, made up and ready to go in a figure hugging mini dress, she looked stunning.

*

Ziggy drove the Bentley aimlessy around the streets, where he was going he hadn't worked out yet. If he didn't have so much on his mind he might have enjoyed the car more, but he had two dead bodies to get rid of, until that was done he wouldn't be able to relax. At least he didn't have to think of the kid for a while. He took a left at Dalston lane, a red light stopped him at the junction of Pond street and Graham road. A police car drew up beside him. This is it he thought, he had been pulled up in Hackney many times, the procedure was always the same. 'Is this your car sir?' was always the first question, followed by 'Would you mind stepping out of the car.' They'd search the vehicle, find the bodies in the boot and that would be it. Ziggy held the Bentley in first gear, his left foot on the clutch, his right hovering about the accelerator. As soon as the cop got out of the car he would speed away regardless of the state of the traffic lights. Hopefully those few seconds it would take for the cop to get back in his car

122

SHADES OF GREY

would give him enough of a start to get away. The odds were stacked against him he knew that, but there was no alternative.

Ziggy watched the policemen from the corner of his eye. The look of amazement on the cops face changed to one of envy and resentment as he looked repeatedly from the car to Ziggy's black face and back again. The cop nearest to him said something to the other cop who looked over. The two policemen were both approaching middle age which was unusual, the cops these days seemed to be getting younger and younger. Ziggy's eye's were fixed on the traffic lights. The amber illuminated, Ziggy waited, His heart was pounding so loud he was sure that they could hear it. His sweaty palms gripped the steering wheel like they were afraid it might take off and leave him. Still the policemen stayed in their vehicle. Ziggy was so geared up to go, that when the green light came, it triggered a reflex response that shot the Bentley forward with an un-harnessed roar of it's 6.75 litre V8 engine. But only for a foot or so before Ziggy had regained control of both the car and his fraying nerves. He looked over to the police car, the policeman smiled as Ziggy allowed them to go before him. He proceeded slowly behind allowing the police car to get well ahead, then took the first left turn he came to.

"That was close."

Ziggy looked in the rear view mirror, suddenly the green and yellow decomposing faces of the dead men leaped up and were crawling over the rear window of the car. Ziggy screeched to a halt. The recoil jolted his head forward spraining a muscle in his neck. He frantically turned to look behind him. There was nothing. He took a long deep breath in an effort to calm his nerves. He was tired he told himself. But he had been shaken up so much that he needed to take a look at the corpses to reassure himself that they were dead, and still in the boot. They were there alright but neither was a pretty sight. Rigor mortis had frozen a wide eyed open mouthed blood curdling look of terror on their mangled remains. Ten grand or no ten grand, this was a dirty job, the dirtiest!

How life had changed in just a few hours. Jess would never believe what he'd been through, he'd almost been killed for

SHADES OF GREY

Christ sake! Jess.... How he wished he could turn back the clock. Things were going to be different from now on, he was going to find himself a job, maybe buy himself a car, okay it wouln't be a Bentley, but still, it would be something he and Jess would be proud to ride in.

Thinking about her seemed to calm his nerves somehow. He missed her, he really missed her. His close brush with death had made him realise just how precious life was. There was more than one way to throw it away, drink drugs and loose women were just three of them. The emotional jolt like the one he'd had that night had opened his eyes to what was real and important in the world. Jess was a beautiful woman, he was lucky to have her. What did she really see in him? Being objective about himself had always been difficult for Ziggy, he'd always seen himself as Gods gift, now suddenly he didn't seem such a hot proposition. He had to admit he had his bad points, quite a few in fact. He began to feel a little insecure. How would he feel if Jess broke off their relation ship? He laughed aloud.

"This is no time to get sentimental." But he was feeling sentimental, vulnerable, alone, and but for the two dead bodies in the boot he was all of those things. He wanted to see Jess, she was his woman and he needed her. He was even prepared to be nice to her mother. He suddenly swung around and headed for her parents house.

Ziggy pulled up into the driveway of a terraced house in East ham. He got out of the shinning black limousine and took a moment to speculate at the reaction of Jess's parent to their much hated son in law pulling up in a Bentley. They'd be so impressed he thought, 'if I had money they'd love me.'

He rang the doorbell, It was answered by the well preserved dark skinned mother in law that he had always found strangely attractive. He might well have sought her as yet another conquest had she not been Jess's mother. Ziggy could never quite work out what it was about this very English black woman with her many airs and graces that turned him on. He had always imagined her to be an animal in bed, though when she spoke you could be forgiven for thinking you were speaking to the queen herself. She was obviously surprised to see Ziggy

124

SHADES OF GREY

"Is something wrong? Is it Jessica?" she squealed.

"Yeah, I've come to take her home" he said. He wanted to say we're going to have children that will look just like me. She would probably have collapsed at that, but right now he wasn't interested in giving the old bat a heart attack. He just wanted to see Jess.

"Take her home? We haven't seen her from yesterday, did she say she was coming over?"

"Come on, I know she's here."

"No she isn't, are you sure she's not at home? Cedric!" She called into the house, "Ziggy's come to call for Jessica."

A middle aged light skinned pot bellied black man approached wearing a puzzled frown. He spoke with a deep heavy Jamaican accent. Ziggy had often wondered how this odd couple had ever got together.

"So wa happen, you two had a row? Well she ain't 'ere mate, she mussa gone by one of she friends."

Ziggy looked from one face to the other, he knew they were not lying. So where was Jess?

*

Ziggy had intended to dump the bodies on the Hackney marsh or in the Thames. Now he just wanted to find Jess. This whole thing was getting more risky by the minute and suddenly he didn't have the stomach for it. Why should he take all these risks just to save Sobers skin. This was his car, they were his dead friends in the back. It suddenly dawned on Ziggy that he could just walk away and forget about the whole thing. It would be his word against Sobers but all the evidence would point to Sobers. He decided that that was what he would do, find a secluded place for the car and dump it.

He drove to an old warehouse in one of the back streets of bow. The place was empty and deserted, he knew it would be, previously it had been used as a drive in disco, but residence from miles around would complain of the noise. The police were always raiding the parties, eventually it was abandoned. He forced open the door and drove in, it was strange to see it so quiet and lifeless. He parked the car got out and began the walk for home.

SHADES OF GREY

*

He had only been in bed about an hour when the police called to take him in for questioning. He went obligingly. playing ignorance. He thought that would be his best bet, deny all knowledge of Sobers, the robbery, the murders and the car and rely on Dexter giving him an alibi.

CHAPTER 22.

Day 4. Saturday afternoon.

When Benjamin got to the station there were two black guys in their late twenties arguing with Franklin. The first guy, a yellow skinned short fat black Billy bunter look alike was making most of the noise. The other guy, a tall thin dark skinned man stood zombified, his eyes were glazed and he wore the permanent, dopey hang dog, brain dead expression of a certified junkey. When Franklin saw Benjamin he looked relieved.

"Can I help either of you gentlemen?" Benjamin said.

"Sure you can help us, by getting this killer off the street. Man, they're murdering us out there man, and we wanna know what you're doing about it," Bunter said. Dopey grunted in agreement.

"You gonna arrest somebody, or you gonna wait until a few more of us get killed?" Bunter went on. Dopey grunted again.

"We are in the process of conducting a thorough investigation, but as yet we have made no arrests." Benjamin said.

"Well don't you think it's about time you did that?" Bunter pressed him. Dopey grunted once more.

"And who do you suppose I should be arresting?"

"Dem National Front guys innit! Everyone knows is dem man." Bunter said. Dopey was grunting and nodding his head emphatically now.

"Look guys, I understand your concern, but you're not helping matters by slinging accusations around. It doesn't matter how you or I feel about the Front I can't lift a finger without real

126

SHADES OF GREY

evidence. Now the best thing you can do is go home and..."

"You're full of shit man! We ain't going nowhere until you arrest somebody," Bunter said.

"Alright, what about your friend here, what's he on? Using narcotics is against the law you know. And who's his supplier? you? If you don't get outta here fast, I'd say you could be on the road to a five to ten year stretch."

Bunters eyes widen, without another word he began backing up towards the door, but after a few steps he had to return for dopey who hadn't made a move.

As the two of them scuttled out like a couple of frightened rabbits, Spikey slithered in looking sassy in an expensive looking full length leather coat. As she walked her thighs parted the wings of the coat allowing intermittent sparkles to escape from the glittering dress she wore underneath. She paraded up and down, twirling like a cat walk model at a fashion show. Benjamin stood mouth agape in astonishment. He wondered what the hell she could be celebrating, the Metropolitan police ball was last week, and he knew it wasn't Christmas. She sauntered in front of the desk and sat seductively on it's edge.

"So what do you think?" she asked Benjamin. Nash was hovering around giving off hostile vibs as usual.

"Yeah, not bad," he said.

"What you doing tonight, maybe I could show you something you ain't seen before."

"Maybe tomorrow Nash, I'll bring my magnifying glass along." Benjamin wanted to get a look at Spikey without the coat, but thought it improper to ask. He stared at her with an obvious look of naked disbelief on his face.

"Spikey?... is.... is that you?... you look..."

"Beautiful?" She prompted.

"Well, yeah" he said hesitantly. "Yeah... So what did you want to see me about?"

"News from the street daddy,"

"What you got?"

Spikey with a look of elation on her face mysteriously held up a pair of diamond earrings. Benjamin frowned, he was obviously none the wiser. For a while they held their poses both waiting for

SHADES OF GREY

the penny to drop.

"They go well with the dress," Benjamin said speculatively.

"I'm not gonna wear them, they're evidence" She could tell from Benjamin's face that he still just wasn't getting it.

"From the robbery," she went on "the King jewellery store robbery?"

"What?!.. Hey!.. Wh... Where'd you get those!?" Benjamin exclaimed.

"Would you believe those hot gems are already in circulation..."

"Any idea where they're coming from?"

"Yup. The same place that sachet of cocaine came from. His name is Conrad Baptist a night club junky, hence the appropriate attire."

Benjamin relaxed, he smiled and nodded affirmatively.

"Now I get it." Benjamin said finally. "When?"

"Tonight," she told him, "Pinkies is the place to be."

Benjamin breathed a quite sigh of relief, that meant his date was on, and Spikey would be out of the way. At that moment he didn't care about the robbery, the department thinking he was a bent cop or even that there was a killer on the loose, he needed a break, a break with a pretty women. Spikey twirled around like a summers day bride.

"You think Baptist will go for it?" she said.

"Eh... that depends," Benjamin answered.

"On what?"

"On whether he likes any meat on his bones...."

"You shut up...!"

"You know I'm kidding. Poor guy, he won't be able to help himself.- Now remember, don't have too much of a good time, if he shows knab him. We need to find out where the bodies are, and where the murder weapon is right? I want a result hear? The last time we were on a stake out I was left alone in the car while you were off gallivanting. Well not this time!"

This time Benjamin had plans of his own.

CHAPTER 23.

Saturday afternoon.

The grey light from an overcast sky blurred through the window and diffused depressingly around sink of dirty dishes. The steam from a boiling kettle rose up forming a misty cloud merging with the day. Agnes had already been up an hour aimlessly browsing through the pages of Cosmopolitan while she sipped a citrus fruit drink. She was an attractive brown skinned woman of 35 with a brown curly shoulder length weave on. Shapely but just a little over weight, she stood 5' 7" from the ground. Her outfit of yesterday, a bright knee length skirt of african influenced design and a simple white blouse rested on the ironing board.

She had already made two attempts at getting Conrad out of bed, and was about to make a third when a sudden sonic blast of screaming female vocal chord emanated through the floor from the flat below. A slightly less audible but equally ferocious male voice bawled in response. Now the two voices crescendoed in an unblending anarchic disorder. No one could sleep through this she thought. She poured the boiling water into a cup of coffee granules, and the rest into a washing up bowl. She stirs milk and three teaspoons of white sugar to the coffee cup. The row from below continued quite audibly and Agnes stopped for a moment to listen. 'The blissful tranquillity of married life,' she thought.

"I can't wait."

A glance at her watch told her it was five minutes past one. She takes the cup over to Conrad, still deep in sleep. She shakes him vigorously.

"Here. You know it's almost two thirty" she lied. Conrad clambers through the blankets and somnolently sits on the edge of the bed taking the coffee that is almost too hot to hold an certainly too hot to drink. There is a loud crash from the flat

SHADES OF GREY

below.

"Conrad this place is a tip, how long have those dirty dishes been in the sink? They smell. Look at the state of the place." She nagged "If I knew you were bringing me home to a flea pit like this I would never have come."

Agnes had been Conrad's pick up the previous night. In her intoxicated state she had allowed Conrad to sweet talk her into coming back to his 'luxury pad.' Now in the cold realism of a sober morning she felt like complaining.

"Listen to those animals downstairs! You should phone the police and report them."

Conrad hung over and drowsy, found the piercing sound of Agnes voice irritating. He reached for his cloths which had been carefully discarded to a heap during the frenzied undressing of the last nights passion. He had learned through experience that during these crucial moments, awkward pauses of struggling with belt clips and shoelaces could have the effect of cooling a girls eroticism. One such girl seemed to sober, up change her mind and walked out the door while he struggled to take off his boots. Another came to realise that she really did love her husband and took the same rout.... out. So he had perfected an undressing technique, taking off trousers and underwear in one movement with the left hand, unhooking her bra strap with the right, while at the same time kicking off his shoes. All things being equal, if drink intoxication had not robbed him totally of his co-ordination they would both become naked around the same time. From there it was plain sailing. In the morning his underwear was still in place within his trousers while his shoes sat at the bottom of the pile, waiting to accept his feet as they popped from each trouser leg. His shirt would have been thrown on top. The whole thing looked as if a body had disintegrated like a vampire in the sunlight, leaving it's clothing to collapse where it stood. It was even possible, though he thought unnecessary to get dressed in one movement also, in a kind of reversal of his undressing procedure. This highly refined technique however had one slight drawback, it made no provision for the removal of his socks. He would be butt naked but for his smelly socks. Not surprisingly some of his conquest had found this a bit of a turn off. By that

SHADES OF GREY

time though, they had usually passed the point of no return. If she complained he would simply slip them off.

Conrad put the coffee down. Eyes still shut, he walks lazily to the sink, splashes cold water on his face then dries it with a dirty looking light blue towel.

"Why don't I drop you at the station," he suggest flatly.

"Just like that!?" she snaps back indignantly. "I thought you were taking me to the fair."

"I'm busy" he said cold and abrupt. He callously threw her coat to her. The coat fell halfway across her face onto her shoulder. For a moment she froze like a statue. She felt insulted, used, hurt. She pulled the coat from obscuring her face and hung it over her arm which felt a more dignified position. A lump in her throat would have prevented her from speaking if she'd known what to say. Conrad seeming insensitively unconcerned, had put on his jacket and was already half way out the door. He looked at her, she stood eyes to the floor failing to take her cue. Finally she said sheepishly,

"Are you going to ring me?"

"Sure." was all he said. They left.

CHAPTER 24.

Saturday Afternoon.

When Dexter left the flat to meet his riot victim clients at the police station, he had no idea that he might be leaving Jess with a homicidal maniac. Jess had tried several times to strike up a conversation with Toby but he arrogantly ignored her, giving his undivided attention to the drinks cabinet.

"You don't remember me do you?" she asked him. Toby turned to face her.

"Yeah I do," he said. "You were that girl in the bar, pretending to be waiting for someone."

"You knew all along."

"It was obvious." Toby turned back to the drinks, he poured himself a brandy.

131

SHADES OF GREY

"No port," he said without looking at her.

"Sorry."

"No sweat," he said cooly, knocking back the brandy in one. Toby began exploring the other liqueur bottles, finally he reaches for the West Indian rum.

"Why didn't you come back?" She asked him, trying to make it sound like it didn't matter.

"Hm? Oh... something came up," he said carelessly.

"What?" she probed, then bit her tongue as soon as the word had passed it. Not cool. Not cool at all. Toby looked at her but didn't answer. Jess turned away a little embarrassed.

"Yeah, your boyfriend's got a nice place.... he's a bit of a dick head mind you, but I suppose you can't have everything."

"He's not my boyfriend."

Toby turned to Jess. There was something about his gaze that made her selfconscious. It had nothing to with sex, he just had a way of stripping her down and looking at her bones, reading her like an open book. He was so self assured it was intimidating, yet she sensed that all was not as it seemed with him on the surface.

Jess picked out a record at random and put it on. Dexter had a large record collection. lots of old and interesting albums, many by people she'd never heard of, mainly jazz from what she could tell. He had quite a few books too, though few novels, mainly law and political text books.

"You like Monk?" Toby asked her.

"What?" she said blankly.

"Thelonious Monk," he said pointing to the record.

"Yeah, yeah," she said "he's great."

Toby gave her a tired look then turned away, making it obvious that he didn't believe her.

"Actually, I've never heard of him before, I've read this though."

She took down the autobiography of Malcolm X. Toby looked unimpressed.

"Well some of it," she confessed. Toby said nothing, he raised his glass to his lips as if it were the only thing worthy of his attention. Jess was annoyed at Toby for some reason, and

SHADES OF GREY

the strain of trying to out cool him was getting too much. She yelped a frustrated cry.

"Christ! Why am I trying to get your approval all the time!?"

"I don't know," Toby said simply.

"You're so bloody smug and judgemental. You make me sick!"

"Maybe you're looking at yourself through my eyes, maybe you make yourself sick."

"And what do you do Mr perfect, if you're so great how come you haven't even got a place to stay?" Toby poured himself another drink, knocked it back then poured himself another.

"God what are you trying to do, kill yourself?" Toby looked at her, he smiled. She felt a quiver run down her spine.

"I'm trying to get somewhere, in my head. Can't always do it with this stuff."

"You'd better eat something," she said. Toby again looked at her but she quickly made for the kitchen to avert his gaze.

"How about a cheese sandwich?"

"Okay," he said. He came to the kitchen door, watching as she buttered the bread and sliced the cheese. The kitchen was small, strictly a one person den, and with Toby obstructing the exit looked even smaller. Jess felt trapped. The sandwich was one of the fastest she'd ever made, she handed it to Toby then clambered awkwardly past him. Toby took hold of her left hand and peered at her wedding ring. She snatched away from him.

"You having an affair with that guy?" Toby asked casually as he bit into the sandwich. She shrugged her shoulders as if to say 'no big deal, who you screwing?' That made him smile.

"Made your mind up yet or you burning both ends?" he said.

Though she was trying to play it cool she couldn't help but feel invaded by Toby's direct line.

"Hey, don't feel bad. It's just a game," he said softly.

"Is it?" she replied. 'Perhaps it was' she thought to herself in answer to her own question, 'perhaps life, the whole world was just a game and I'm just a bad player.'

"I'm just a bad player in the game of life," she said aloud without realising.

"But the game is never won or lost until the final whistle," he

SHADES OF GREY

said. Jess smiled in amazement that he had appeared to read her mind.

"So what's my next move coach?" She said spiritedly. You seem to have all the answers to everything."

"Forget the rules, they're only to help beginners, learn the tricks and plan your strategy. No use expecting all your life, few get what they deserve, nothing comes to she who waits, but all is there for she who takes. You believe that, but you don't live by it. You're soul is a slob. Your heart is a slug, your spirit is dead and your life is a lie."

Although he spoke with a easy smile, his tongue was a razor blade of truth. She felt the sharpness of his callous words cut through her like a 'Bic' through melting butter. Jess felt as ashamed as if caught stealing from Sainsburys, and as exposed as if the store detectives had stripped her naked on the crowed high street. It made her angry.

"So you're different are you?" she attacked.

"Yeah, but not because I do the thing you want to but don't. I play a different game.- It's called re-addressing the balance."

Jess stared at Toby, she was mad at him herself and the world. But slowly her anger subsides.

"You're right, my life's a mess. I don't even know what I want. I hate my husband, he makes my skin crawl, but you know, when I'm with Dexter I pretend he is Ziggy! Oh, it's not as difficult as it might seem, they're twins you see. I just pretend that Ziggy has finally got his act together, got himself a good job, a new flat and all these nice things."

"Poor old Ziggy," Toby said. He suddenly hurls the cup into the drinks cabinet smashing bottles and glasses. Jess watches frightened and amazed as he kicks over the record player. A single but very audible scratch and the crash of the turntable brings an abrupt end to the music. He shoves the records from the shelves smashing everything in sight.

"This is called re-addressing the balance, evening the odds." Toby kicks the TV over, and smashes the cabinet to the floor. He grabs the knife from the cheese spread and begins slashing the leather upholstery and stabbing the walls. Jess runs to the phone but Toby is there before her and rips it from the wall. Then

SHADES OF GREY

suddenly he freezes. Jess looked on petrified, not knowing whether it was safe to move let alone make a run for it. Toby's body had stiffened, he stared straight ahead, his eyes deep and fretful as if witness to a horrible scene. He struggled to open his mouth, then to speak. The sounds he made were un-intelligible to Jess but expressed a pain that words could not. His eyes watered, his face contorted from rage and agony. For a while Jess watched curiously, she wanted to touch him, ask him what was the matter, but was uncertain of that approach. She slowly turns his chin to meet the glaze of his tormented eyes. The inquisition in her face posed the question without her needing to speak.

"The world's fucked man," he said. He looks at her a madman, enraged and fuelled with the poison of paranoia. "You want them to get me don't you?" his word are cold and deadly. Jess huddles up to the wall in fright as he encroaches upon on her.

"No! I don't want them to get you we're friends remember? Remember!?"

Toby no longer seemed to recognised Jess, he snarled at her like a predator to it's prey, ready to kill. Then, as suddenly as the rage had possessed him, it left him, he smiles to himself. Jess had slowly begun creeping along the wall toward the door. She was out of his eye line now and just inches away from escape. She thought about making a run for it but was sure he would catch her. She crept a little more, but with just a few inches to go she felt his hand grab her shoulder.

"They threw me out of the Posse man, can you believe that? I was a founder member, yet they kicked me out. But it don't matter, they did that to Malcolm too right? I'll just start again.- You want to be my first member?"

Jess frightened for her life, nods an emphatic 'yes'.

"Come on, we're getting out of here."

Toby takes her by the wrist, they exit the flat.

SHADES OF GREY

CHAPTER 25

Benjamin pulls up outside Spikey's house carrying a cheap bunch of flowers and a box of out of date chocolates, both bought from the petrol station. Jeraldine is wearing an executive styled blue suite with matching shoes and hand bag. Benjamin is looking the best he can, he'd showered and shaved and was wearing a musty cologne. His jacket had just come from the cleaners, but his trousers needed pressing and his shoes could have done with a good polish. Benjamin opened the passenger door for her then ran excitedly around the car and gets into the drivers seat. As soon as Benjamin sat in, he realised he should have given the car a good clean. Jeraldine looked like a princess on a rubbish tip. Empty beer cans, cigarette butts and sweet wrappers had all been discarded indiscriminately around the cars interior, there was even a half eaten steak and kidney pie on the dashboard. Benjamin began to see everything through Jeraldine's eyes, and it looked like shit. He threw the pie out of the window and immediately thought 'shouldn't have done that.' He got out of the car picked up the pies remains and put them in a bin across the street. When he came back to the car Jeraldine could see that he was embarrassed. Benjamin began collecting up the empty cans, sweet wrappers and cigarette butts.

"You don't have to clear up for me," she said.

"Yes I do," Benjamin replied, "and I want to apologise for being such a slob, I should know better than to pick you up when my car is in such a mess, but the truth is until I saw someone as beautiful as you in it, my car looked good. I swear I never noticed it looked like such a dump inside, but next to you a palace would look like a dog kennel. I'm just sorry you had to see me in my squalor, but I'm grateful to you and your beauty for showing me how low I'd sunk." Jeraldine was near to tears.

"Well why don't I go back inside," she said, "we'll pretend you haven't arrived yet and you can called for me in say, ten

SHADES OF GREY

minutes?"

Benjamin smiled, he ran to the passenger door opened it and escorted Jeraldine back to her front door.

"You're beautiful," Benjamin told her as he backed off down the path.

When he got back to his car he continued frantically collecting up rubbish, but then he stopped and gave a gratifying smirk,

"You smooth talking bastard," he said to himself.

After having cleared out all the crap, he drove around to a petrol station, bought a can of air freshener and completely fumigated the car, he also bought a little green frog scented car mascot. When he called again for Jeraldine they both pretended it was for the first time.

"We can have some dinner then go see a movie," Benjamin suggested.

"That sounds nice," Jeraldine said with a smile.

As Benjamin opened her passenger door, a powerful thick eye watering fragrance of lavender wafted up, Jeraldine is at first taken aback but then proceeded as if all is normal. Benjamin ran excitedly around to the drivers side. Once in he gives Jeraldine an admiring look, she blushes.

"You are beautiful," he tells her again, then finally they are away.

They had dinner at Bella's Ital food restaurant. Bella looked approvingly at Jeraldine, and gave Benjamin an exaggerated wink when Jeraldine wasn't looking, but nothing else was said. Bella's cooking as always was wonderful.

"What is it you do?" Benjamin asked Jeraldine as he shovelled a spoonful into his mouth.

"I'm a school teacher."

"Your daughter's a clever girl," Benjamin said through a mouth of rice.

"She got the brains from her father," Jeraldine smiled politly.

"And the beauty from her mother?" Benjamin added as he swallowed. "He was a very lucky man is all I can say."

"Not so lucky, he died when she was three, then Kelvin.... did Catherine tell you about Kelvin?"

"Catherine?" Benjamin enquired.

137

SHADES OF GREY

"I think you know her as Spikey? Brains but no sense. Kelvin died when she was seventeen."

"I'm sorry," Benjamin said, "it must have been tough on you."

"It's been tough on her losing a father and a brother, I try to make up for them but it's hard."

"I can imagine, I've never lost anyone, touch wood, not from my immediate family you understand. But when my wife divorced me...."

"Oh but they say that a divorce can be just like a bereavement, you go through the same grieving when you lose someone, it doesn't matter how they are lost."

"Well that's exactely how I felt when she left me, just like she'd died."

"Are there any children?"

"Two beautiful girls," Benjamin beamed with pride. "They're the only thing that has kept me going."

"You see them quite often then?"

"Oh yes, every day. I have custody you see."

"Really, that's unusal. Does their mother visit often?"

"Never. You see she abandoned them, took off with some rough neck and went to America."

"How awful! Those poor girls." Benjamin takes a little offence at the suggestion that his girls might be suffering with just him as their father.

"They aint so poor, in fact they're fine. I give them the best I have and anything they want."

"I'm sorry, I didn't mean it to sound as if they were depraved in anyway...." Benjamin bites his tongue.

"Don't apologise, I'm sorry if I appeared... well you know. In fact I didn't tell you the whole truth. She didn't really abandon them, the fact is I wouldn't give her a divorce unless she agreed to leave them with me. Her rough neck didn't want them, and with school and things,- and I suppose the fact that she didn't want to leave me entirly alone,- anyway she agreed. I was just being bitter that's all."

"You still miss her don't you?" Benjamin met Jeraldine's sincere gaze with his own, then looked down.

"Sometimes. I suppose it takes time to get over something

SHADES OF GREY

like that." Benjamin began eating again, Jeraldine sensed that he didn't want to talk about it anymore and began eating too.

*

They had left Bella's and were just cruising on their way to see a movie when suddenly Spikey's voice comes over on the bug receiver.

"Daddy I've just seen Conrad, I'm all decked out and I'm going after him so stay with me."

"Damn! not now." Benjamin said.

"That sounded like Catherine. Is there anything wrong?"

"Eh, no... no everything's fine, eh... it looks like something may have cropped up... eh... you know how it is, a policeman's never off duty."

CHAPTER 26.

Toby and Jess walked to Stratford tube station. Toby seemed much calmer, so much so Jess didn't feel threatened at all. He no longer held her wrist, so she could have escaped at any time, but didn't. They caught the central line all the way to Totenham court road, where they shuffled through the scatters of discarded litter on a dirty Soho back streets in silence. Toby wasn't looking too good.

"What's up," Jess enquired.

"Nothing," he said. That was enough for Jess, she didn't want to trigger another of his raging tantrums. If he didn't want to talk about it the safest thing would be to leave it alone she thought. They came to a phone box and stopped.

"Wait here," Toby said "I've got to make a phone call."

"I've heard that one before," she joked. Toby didn't seem to hear her.

Inside the box he dialled a number written on a scrap of paper he drew from his pocket. A woman answered, Toby asked for Harry. A moment later Harry came on the line.

"Harry I've got the stuff, you're gonna like it man there's lot's of chunky bits here" Toby was trying to sound cheerful but he felt

139

SHADES OF GREY

like crap.

"Hey Toby, I hear you're in deep shit with the pigs."

"Nothing I can't handle." Toby said.

"All the same I wanna let this thing cool a couple days. Here's what we do, friday you bring the gems to Mile End tube at 10.30. I'll bring the money. You got it?"

"I got it, and hey, don't worry, even if I get caught you're safe. I forget all about you." There was a silence then Harry spoke, slow and deliberate.

"You'd better, 'cause you know what happens to squealers, who talk to the pigs? They get cut up for bacon."

"Don't worry," Toby said brushing his threat aside. "Hey wait till you see the gems, you'll love 'em."

"Good," was all Harry said before he hung up. When Toby came out of the phone box he was smiling, but Jess knew underneath he was angry.

"Everything alright?" she asked.

"Fine, I've just been speaking with the enemy."

Next stop was an amusement arcade. Toby's eyes danced busily around the place like a butterfly in a rose garden, he looked mesmerised by the flashing lights, Zaps, bangs and explosions of the games machines. Jess supposed he was just another video game freak addict looking for a fix. She was right, he was a video game freak, and he was an addict looking for a fix, but she was wrong about the type of drug he needed. She watched him dig deep into his pocket for change, his hand came up with a wad of fifties and twenties, he quickly shoved them back in, looking almost embarrassed when he realised that Jess had seen. He put a pound coin into the martial arts tournament machine and started the game. He seemed to Jess to be playing little attention to the action, instead he watched all around the room as if looking for someone. His karate opponent was kicking hell out of him. Before very long all his lives were gone, he put in another pound coin, this time he played a little, and for a while displayed much expertise in giving a japanese black belt a good hiding.

A short white guy in dark glasses and trilby hat beckoned to him from the back of the arcade, he reminded Jess of the little fat

140

SHADES OF GREY

guy from the blues brothers movie whose name she couldn't remember. Without a word Toby went swiftly to the guy, the two of them disappearing through a black door discreetly located in a dark corner behind the counter.

A few minutes later Toby emerged looking like a different person, gone was the drowsy and depressed look. Now he seemed elated and alerted, the transformation was astounding. They walked towards Covent garden, where they stopped at a bar. Toby had ordered two port and brandies, when they came he knocked his back in one then looked to Jess expectantly, she responded by doing the same. She came up coughing, having to draw in gusts of cool air to soothe her burning throat. Toby started to laugh as did Jess... eventually. He ordered two more of the same even though Jess, still unable to talk was waving her hands and shaking her head negatively, she'd had enough. Toby took no notice, sunk his second drink in a similar fashion to the first then looked to Jess as before. She stepped back to decline the challenge.

Toby shifted his attention to a pool game that was just coming to an end. As the last ball was sunk Toby issued a bold challenge to the winner. After some consultation with his mates the guy, a pot bellied white man of around thirty accepted, producing a crisp twenty pound note from his wallet. Toby matched it with a mangled twenty from the much depleted wad Jess had seen earlier. Toby would pot a series of balls, fast and furiously leaving the cue ball awkwardly on the cushion or close up behind one of his own. Within a few minutes he had snatched up the victors prize money. Next Toby wanted to eat, They went to the finest restaurant they could find, he ordered two steaks and champagne. Toby was loud and obnoxious and drew much amusement from the disapproving looks he got from the white well dressed and well to do patrons whose tables surrounded theirs. Jess was on a cloud, her head was swimming from an abdominally mixed cocktail of wine, brandy, port and now champagne, but she was having fun. Toby was just tripping out! Jess had never before seen anyone so crazy. He fooled around the whole time, an hour later they were ready to leave but he had hardly eaten a thing.

SHADES OF GREY

As soon as they'd hit the fresh air Toby felt sick, exuding an empty vomit to the pavement much to the disgust of an old asian lady whose dog had to be restrained from lapping it up. Almost immediately afterwards Toby was again raring to go. Calling in an off licence for more booze. Jess suggested they slow down, but was soon made to feel a party poop by Toby's boundless enthusiasm. They were heading for the bright lights of Liecester square and a movie at the odeon.

"I want to see a 3D film," Jess said excitedly. Toby, his mood as boisterous as ever, was unusually thoughtful for a moment. He stared at Jess. She knew her selfconscious was evident. She felt herself fidgeting, rocking from heel to toe, tying her fingers in knots. Her face hung tilted to one side smiling involuntarily like a little girl after having been kissed for the very first time in the playground.

"What?" she said finally when the embarrassment became too much.

"I know how we can see a 4D film! I've got something that will make you fly, float in sea of coloured bubbles and touch the the moon!"

"What are you talking about!?" she exclaimed.

"Bring it down to earth!" he continued." Wacky eh?"

Toby laughed broadly, Jess joined him nervously, though she wasn't sure why. Toby took her hand and led her through the underpass at Totenham court road tube station. He was heading into the Gents with Jess still on tow when she stopped him suddenly.

"I can't go in there!" she said. Toby looked at the stick like male figure emblem under which was clearly marked GENTS. He glanced across to the skirted stick figure of the LADIES. His face turn from one facing dilemma, to one which had solved a problem. He pulled Jess in the direction of the ladies loo.

"You can't go in there!" she cried.

"Don't worry about it," he said.

She was as embarrassed as if she'd been found peeing in the gents urinal. Once inside Jess was relieved to find the toilet deserted. He took her into a cubical and locked the door. Jess watched as he prepared two thin lines of white powder on a

SHADES OF GREY

piece of card from a packet he had been carrying. He the took a straw and sucked the powder up through his nose after which he sniffed repeatedly opening his eyes extremely wide then blinking them tightly. He then prepared another two lines, handing Jess the straw. She held it lightly between her fingers as if it were a squiggly slimly worm from which she feared for her life. This was her first cocaine fix.

*

Jess thought the movie was all that Toby had promised it would be. Toby seemed calmer now as if satisfied or perhaps burnt out, any way he no longer wanted to touch the sky, she was relieved at that.

"Where are your parents from?" he asked her.

"Why do you want to know?"

"Just curious," he assured her.

"I'm not telling you," she said.

"Huhm, must be a small island," he quipped.

"Suppose that means your from Jamaica?"

"No, I'm a smally too," he said simply, they laughed a little. He held her hand affectionately though without sexual connotation. The night air felt crisp and fresh in their faces, as they walked among the flashing coloured lights of the square. They sorted through souvenir stalls with glaring fascination, stood in awe shoulder to shoulder with the musicians of the street in Covent garden, and marvelled at the sights like a couple of tourists. They arrived bone weary at a wine bar off piccadilly and sat at an empty table. Toby humbly, by earlier standards at least, ordered a bottle of house white. Jess had forgotten all about Toby's deeply emotive outburst of an earlier hour. Now she thought about it, it felt like someone else, somewhere else of a different time. It made her think of Ziggy and Dexter, she didn't want to. She blotted them from her mind and thought only of the moment. Jess could see that something in Toby's thoughts was bothering him too. She held his hand and peered into his eyes across the dancing candle flame and smiled. Her smile melted his gloom.

"Whatever it is there's a simple solution, you taught me that remember?"

143

SHADES OF GREY

A black jazz trio, guitar, double bass and tenor are cutting some swing reminiscent of early Lester Young. Jess nods her head and taps her feet in time, Toby looks on expressionless.

"Look what my brothers are reduced to, minstrels, singing for their supper. Nothing changes."

"But they're good!" she exclaimed.

"But black," he countered.

"There are no black people, there are no white people, just grey people of different shades." Toby looked at Jess as if she were an alien from space.

"That's bollocks and you know it. One of those pretty phrases that sounds good but don't mean shit. Blacks invented the music yet it's the white imitators that are up there making all the dosh and you're trying to to tell me it don't matter if you're black or white? Do me a favour. Harlem in the twenties, London in the ninties, the same shit"

"Yeah, you're right. Nothing's really changed has it."

"We've got to smash this system babe...." Toby begins to ramble, his eyeball shuttle frantically from side to side as if in a state of delirium. "We've got to smash this system, or we ain't going nowhere. Smash it up. Crush it. Fucked and brain-washed man! White's and, Tom nigger and women, and mothers, and fathers and... and..."

His brow was now beaded with sweat, he looked to be either on the verge of a tearful breakdown or a highly emotive raging outburst.

"People shouldn't fuck with me man, 'cause I ain't gonna take it. They try that shit with me they're fucked. I shoot 'em man, I shoot 'em dead you know. Dead means they can't fuck with me anymore."

Jess withdrew her hand from his clasp and sat back turning her head away. She didn't know what to make of Toby, sometimes he was so totally aware, sounded like he was in total control of not just himself but of others around him, then other times he sounded disturbed and in need of help. Toby seeming to get a hold of himself leant back also. He knew he'd just laid something heavy on her, he didn't want to push. She tried again to get her head around it, but it was no good, maybe later she

SHADES OF GREY

thought. She pretended she hadn't heard him, he pretended he hadn't said it. They pretended that nothing out of the ordinary had passed between them. They tried to act normally. But for the remainder of their time in the bar they spoke very little.

CHAPTER 27.

Saturday night

Spikey sat cross legged on a high bar stool, puckering her bright crimson lips around a candy stripped straw, through which she sucked a coconut rum punch cocktail. The coat had gone revealing a sparkling red low cut off the shoulder dress that hugged her hips, then sprayed out from just above the thigh stopping two inches short of her knees. The shiny satin frock suggested in Spikey a latin temperament that said I'm hot, spicy and wild, try me.

Truth be told her boyish contours struggled to fill the garment, but what she lacked in substance she made up for in spirit. She swivelled her hips like a fifties movie queen, posed and pouted like a penthouse hussy and adopting a permanent tits and ass posture she wasn't sure her back would be able to sustain the whole night. Yeah, what she had she flaunted like a pro, she was oozing sex. She felt the eyes of several guys following her every move, every time she looked around she caught the hungry gaze of a man wanting her. She felt good. Suddenly she had found herself, never mind being a detective, this was it. Sassy cloths, nightclubs, loud music, and guys swooning at her feet.

"I was made for this, I've missed my vocation," she said to herself.

She could see Conrad across the noisy bar, mouthing words and gesticulating to a busty red headed white girl. The girl was certainly curvy, and her tight bright yellow dress, which Spikey thought at least two sizes too small, was saving nothing for later. Spikey looked through a sea of liqueur bottles at her reflection in the bar mirror. She was slim by comparison, in fact skinny she thought. She looked down into her non existent cleavage, all she

145

SHADES OF GREY

saw was a microphone taped to her almost breast-less chest. Spikey was wearing a bug. All she had to do was get Conrad to tell her where the bodies were and it would be all on tape. Nothing to it she'd told Benjamin. Now she felt to eat those words. Seeds of doubt had begun to grow in Spikey's head, 'what if he doesn't fancy me?' she thought. What if he's the type of black guy who only goes for white women, with huge breast and soggy butts. She quickly turned away, slouching over the bar, embarrassed by her sudden loss of confidence. Now it seemed the whole case would depend on whether or not he found her attractive. The burden of responsibility weighed heavy. Her flirtatious bravado had deserted her completely now, and she wished she'd read more of those girly magazines that tell you how to turn a man on from fifty paces, with just a shimmer of a shoulder blade. What was she to do? She'd already had three dutch courage glasses of wine, anymore and she couldn't be held responsible, and would probably need to be held up. It's alright for Benjamin, she thought. How he'd laugh if he could see her cowering right now. But would he make out any better dressed as a christmas tree fairy with a microphone gaffer taped to his tits? She smiled. The thought of Benjamin's ample folds of flab being forced into the skimpy red dress drew a tear from her eye as she suppressed a raucous belly laugh. Ah what the hell she thought, Conrad was no oil painting. Would a girl like her, young slim, pretty and smart normally bother with a loser like him? Not even on his lucky day she concluded with satisfaction. New resolve had arrived to bolster her self esteem.

"You're here to do a job girl, now go get your man."

She watched the vivacious red head enjoying the titillation of Conrad casually running his palms up and down her thighs and occasionally around her buttocks. Normally scenes like that would have outraged Spikey, but now her mind was totally preoccupied with the job in hand.

She swaggered passed Conrad purposely jogging his drink causing some to spill on to his shirt front.

"Oh I'm sorry" she said rubbing her palms provocatively across his wine drenched chest.

"I didn't see..... you..." She broke her sentence with a pause

SHADES OF GREY

just as her eyes met his. A subtle breathless quiver broke her last word. She swallowed, then allowed her bottom lip to fall, opening her mouth just slightly for the vulnerable heart fluttered and helpless look. Her face told the lie of a longing that was but a masquerade. She broke eye contact throwing her gaze timidly to the floor. This was Police academy seduction training in action.

"Works every time" Benjamin had assured her.

"It's okay" Conrad said. His eyes gave her the once over, she passed. He knew she was coming on to him, she wasn't even subtle he thought, but it didn't matter. He quickly decided that the red head was old meat for roasting another day, Spikey was fresh, a new conquest ready and willing, so it seemed. If she was offering he'd take it, it was as simple as that. The redhead seemed to get the hint and sauntered away out of the picture. "Let me get you a drink," he said. He touched his palm on her bare back, it sent a horror'd shiver through her body. She flinched visibly.

"Oh I should be buying you a drink" Spikey replied. Conrad smiled fiendishly. He leaned over and lowered his voice as if about to deliver a filthy proposal.

"You owe me a clean shirt, I owe you a drink. I'll pay my debt now, you can settle up later," he suggested cheekily, and slide his sweaty hand round her waist. Spikey felt her guts churn, she wanted to spew up in his face, there and then but she managed a teasing smile of gentle reproof. He offered her his arm, she accepted, and so the two of them walked to the bar like bride and groom to the alter. This guy was repulsive to her, no mistake, this was a tough assignment.

"What would you like?" he asked, touching her arm.

"I'll just have a lemonade," she said. Now more than ever she knew she needed a straight head to keep this lech from taking advantage of her. He ordered a lemonade, and a rum and coke for himself.

"I'll be back in a minute, I just need to go to the bathroom and freshen up."

She needed the bathroom alright, but more than that she needed some space, away from Conrad. The feel of his cold

147

SHADES OF GREY

soggy hands slobbering all over her was unbearable, she wanted to spend as little time with him as possible.

"I'll be waiting" he said with a sickly smile.

As soon as Spikey was out of sight he had the barman put a quadruple vodka in her lemonade. As soon as Spikey got into the loo she slammed the door shut, then leaned back to rest on it in tired exasperation, just as she'd seen them do in the movies.

"I hope you're listening to this creep" she bawled into the microphone. "Boy, the things I do for the force. Now I'm relying on you to come get me if things get too hairy, so keep listening. The speed he operates he'll probably be trying to get me round to his place in a couple of minutes, so keep listening!" she stressed.

Just then the red head came into the loo. For a few tense moments she just stared. Spikey wasn't sure if it was because of the way she'd moved in on Conrad, or whether it was the way she had been apparently screaming to no one when the red head came in. Either way Spikey felt the need to say something to alleviate suspicion.

"I'm a singer," she said. "I just can't resist bathrooms and toilets and things- it's the acoustics."

The red head said nothing, but went to a mirror. She took out a face pack, and started re-touching her makeup.

"Conrad's a nice guy." Spikey added hesitantly.

"What's your thing bitch?" the red head snarled.

"I'm sorry." Spikey asked, genuinely bewildered.

"You picking on a trick, or you just looking for a sugar daddy?"

"No, you don't understand, I like him," Spikey said trying to sound as convincing as possible. The red head looked amazed and amused.

"Well ain't that cute." She packed away her make up and began walking towards the door, she had heard all she wanted to hear. But just four steps from the exit she was stopped by a thought, she turned looking sympathetically at Spikey.

"You're young and pretty and that's good, trouble is you're naive too.- I was like you once, starry eyed and innocent and in lo...."

SHADES OF GREY

She stopped suddenly as if the pain of remembering was too much. She looked at Spikey, wanting to say but unable to.

"You wouldn't want to know anyhow." She said dismissivly. "When I was you're age I didn't wanna listen either."

There was a sorrow in her eyes that made Spikey want to hug her and say it was alright to cry. The redhead dabbed a tear from her cheek, took a quick glance into the mirror, then took three steps towards the door with the bounce of a carefree playgirl Spikey wasn't sure she believed.

"See you later honey." She tossed the phrase carelessly over her shoulder as she reached for the door handle. But then again she stopped. She turned slowly, this time her face bore an expression of a deep maternal concern. She seemed older, as if her youthfulness had been acquired only by forgetting the past she was now remembering. This was truth Spikey thought.

"Don't let him break your heart." The red head said mournfully, then turned away and walked sadly out into the club.

"Now wasn't that sad" Spikey said into the microphone trying to sound unaffected. Daddy if you could have seen her you wouldn't know whether to kiss her or cry. If Benjamin could have seen Spikey at that moment he would have hugged her and told her it was alright to cry too.

Now Spikey knew she had not missed her vocation. This lady was not going to wind up tramping these floors ten years from now and well passed her sell by date the scorned love of a bum she told herself. Spikey pushes the door to one of the cubicles and enters. She pulls down her panties and sits.

"Now Benjamin, I know I just said I wanted you to keep listening,- but, I wanna take a pee. Do you mind turning off for about twenty seconds?"

When Spikey came out of the ladies the eyes of Conrad were waiting expectantly. He looked to have been looking at the door so long and hard she imagined he'd drilled two holes in the wood. Spikey met his glare, a dirty grin exposed a shiny gold tooth, she hated gold teeth. Conrad handed her the heavily laced lemonade. She took a swing and coughed. If that was his game she'd be better off going on to the the next stage while she still had her sobriety.

SHADES OF GREY

"Your place or mine?" She said. Conrad choked on his drink just as Spikey had before him.

"I'm sorry, am I going too fast for you?" she said faking innocence.

"No no. Your place my place I don't mind," he said. She had merely surprised him. Now he'd regained his composure, no girl could be too fast for Conrad. Spikey resisted the temptation to say, 'my place pig, so I can lock you up and throw away the key.' Because for that she'd need just a little evidence. She hoped to find it at the sty this hog hung out in.

"Your place" She said with a smile.

*

As Conrad's black BMW sped along the west way Spikey resumed her game of seduction. She ran her fingers through the hairs of his chest and along the back of his neck. Then she leant over to whisper into his ears resting her palm on his thigh. She absent mindedly began flicking into his crotch with her finger tips while allowing her lips to caress his lobs as she spoke, breathlessly.

"Are you a wild man? I like wild men." Conrad was hot and getting hotter, he increased his speed another 10mph. Benjamin following in his Cortina did the same. A panda car police siren began to wail.

"You're gonna get me arrested" Conrad said looking anxiously in his rear view mirror as he slowed down. "It's okay" he sighed relieved, "they've stopped the bloke behind."

The panda car swung in front of Benjamin forcing him to stop. Two uniformed policemen rushed out.

"Would you hand me the keys," one of them said.

"I'm a police detective," Benjamin began.

"Just give me the keys nigger!"

Benjamin made a mental note of the cops number then handed him the keys.

"Right now step out of the car. Hands on top and spread your legs," the policeman ordered with the raucous voice of an army sergeant.

"What do you think you're doing!" Jeraldine protested.

"It's alright Jeraldine, I'll handle it," Benjamin said.

150

SHADES OF GREY

Benjamin reached into his inside pocket for his badge.

"Look I'm a cop, now get your car out of the way...."

"Keep you're hands where I can see them!" The policeman screamed pulling his truncheon.

"Don't let them humiliate you on the street, stand up for yourself."

"Jeraldine do you mind? I said I'd handle it," Benjamin said firmly. The policeman pushed Benjamin up against the car and spreaded his legs. Benjamin felt the end of a truncheon being pushed hard into the base of his skull while the other policeman searched him.

"Well if I might say so, you're not handling it very well, and you're letting that man get away with Catherine..."

"Jeraldine, shut up!" Benjamin bawled at her. The policeman looked in at Jeraldine and gave her a dirty smirk but said nothing.

"Look I'm a detective Benjamin pleaded, you're letting them get away..."

"A nig-nog detective a?" the policeman sounded amused as he turned the truncheon like he wished it was a knife, applying more pressure as he spoke. "Okay if I call you Shaft?" He started laughing through gritted teeth at his own joke. Just then Benjamin felt the policeman pull out his gun.

"He's got a gun!" The two cops look to each other in panic."

"I told you I'm a detective, my ID's in my breast pocket." Benjamin reaches for his ID. The policeman nervously points the gun at Benjamin. Benjamin shows his ID and snatches the gun from the frightened cop almost with the same movement.

"I got your number, you'll be hearing from me. Now get that fucking can from out of my way!"

"Y... Yes sir!" The two clambered back into the panda reversing it from Benjamin's path.

Benjamin stepped on it as best he and his clapped out Cortina could. He was hoping they hadn't got too far out of range.

"Can't you go any faster?" Jeraldine nagged.

"If you don't shut up I'm going to put you out and leave you! Now I mean it right?!"

151

SHADES OF GREY

For a moment there was a stoney silence, then Jeraldine let out a disgruntled mumble.

"No wonder your wife left you."

*

Conrad showed Spikey into his dingy little flat. A thick and sickly stench congested her nostrils. 'I was right,' she thought, 'smells just like a pig sty.' For a while they were in darkness as Conrad went for the light switch. It was a while before it came and for a moment Spikey thought it might be a ploy. She was right. Conrad had manoeuvred around silently in the darkness until he was behind her. He was about to put his arms around her and kiss her neck, but as soon as he'd touched her, Spikey sang out one almighty scream, genuinely terrified.

"What's wrong baby," He said in a panic, the last thing he needed was a rape rap. Spikey was surprisingly glad to hear his voice.

"Nothing," she replied shakily.

"I guess I'm just a little afraid of the dark." Spikey kept on talking, partly to let Benjamin know she was still alive, and partly because she was as nervous as a turkey on christmas eve. Finally light came, a bright and un-seducing naked bulb hanging from the centre of the ceiling. As before, a pile of un-washed crockery to which clung scraps of decomposing left overs lay in the sink, submerged in a shallow swamp of stagnant water. 'Looks like a pig sty' Spikey thought. Spikey felt insulted. Had this been a real date she would have slapped his face and left.

"Nice place," she said.

Conrad took her into his arms and gave her a long hard wet kiss. She breaks off.

"I'm hungry." She blurted out suddenly.

"You're hungry!?" he exclaimed exasperated.

"When I'm hungry I think of food and I just wanna think about you," she smooched. "Besides, chicken makes me feel kinky," she added with a kind of sexual dominance. Conrad's eye's lit up, Spikey was really turning him on.

"Chicken huh? Kentucky? indian?" he said eagerly as he retreated to the door. Spikey went for the an indian. She knew the nearest fried chicken shop was in the high street, a ten

152

SHADES OF GREY

minute round trip at the most. He'd have to wait for an indian.

"Vindaloo? Korma?...."

"Either" she said without thinking, it didn't matter to her as she had no intention of being there when he got back. Conrad thought it strange, a Vindaloo was very hot and a Korma very mild, he'd have thought she'd have had some preference. But what did she say? Chicken makes her kinky? Maybe she wasn't going to eat it he thought. He decided to get a Korma to be on the safe side.

"He's gone daddy, I'm gonna take a look around. He isn't carrying a gun, I frisked him while he had me in the clinches, so let's hope it's here somewhere, I deserve a break. The way this place smells, who knows I could even come up with the bodies."

She went to the window, she saw Conrad pulling away. She'd expected Benjamin to have parked just across the street receiving her loud and clear, she couldn't see his car so thought he must be down the road a little. Little did she know she was on her own. She searched the chest of draws.

"Starting from the bottom to the top. That way you don't need to close each draw when you've finished." she said into the microphone. It wasn't academy training, she'd got that from a movie.

"Socks and underwear is all that's here. I'm gonna check the wardrobe now."

The wardrobe was full. Suits, shirts, jackets trousers. She started going through all the pockets.

"Daddy, If this guy has a gun it ain't here. Why don't you drive round front and pick me up before he gets back, I've left the place in a bit of a mess so I wanna get out before the chicken comes."

Spikey goes to the window looking out for Benjamin. Instead she sees Conrad getting out of his car with two boxes of chicken. Frantically she begins stuffing his cloths back into the draws and wardrobe. But it's a hopeless task, cloths are everywhere. She freezes as she hears a key turning in the lock.

*

Benjamin was cursing those cops. He had been driving round a good ten minutes but still couldn't pick up a signal. He was

153

SHADES OF GREY

gonna have their asses first thing in the morning. Racial harassment and abusing a police officer at least, and if anything happened to Spikey he'd get them bummed out of the force.

*

Conrad didn't go to the indian. Spikey didn't seem too worried about what kind of chicken it was so he went to the kebab take away and bought a couple ready cooked pieces of breast and some chips. He stipulated no pepper! Kinky was kinky but pain was still pain. He got radish, onions, and cucumber in fact all the salads which were supposed to have aphrodisiac qualities, and of course he had his stud spray.

When he'd unlocked the door of his flat, Spikey was still trying to look as if all was as when he had left. But Conrad could see his cloths all about the floor.

"What have you been doing?" he said dangerously.

"Okay daddy," she cried into the bug. Conrad smiled and started walking slowly towards her.

"So you want me to be your daddy huh? Okay you kinky bitch," he said grinning. "You've been a naughty girl haven't you? Now daddy has got to punish you."

"Stay away from me you ugly pig!" Spikey cried venomously then called, "Hurry up daddy, he's here, he's gonna get me," into the microphone.

Conrad was confused about how to play the game, but from what he could gather she was a naughty schizophrenic who wanted discipline. He slapped Spikey across the face sending her painfully to the floor.

"You liked that didn't you huh? huh? You want me to do it again?"

He walked towards her ready to deliver another blow, Spikey catches his arm throwing him judo style onto is back, as he was getting up she delivered two short kicks to his belly.

"Come on baby, don't get mad, I thought you liked that stuff!" he gasped. Spikey didn't bother trying to explain, instead she called to Benjamin for backup. Conrad backed off looking worried.

"What are you, police?"

"That's right pig," Spikey said confidently as she delivered an

SHADES OF GREY

eye watering kick to his groin, "and you're under arrest."

"What for?" he gasped painfully.

"Let's start with striking a police officer." She hadcuffs Conrad's wrists together while he was still clutching his balls.

Just then Benjamin burst's in gun cocked at the ready. Spikey poses one foot up resting on Conrad back her heel dug in his spine while ceremoniously dusting her hands.

"Where you been daddy?" she said cockily.

Jeraldine pushes past Benjamin. Boy was she mad!

CHAPTER 28.

Saturday night.

When Dexter left Jess to meet his clients at the the police station he hadn't expected to meet Ziggy there. Dexter gave the desk sergeant his name and told him that he was a lawyer come to represent those who were arrested at the anti racist demonstration. He also added that if any of his clients had been miss treated he would be pressing criminal charges against the officers responsible. Dexter was determined to come off looking like a hardened criminal lawyer. He visualised the headlines, RADICAL BLACK LAWYER TAMES RACIST POLICE FORCE. His hard man technique was obviously working so far as the desk sergeant was concerned. Franklin was stuttering and stammering a carefully worded response as Benjamin and Spikey walked in with Conrad still in handcuffs.

"It's alright Frank, Mr Sinclair won't be seeing his clients, not today anyway." Benjamin turned to Spikey. "Why don't you lock him up while I deal with this guy. Are all the cells taken now?"

"No there's still one free," Spikey replied.

"Good." Benjamin said as he turned to face Dexter.

The two men stood head to head, toe to toe, they held the stalemate for a moment but then as Dexters resolve began to wilt visibly he took a step back.

"You... you can't do that, I need to see my clients."

Dexter wiped his sweating brow with a handkerchief from his

155

SHADES OF GREY

breast pocket, Benjamin stood his ground, sizing Dexter up as another murder suspect.

"I think perhaps your brother is in greater need of you right now."

"My brother?"

"Mr Sinclair would you mind stepping this way?" Benjamin said.

"What's this all about?"

"I'll tell you what it's about, your brother Mr Ziggy Sinclair says that he spent last night with you playing cards. If you can confirm that then fine, if not your brother could be facing a murder charge."

Benjamin takes Dexter's arm and leads him to an interrogation room, where he is left alone to sweat a little. Benjamin went back to his office to ponder.

*

They had turned Conrad's flat upside down, but it turned out to be clean- metaphorically speaking. The guy would have been off the hook had he not been stupidly peddling hot gems on the street. What a fool Benjamin thought. Conrad wasn't saying anything. But that didn't worry Benjamin, he knew the type, given time, he'd be begging to make a statement. Sobers had come in off the street claiming that Ziggy had stolen his Bentley, who was he trying to kid. The way Benjamin had it worked out they were all in it together. They'd probably taken the guns along just to scare people. One of the hot heads had killed somebody, and now Sobers was clumsily trying to exonerate himself while incriminating the others. Benjamin often played a mental game of who did what with whom and when, and though he wasn't always right, this time, he was as sure as a bishop on a Sunday. Ziggy's prints were all over the jewellery shop for christ sake! Benjamin couldn't believe it, whoever it was said the black people were natural criminals should take a look at this bunch. They had to be the most amateurish outfit he ever heard of. If this were a movie script he'd have thrown it straight in the bin. Benjamin figured Sobers as the boss, for no good reason other than that he looked the part. The rest were much of a muchness he thought. Anyone of them could have been the get-away car

156

SHADES OF GREY

driver, but he gave that part to Ziggy, if only because of what Sobers had said. He cast Conrad as the cold blooded killer even though they couldn't find the gun in his flat. That left Dexter as the safe cracking explosives expert or what ever it's equivalent today. Yeah, he had them all down pat. Dexter was the only one that bothered him, he didn't look like good criminal stock at all, more the nervous bookworm type.

The interrogation rooms were full. Dexter, Conrad, Ziggy, and Mr Sobers occupied one each. All suspects to armed robbery and multiple homicide. But without the bodies or a murder weapon, Benjamin wasn't sure he had enough evidence against all or in fact any of them, to ensure that they got what they deserved. Benjamin and Spikey knew they still had their work cut out. Individually each of them stuck to their story. Dexter was definitely the weak link. He looked more jumpy than a kangaroo on a hot tin roof, either that or he was the best actor of them all. His claim that his brother Ziggy was with him at the time had to be the easiest to crack.

Benjamin offered Dexter one of his favourite cigars and brought out his bottle of ten year old whiskey from the filing cabinet. He talked about his wife and two kids, what it was like being a black cop and where he planned to take a holiday that year. He was being so friendly you'd have thought he was trying to persuade St Peter at the gates of heaven to let him in. He told Dexter that he didn't think that he had anything to do with it, but if he didn't talk he'd become an accessory to armed robbery and cold blooded murder, and would spend the rest of his life in jail. But Dexter wouldn't budge from their card playing alibi, a lawyers instinct maybe. Too frightened to think straight sure, but he wasn't going to incriminate himself by saying anything other than what he and Ziggy had worked out. He hopped to God that Ziggy was doing the same. Benjamin decided that he might as well try interviewing the brothers together. Ziggy's finger print match was the one piece of concrete evidence they had, and in the light of that fact their story just didn't hold up. It would be interesting to see how it might change once they were made to realise that.

Nash asked Benjamin if he could sit in on the interrogation if he promised not to interfere. Although Spikey objected Benjamin

SHADES OF GREY

agreed, but only because he didn't want anybody thinking he had something to hide.

The brothers looked relieved at the sight of one another. Ziggy, the calmer of the two gave his brother a reassuring look that was meant to re-affirm their solidarity. When Spikey came in with a sandwich and a coffee, Ziggy became suspicious and refused them, perhaps fearing they'd been drugged or something. Seeing that, Dexter sheepishly followed suite. Nash took and instant disliking to Dexter fixing him with a mean cold stare that made Dexter even more nervous. Benjamin asked them each a series of questions, each of which he had asked previously. Each responded with identical answers, each feeling more secure having heard their apparent air tight alibi reiterated.

"Can we go home now?" Ziggy sighed tiredly.

"I'm afraid not." Benjamin said cooly.

Ziggy was getting mad. His eye's widened, his lips stiffened to a fine line and his nostrils flared up like the bell of a trumpet.

"You can't keep us here for ever." Dexter winged. Ziggy suddenly jumps violently to his feet.

"The law says you have to charge us or let us go!"

Ziggy and Benjamin stood just inches apart, seething, nose to nose, eyebrow to eyebrow, each wanting to man handle the other, but each exercising restraint, if for different reasons.

"That's right," Benjamin said finally, "so I'm going to charge you."

Dexter who already looked as if he had peed his pants buried his face in his hands. Ziggy laughed mockingly.

"And what the charge?" he said.

"Murder." Benjamin said flatly. Dexter shouted out "No!" in panic to which Ziggy bawled "Shut up!"

Dexter's cries were instantly muted. Ziggy turned back to Benjamin, his face stiffened with a cold sternness, like a venomous snake.

"You can't prove a thing," he said forcefully.

"We have your fingerprints, they were all over the joint!"

Ziggy was mortified, he simply sat down, thinking back he knew it was true.

"I want to speak to a solicitor," he said flabbergasted.

158

SHADES OF GREY

"Fine," Benjamin said "And what about you?" Dexter was frantic, what had he got himself into!?

"I don't need a solicitor I had nothing to do with any of this!" he pleaded.

"Where were you at the time?" Benjamin interrogated.

"I... I was with a girl, the whole weekend!" Dexter cried.

"You can prove that can you?" Benjamin asked.

"Yes, yes of course I can."

"Okay give us her name, if it checks out your free to go."

Dexter froze. The frenzy that was with him had disappeared, he looks apprehensively at Ziggy who was now subdued to the point of zero reaction.

"Well come on, give us her name," Benjamin presses.

There was a pause, Dexter bows his head like a man ashamed and whispers Jess's name. It was not loud enough for Benjamin to pick up on, but Dexter knew that Ziggy had heard. He could feel Ziggy astonished glare burning at the side of his face.

"Who?" Benjamin asked.

"Jess... Jessica Sinclair."

"And you say you spent the whole weekend with her?" he asked tactlessly.

"Y.. Y... Yes," Dexter replied.

"Sinclair? Is she a relation of yours?"

Dexter could feel his brother glaring at him, Ziggy's breathing was deep, long, loud and erratic. He slammed his fist down hard and noisily on the table right under Dexter's nose. All three policemen grimaced as if the blow to the table had somehow ignited a sharp pain in their heads.

"She's my wife," Ziggy interrupted coldly, still glaring at the side of Dexter's bowed head. "You bastard. You dirty stinking bastard!"

Ziggy lunged at Dexter, gripping his neck and squeezing it as tightly as he could. Nash leaped in among the scuffling. He and Benjamin struggled to separate them, Nash hits a blow to the back of Ziggy's neck, Ziggy crumbles to the floor.

"I'm sorry, I said I wasn't going to interfere didn't I." Nash said apologetically as he threw a smug look to Spikey, "It's a good

SHADES OF GREY

thing I was here though Bengy, this could have developed into quite a mess, quite a mess. But please don't thank me, it was nothing really,"

Nash, with a beaming self-satisfied smirk on his face, licked his index finger and chalked a 'one up' on an imaginary blackboard in front of him. Then as if to ram home the point he sat back in silence like a subdued alter boy. Benjamin would normally have been grateful for the help had it been given by anybody else. But he hated being indebted to Nash so much he wanted to puke. For Ziggy that was it. What the hell, nothing mattered now. They could put him away for thirty years and he wouldn't feel as devastated as he did at that moment. His wife and his brother had been having an affair. He kept saying it to himself over and over, but somehow it didn't seem real. Benjamin sensed that this was the time to probe. Benjamin looked at Ziggy, a man broken inside.

"You wanna tell me about it?"

"My brother persuaded me to impersoniate him and drive his boss, Mr Sobers to a meeting." Ziggy began. "We were driving along, we saw this guy, a kid, robbing the jewellery store. One of the guys in the car with us had an office above or something, so we pulled over and went into the store.- He shot them."

"Who shot who?" Benjamin asked.

"The kid, he shot both of them, then..... he kind of broke down. Mr Sobers didn't want any scandal because of some election, so we decided to hush it up."

"He also killed two people in the broadway pool hall that very night, and a guy in a club the night before, I think the kid must be crazy. Where are the bodies?" Benjamin asked.

"In the boot of the Bentley." Ziggy replied.

"Have you any idea where the kid might be?"

"I took him round to Dexter's before I dumped the car," Ziggy said as he slowly realised the implications.

"My God!" Dexter exclaimed "He's with Jess!"

"Okay, let go," Benjamin said.

SHADES OF GREY

CHAPTER 29.

Saturday night.

When Toby and Jess finally emerged from the wine bar it was pouring with rain. They tried to get a cab but it was the same old story. It wasn't long before they were both soaked to the skin. Though a fleet of night buses were due to take to the streets soon Toby negotiated a £12 fare with a brother in an F registration Ford Sierra.

"Stratford," he told the driver and they were on their way.

Toby paid the driver and took Jess to the front of a dingy deserted house. He climbed over around the back, a moment later he appeared at the front door. Inside Jess looked around, something didn't add up. After all the high living Toby had enjoyed that night he was apparently happy to come back to this dilapidated squat.

"I must apologised for the state of the house," Toby said, "If I knew you were coming I'd have baked a cake." Jess made no response to the old joke, Toby winced an apology. He threw some logs into an old victorian fire place and proceeded to light them. He then threw a look over his shoulder just in time to see Jess shiver.

"Cold?" he asked her.

"Just a little," she replied. Toby left the fire ablaze, went to Jess and wrapped his arms around her, rubbing her back vigorously.

"Better?"

"Ooh yeah," she said.

"We'd better get out of these wet cloths."

Jess suddenly realised her vulnerable position. She was in a deserted area in a derelict house, with a man of questionable mental stability whom she'd only just met. Nobody even knew where she was, and now he was asking her to strip off! 'If he were to murder me now it probably wouldn't make the news for weeks' she thought. Toby got two blankets, gave one to Jess,

161

SHADES OF GREY

wrapped himself in the other and began undressing. Jess hesitantly wrapped herself in the other blanket an slowly began to peel off. Soon both stood naked but for their blankets.

"It's been quite a day," Jess said nervously, trying to add a normal conversation to an odd situation. Toby didn't answer, he'd found a cigarette on the mantle and began lighting it in the fire.

"I didn't know you knew Ziggy, coincidence that, the way we found ourselves together in the......" She stopped herself abruptly deciding that it would be better not to talk anymore about what happened in Dexter's flat, for fear of provoking another outburst.

"I've never had cocaine before," she said, "it certainly made the film go wild...."

Toby turned towards her, he stared in her eyes for a moment then stretched his arm out to offer her a drag of the cigarette.

"No thanks," she said cautiously, "I'm trying to give them up." Toby said nothing but cooly took the cigarette to his lip and drew in long and deep. He was again the cool guy she'd met in the pub, she hadn't seen him since he went to make the telephone call. Toby appeared to have many identities she'd decided, she now knew at least four. The raging neurotic, who smashed up Dexter's flat and talked of murder. The the happy drugy, with an inexhaustible zest for life and money to burn. The tearful problem kid on the verge of a nervous broken down, and Mr cool, the man of few words.

"I don't know about you," Toby said "but I'm wacked." he gave the air a loud yawn then looked down at an old mattress sprawled across some old fruit crates from the market, this was his make shift futon. It reminded Jess of the mattress on her bed back home only worse, she would have laughed but she didn't feel like joking.

"You can have whatever side you want," he said.

Jess watched in amazement as Toby unveiled himself from the blanket revealing his butt nakedness, and crept under a double quilt without saying another word. Jess was frozen for a time wondering what she should do. A moment later, and Toby began drawing snores. Jess was beginning to feel pretty stupid, naked under a blanket in an old house in the middle of nowhere. And in spite of the fire she was cold. She did not relish the

SHADES OF GREY

thought of standing there all night, but surly getting into bed with Toby would be asking for trouble. She imagined herself in Pinkies telling the girls about it, they would be mightily impressed. Then she imagined them each in her situation, telling the story. Roslin said she just climbed in, no problem, in fact on a scale of one to ten this story would rate a tame two by Roslin's standards. Maxine would definitely have climbed in, so too would Sharon she decided. Jess took off her blanket and joined Toby under the quilt. Before she knew it they were both snoring.

*

Jess woke up in the middle of the night. At first she payed no mind especially as to where she was. She felt a naked body next to hers and thought in her drowsiness that it was Ziggy. She opened her eyes. The room looked strange, then memories of the last couple of days came flooding back to her. She peeped across the bed and saw Toby's face in the orange light of the smouldering wood fire. He was awake and just staring at the ceiling, he caught her gaze.

"What time is it?" she asked.

"About 3.30 in the morning."

"How long have you been awake?" she asked him.

"I haven't been asleep." he replied. "I haven't slept in three days."

"I heard you snoring, as soon as your head hit the pillow," she accused lightly. Toby smiled

"I just did that so that you would come to bed."

"Oh...."- Jess suddenly realised that her naked thigh was wrapped across his waist. She wondered if she should move it but decided that keeping still might be safest for the moment.

"What are you thinking about?" Jess inquired.

"Things." was all that Toby said, he continued to stare up at the ceiling. His silence made her nervous, she thought again about moving but thought it less conspicuous if she did it while in mid conversation.

"Don't you feel like talking?" she asked him.

"I don't mind, what do you want to talk about?"

Her head was a mass of questions. What was the Posse, why had he smashed up Dexter's flat, what was the new

163

SHADES OF GREY

tomorrow?

"Earlier on, did you mean what you said... I mean is it true?" Jess asked.

"Is what true?"

"About shooting people... I mean is it true, you...?"

"No, of course not," he said with a chuckle.

"So what were you talking about in the bar tonight?"

Toby is thoughtful, Jess is silent as she wait his reply. Toby, looking cool calm and self assured seemed a million miles away from the troubled fretful state he was in at the bar, yet Jess was convinced there was something amiss.

"Don't you ever feel that things aren't right, that they have to be changed no matter what?" Toby asked her.

"What do you mean?"

Toby again pauses for though, he appears to be searching for words, the right words.

"You hear people talking about there being two sides to everything, and like everything not being black and white but shades of grey, like plain old right and wrong don't exist. But me, I got a clear sense of what's right and what's wrong, I see it everyday, as clear as day and night. If I can see it, why can't they? Huh? Funny how it's always the blind one's that are doing the wrong. They should step on this side of the fence, the side where you get shat upon, a little bit of shit I reckon would open their eyes."

Toby looks for some response, there is nothing.

"Ah you wouldn't understand, pretty girl like you? Guys be falling over themselves to spread their overcoats on the floor so you can trample them into those puddles.- Maybe you need to have suffered to see."

"Re-addressing the balance, what's that?" Jess asked.

Toby's eyes wander the darkness in search an explanation. Again there seems no simple answer, Toby struggles for a beginning, then speaks as if in verse or prayer.

"It's like Robin Hood. It's like two wrongs make a right. It's like taking the system, the power structure, shaking it up and turning everything upside down."

"It sound good.... sounds right. I want to be apart of it."

164

SHADES OF GREY

"Like one of my merry men or something?" he says jokingly.
"Don't make fun of me!"
Toby sees that Jess is deadly serious.
"Why not," he says, "why not."
Toby rolls away onto his side alleviating for Jess the problem of breaking physical contact without making a big thing of it. For a while they lay in silence. Toby thought that Jess had fallen asleep when suddenly she spoke.

"I was raped once.- I was just twelve years old... just a child. My uncle, my mothers brother... I would often babysit my little nephew whenever my aunt and uncle went out. One day I called and my uncle was alone crying, my aunt and my nephew were gone. He was crying like a baby, he started telling me about auntie May.... confiding in me like I was an adult. She'd apparently ran off with another man. Then he hugged me, that wasn't too strange we had hugged before, but this time he was so distraught he... he began crying on my shoulder, squeezing me tighter and tighter crying harder and harder. He was calling me May, my aunts name. He started getting mad, I... I started to struggle I wanted to get away, I'd never seen him like that before. He was crying and shouting, mad, like he wanted to kill somebody. Then he hit me, hard.- I must have passed out... when I came to I was naked... he was on top of me..... Afterwards he kept apologising, saying he was sorry he'd hit me and.... It wasn't long after that I found out I was pregnant. My parents were furious. But you know what? They were more concerned about who the father was than how I felt. I never told them, I never told anyone... No one.... They made me feel so dirty, guilty... but it wasn't my fault, it was him, and yet..... It felt as if I was to blame somehow..... Where was right and wrong then? I couldn't see them! Why couldn't I see that it was him, him and not me?- My whole life I've been punishing myself, and every man I've met since, why couldn't I see that it was him?! Why!? Why!? Why!?" Jess breaks down. Toby turns over towards Jess, holds her, tries to comfort her. "Why?!... Why!?" she cries.

"I... I don't know," Toby says blankly.

After a while Jess stopped crying, the two of them lie huddled together in silence for what seemed like a long time. Toby still

165

SHADES OF GREY

with his arms around her. Finally he spoke.

"I don't know, maybe you..... Maybe I... Maybe for you I was wrong... but for me...."

"No," she stopped him. "You were right.... You're absolutely right. I should have blamed him. I should have blamed him instead of myself and everybody else. He was wrong, I see that now, right and wrong, black and white as plain as day and night."- She takes a deep breath, then sighs heavily, as if relieved of a heavy load. She smiles at Toby and gives him a brotherly kiss which says 'thankyou for listening, I'm alright now.'

"I wish I'd known you when I was twelve."

"I'd have just pulled you're hair and ran away." he told her. They laugh a little. A moment later they were both asleep.

*

Spikey, Benjamin, Dexter and Ziggy arrived at Dexter's house along with two uniformed policemen. The way the flat had been busted up instilled fears that Jess may have met a similar fate. Ziggy and Dexter were devastated, but both bore a sense of guilt, it was their betrayal of one another which had led to Jess's life now being in Jeopardy, that is if she were still alive. Had Ziggy been honest with Dexter about Toby, Dexter would never have left Jess alone with him. Had Dexter been honest with Ziggy, he and Jess would not have been having an affair and so she wouldn't have been there in the first place. Neither could bring himself to look the other in the eye. Benjamin looked at the brothers.

"Any idea where he might have taken her?"

Neither had a clue.

"Think!" Benjamin urged insistently, "remember this kid has already blasted five people!"

At that Ziggy broke down, Benjamin bit his lip, maybe he had been unnecessarily reckless with his choice words, but he was a cop with a job to do, and if it meant saving a young girls life he'd interrogate her mother.

They combed the house for clues but came up dry. There didn't seem any point to hanging around any longer, Benjamin didn't think they'd be back, and he knew they were not going to find them with a fibre of tweed from Toby's jacket, or a single

SHADES OF GREY

discarded strand of hair as Batman or Sherlock might have done. There seemed little point in dusting down for finger prints like some house proud char woman either. Out there somewhere a crazy kid with a gun was holding a young women and he feared for her life. The next logical step was to recover the bodies from the Bentley. Dexter and Ziggy were placed under house arrest while Benjamin and Spikey went to the warehouse.

*

Inside the Bentley waited just as it was left, just as Benjamin had imagined it would be.

"Like a big black panther sleeping in a deserted lair," he surmised. Spikey likened it more to a big fat brooding cow waiting to be milked. Benjamin couldn't see the connection. They opened the boot, the smell was almost unbearable.

"I'm glad my morning pinta comes from the Unigate man." he quipped.

Benjamin couldn't get the thought of jess and the possibility they she may already be another corps out of his mind. Spikey was more optimistic. She pointed out that they now knew who the killer was and they had the bodies. Conrad, Dexter, Ziggy and Sobers would be charged as accessories to murder and armed robbery after the fact and for handling stolen goods.

"All the loose ends had been tidied up, now all we need is to bag the big knot, the largest piece of the jigsaw, the missing link." She said.

"And hope nobody else gets dead," he added cynically.

CHAPTER 30.

Saturday night.

When Benjamin got back to the station the first thing Franklin said, was that the captain wanted to see him. Benjamin went to the captain's office, the door was already open. The captain was sitting in a smoke filled room, hunched over his desk with a grim expression on his face, it looked as if he had been waiting for Benjamin a while.

"Come in Benjamin," he said.

Benjamin walked to the centre of the room and stood directly in front of the captain. The captain's face was enough to depress santa claus on his birthday, you'd have thought his mother had passed away that morning or maybe he knew that the world was to end that night. Anyway from the sour looks Benjamin was getting he was expecting bad news, very bad news.

"This case too much for you Benjamin?"

"What do you mean," Benjamin asked.

"I mean do you think you can handle it?"

"Give me a break..."

"A break!?" the captain exploded, "We've got five unsolved murders. Five! And in case it hasn't sunk in your thick skull yet, we also have assault charges pending, and allegations of corruption against the investigating officer, which happens to be you! We have a jewel robbery. A maniac has kidnapped the wife and mistress of two of your suspects, six people dead and you wanna break!..."

"Six dead? Wait a minute, what are you saying? There's only been five murders."

"Haven't you heard? One of your suspects, a Mr Conrad Baptist O'deed in his cell.... What did he do threaten to talk?" The captain accused.

"What!? Now wait a minute. Are you saying what I think you're saying?"

"I'm saying what a prosecuting lawyer could soon be asking

SHADES OF GREY

you. You were the last person to see him alive. I'm saying did you bump him off because he threatened to expose you?!"

Benjamin was speechless, he could not believe what he was hearing.

"Now, you know I don't believe that shit," the captain said. "I'm only trying to show you how it could be made to look if this thing get's any messier. God knows it messy enough."

Benjamin sits down and let's his head fall into his hands.

"Is it that bad?" he says to the captain.

"Let me put it like this, the guys upstairs, they look at it this way, there's no smoke without fire. Now they are not going to bare the brunt of any slur from their superiors, somewhere along the line there has got to be a scape goat, and since you fit the bill perfectly why go shopping around. Let's face it, you know it and I know it, you're black. And while it suited their purpose they were glad to have you around, but the minute you become an embarrassment... You're guilty until proven innocent, and it's up to you to prove it. Which means bringing the two of them in alive, and hope they have the good grace to clear your name."

"Or what captain, give me the bottom line."

"Well to tell you the truth, they'd like to fry your ass, but even if, God forbid the worst came to the worst I don't think they'll have enough evidence. But it will mean the end of your career as a policeman, and there can't be too many YTS places for a man of your age." Benjamin rises from his chair.

"Tell me something, are you in on this too or does Nash have this much pull?" The captain stays silent. "What about my pension?" Benjamin inquires.

"If this thing blows you can forget it," the captain replied firmly.

"Hm, everything to lose and nothing to gain. Well I might as well get on with it then."

Benjamin walks dejectedly from the office. Spikey approaches looking anxious.

"Boy, do you look depressed, or have you just seen the canteen menue?- What did he want?"

"He had a message for me, my heads on the block.- Once upon a time I had everything, a family, a career.... Everything

169

SHADES OF GREY

seems to be slipping away. Milli's... I lose this job I wont even have a pension."

"Don't give up daddy, never give up, we got this thing licked man."

"Yeah?" Benjamin said, sounding defeated.

"Yeah. What about your kids man?" As if hit by a bolt of lighting Benjamin snaps from his melancholy mood.

"How could I forget my little girls? My sweet little girls... Huh, even if I do lose this damn stinking job I could become a private eye, just like that guy in the movies, what's his name?"

"Sam Casy?" Spikey enquired.

"Sam Casy yeah. I just get myself a hat a raincoat and a broken down car..."

"You already have a broken down car." Spikey quipped. Benjamin chuckles.

"Yeah, I do don't I.- Yeah, a private eye.... but before I think about a new career, I'm gonna give my old career one last shot, just for the sake of my little girls and my pension." Benjamin walks briskly towards the main desk.

"Franklin I want you to let all the suspects go."

"All of them?" Franklin asked.

"All of them," Benjamin confirmed, "if they're gonna kill themselves let 'em do it at home."

"What are you up to daddy?" Spikey enquired curiously.

"I don't know, but if one of them knows where the killer is they're not going to lead me anywhere locked up in a cell. Get a phone tap on all their lines, and a twenty four hour surveillance unit on it."

"But that will break the over time ban," Spikey said.

"To hell with the over time ban, what have I got to lose, my job?"

Just then Nash walks into the station. On seeing Benjamin he grins, then starts whistling like a lark. Benjamin's blood begins to boil, he fixes a mean stare at Nash and takes a step towards him. Spikey takes a hold of Benjamin's sleeve but is shrugged off. Franklin calls to Benjamin, but his voice falls on deaf ears.

"Hey Nash, I wanna talk to you." Benjamin said and grabs a hold of Nash shoving him up against the wall.

170

SHADES OF GREY

"You don't wanna talk to me black boy, you wanna hit me don't you?" Nash sticks his grisly chin out as if about to kiss Benjamin on the lips, but instead breaths his stale bad breath into Benjamin's face as he taunts. "Come on, hit me, come on black boy, hit me."

Benjamin eyes are red with rage, he squeezes his clenched fist tighter and tighter as he fights an angry compulsion to smash his knuckles into Nash's chops.

"Don't do it daddy!" Spikey calls out, "that's what he wants. You hit him you're out, then he can say what he like about you and you won't be able to do a thing about it. Your name will be dirt. You hit him and he's won."

"I know," Benjamin seethed, "but right now I want to hit him so bad I'm thinking it might almost be worth it."

Benjamin breaths in long slow and deep, trying to quell a violent fury that is almost in control of him. He slowly begins to relax his grip on Nash. But Nash is determined to goad Benjamin into punching his way onto the dole cue, he laughs in Benjamin's face.

"That's bullshit man, you just don't have the guts. Hey I seen your two little girls today, and you know what I think? They're gonna grow up to be just like Marsha, and then I'm gonna have them...."

Benjamin slams a blow into Nash's face so ferocious, it crushes the bones in his nose splattering his cheeks in blood. Nash cowers on the floor a moment, but then taking his hands from his face begins to smile at his blooded fingers.

"You've done it now Bengy boy, and in front of witnesses too, huh Franklin?"

Benjamin towers above Nash trembling mad and barely able to resist a powerful urge to crash his left boot into Nash's bollocks. Franklin looks from Benjamin to Nash and back, then to Spikey, then finally back to Nash.

"All I seen is you running into that door," Franklin said. The smirk fell from Nash's face.

"What?" he said in disbelief.

"I said all I seen is you running into that door."

"And I seen it too," Spikey added.

171

SHADES OF GREY

Nash looked into their faces, Franklin was trying to hold on to the innocent look he knew would be good enough to convince the captain. Spikey who had been fighting hard to keep a straight face had lost the battle, and had now cracked open a grin so wide it looked as if she had a piano keyboard in her mouth. Benjamin who looked as if on the verge of losing his battle to keep his boot out of Nash's crutch, was quickly ushered away by Spikey to a nearby chair. Nash peels himself from the floor and makes for the exit now nursing his newly acquired broken nose.

"You assholes," he said painfully.

"Big mistake Franklin, big mistake."

CHAPTER 31.

Sunday morning.

Jess woke up encased in Toby's body. She felt like nestling in his arms but resisted the temptation, instead she weasel'd herself from his clasp and got out from under the covers. Toby dreamt that he and Jess were playing on a giant chocolate roundabout. There were lots of old school friends he hadn't seen in years, Patrick Chambers, Judy Parker, Paul Roberts, all singing shouting, screaming and having a whale of a time. Then the roundabout started to fly, up high into a rainbow'd sky. Everyone except Toby and Jess then disappeared. They were laughing and singing. Toby could see Jess was slipping off the roundabout. He called to her

"Jess hold on!" but she continued to slip apparently unconcerned and still singing. Toby called to her

"Jess! Jess hold on!" but still she continued to slip away until she finally lost her grip all together and began to fall. Now her face seemed petrified and she called Toby's name as she descended into a flashing psychedelic whirlpool, finally she disappeared. Toby screamed

"Jess! Jess!." He jumped up and out of sleep, panting and sweating as if he had just run a four minute mile. He looked for

SHADES OF GREY

her warmth with his out-stretched arm, but a note had taken the place where Jess had laid the night before it read;

There is no food in this house! If you wake up before I get back, don't worry I'm out looking for a corner shop or something. If you're still asleep when I get back I'll wake you up with breakfast in bed! Lucky you! love Jess.

Her note made him feel good. He felt good about Jess. He shut his eyes and lay still, it was silent but for the sound of the empty room. He had emptied his mind. For a while he thought of nothing. The silence grew louder and louder as his concentration began to wane. Now he became aware that he was thinking of nothing. Which made it something. The thought brought on a reluctant smile. To think of nothing, was it ever possible? He blanked. A few seconds. The clock began ticking. It's tick was louder than it's tock. He concentrated, it faded to a musty knock but only for a moment. Now came the tock, louder than the tick. Then un-invited he began to hear the street in all it's detail, the traffic, the hubbub of daily life.

Sometimes he would shut his eyes, lie still, empty his mind, block out the light, the clock it's tick, it's tock, the street, if only for a moment. But there was always the sound of the room.

His eyes fall on a partly crumpled sheet of yesterdays paper discarded to the floor, and in particular the cartoon at the foot of the back page, two oversized circular smiling faces that he guessed were gardening. The toon with a single squiggle just above his forehead was mowing the scribble they stood on. The other toon was obviously pruning a flower. The caption read 'love is.... working together, happily.' He imagined what they would look like if the toon were black. A bit gollyish he decided. Maybe that's why they weren't. He thought sarcastically. Not because black people don't work happily together, or love. Or that the extra ink involved multiplied by however hundreds of thousand copies would have been a significant extra cost to the paper. 'It was because they wouldn't have been able to make us look good.' He smiled to himself then read the caption aloud.

"love is.... working together, happily.

A glance at his watch told him it was 7. 45am. As tired as he was he had only managed a few hours sleep, but it had been his

173

SHADES OF GREY

first hours in days. He was sure it was only because of Jess that he'd gotten any at all. His head began throbbing with a migraine. He got up and went into the bathroom in which he had already set his toiletries. He stood over the sink and turned on the taps. He watched his face in a cracked mirror directly in front of him. He looked drawn. He smiled at his distorted reflection, then wet his face. It seem to soothe the pain. He plugged the bath then turned the taps on full. He then submerged his naked body in the freezing cold water.

The bathroom was surprisingly clean for a derelict house. The walls were of pale blue ceramic tiles, of which all but a few were intact. The fittings though had been removed, leaving holes in which old wall plugs that once held a shower curtain rail, a soap dish, and other accessories sat. The floor was just bare boards. As he dried himself he heard the back door open and shut. Jess had returned with a bag full of groceries. Toby emerged from the bathroom wrapped in a dark blue bath towel.

"You've had a bath. Did you leave any hot water for me?"

"There wasn't any hot water, but the cold feels nice, try it."

"Cold water!? Forget it. I like my baths steaming and hot."

"You'll love it," Toby assured her as he disappeared into the bathroom. Jess heard the sound of running taps. Toby again emerged, half dressed and dressing.

"If you want to be one of my merry men you'll have to learn to deal with more than cold water."

"How long have you been staying here?" she asked changing the subject.

"A few months, off an on. It's been a kind of refuge from... everything really." She knew exactly what he meant, and he knew he'd said enough for her to have understood, such was their understanding.

"It's a wonderful day, why don't we go to the park?" she said. Toby looked apprehensive,

"I don't like to go out during the day."

"Are people looking for you?" she asked him. Toby didn't answer. "We can't stay in hiding for ever, what about the new tomorrow? How do we shake things up from here?"

Toby picked up the black bag, unzipped it and showed Jess

SHADES OF GREY

the guns inside. Jess was flabbergasted.

"With these," he said. He hands Jess one of the guns. Jess is entranced by the weapon, the feel of it's power surging through her body excites her.

"This thing is bigger than this room, this house, this street, this town, this country. It's a worldwide operation, that's why I'm getting out. Out of this place." He hooks his thumbs and flaps his fingers simulating a flying bird. "Out of this country, go see my radical brothers in the states. That's where it is man. The posse? I tried to make them into something, but the guys over here ain't happening, when it comes to thinking ahead they're just dead meat."

Toby shows Jess the jewels, but it is the gun that hold her attention.

"In a few days I hand these to a guy I know, he gives me tfifteen grand. This time next week I wave goodbye to Britain. Yeah, visit some of my radical brothers, check out how the wars going on, then I'm coming back here to resume my mission."

Jess said nothing.

"You coming with me?" Toby asked her.

"With you?"

"Yeah, Robin don't go nowhere without his merry men."

Jess turned away and walked towards the window. It had started to rain.

"What is there in England for a black man, or woman for that matter. All you've got to look forward to is grief from Zig and Dee. What's the point? You'd love to get away, you said so yourself."

Jess turned to face him. Yes, she had said she wanted to get away, and the thought of facing the righteous brothers right now was more than she could stand. She wanted so much to be a part of Toby's dream too, but a part of her was still in a rut, part of her was still this little girl with the boring life, boring but safe. Did she have the courage for a life fraught with risk and danger?

"Shake it off and start again," she heard him say, "we can check out the Indies if you like. Imagine, lying in the sun, with people who don't hate you cause you're black. Them Jamaican guys don't mess either man. Yeah, think about it."

Jess was thinking about it. She'd always thought herself

SHADES OF GREY

impulsive, but Toby was too fast for her. He stood there with an expectant glow awaiting her answer. 'Surly he doesn't want me to decide now, on the spur of the moment,' she thought. He'd made it all sound so good so easy. But she couldn't just leave everything, without a word to even her parents and take off with a guy she'd known for only a day.

"Well?" Toby said.

"Okay!" Jess heard herself say.

"Alright!" Toby cried out Yanky style bouncing up and down with excitement. Then he was suddenly calm but serious. Jess looked apprehensive, preparing herself for bad news.

"Look," Toby began. "I want you to know it not always gonna be easy, there's gonna be stuff you'll have to face up to, times you'll have to make up you mind to go with it no matter what. Now I don't want to make you feel like I'm forcing you but.... the bath is ready. What's it going to be?"

Jess's laughter was more in relief than at Toby's sense of humour.

"Oh I suppose it won't kill me." she said walking into the bathroom.

Toby could hear Jess getting undressed. He waited for her reaction to the cold water but it never came.

"How is it?" He called to her.

"It's cold," she called back in a moany voice.

"I haven't heard you get in it yet how do you know."

"I'm in it," she protested.

"Get in the bath," he called to her.

"I'm in it!" she called back "Listen." Toby could hear the sound of splashing water, but he wasn't buying any of it. He walked into the bathroom to find Jess naked but bone dry splashing the bath water with her hand. When she saw Toby she broke into nervous giggles at being found out.

"Get in that bath," he ordered.

"I can't," she whined.

"Get in that bath,"

Jess deciding that the best form of defence was attack started splashing Toby with water.

"Right you asked for it," he said. Toby picked her up and held

SHADES OF GREY

her above the water so that just her backside was submerged. Jess winched, and fought hard to suppress a scream. She pleaded with him not to let her go, but Toby mercilessly lowered her slowly into the tub. Her eyes were agog, her mouth open wide but no sound was heard, she was in shock. Toby swaggered from the bathroom with a smile on his face.

The sound of a break beat being slapped against the back door broke his smile to a grin. It was a password that told him that it was okay to answer the door. It was a double security code because they figured that even if a cop knew about it he wouldn't be able to make it sound convincing unless he were a brother, or maybe an ex drummer.

"Who is it?" Toby called out.

"It's me, Ricky," a voice said. Toby opened the door.

"Long time no see man," Ricky said as he greeted Toby with a five part hand gestured sequence,

"What's happening?"

"Ah, nothing much. What's with you?"

"Well, you know, the thing about Conrad's got everybody down."

"Conrad!?" Toby asked.

"Oh man don't you know? They picked ma man up a few days ago 'cause he was trying to push some heavy stones on the street. They found him dead in his cell yesterday."

"He's dead?" Toby had to sit down.

"They say he O'deed on some shit and choked on his vomit in the middle of the night, but I don't buy that. I think they killed him. Was he pushing them stones for you? If that the case I wouldn't go looking to collect no money. If I were you I'd forget about that and get as far away from this place as you can, 'cause you's next man."

There was a long silence as Toby mulled over the shock of Conrad's death. Jess emerged from the bathroom.

"You alright man?" Ricky asked him.

"Yeah.... sure I'm cool... I er...."

"Anyway business is so bad I've taken to making house calls, and seeing as Conrad's out of circulation I thought I might include you on my milk round." Toby exchanged a look with

177

SHADES OF GREY

Jess.

"It's okay man, thanks, but I don't use that stuff anymore."

"No shit!" Ricky exclaimed with a kind of admiration, he threw a glance over his shoulder at Jess then back at Toby, he smiled to himself. "News like that is good for the soul but bad for business, I don't know whether to laugh or cry." Ricky slowly got up from the chair. "Well I'd better be getting round to the customers that need me. You take care now man, I'll see you around."

"Probably not for a long while," Toby said "We're leaving the country, end of this week, somewhere hot."

"Good for you man. Good for you. As soon as I get my shit together I'm gonna do that too."

The two men touch their clenched fists.

"Take it easy bro."

"Safe." Ricky said, he gave Jess a wink and a smile on his way out.

*

For the next three days the couple hardly left the house. They began a rigorous training schedule, like an SAS combat course. Toby had not had a fix in all that time but it didn't bother him. They bathed together in cold water each morning and slept naked at night. But there was never anything sexual about their relationship. Sometimes after their long training sessions they'd read to each other in front of the fire. They lived for one another, neither demanding anything of the other.

The purest relationship either had ever known.

CHAPTER 32.

Thursday evening.

It was the end of another long frustrating and fruitless day for our detectives. Benjamin's Cortina pulls up outside Spikey's house.

"Another day of nothing," Benjamin said wearily. "Where are they Spikey? Manchester? Liverpool? France? Spain? Dead? Alive?"

"Do you think he might of killed her already?"

"I don't know. But then I don't know too much about anything anymore."

"Don't worry daddy, we'll find them," Spikey said trying to sound positive as she opened the car door.

"How's your mother?"

"Okay. I never knew you were sweet on my mother."

"There's a lot of things you don't know," Benjamin said disgruntled.

"I guess I did mess it up a little for you didn't I?"

"No, not really. I managed to do that okay, all by myself. She say anything about me?"

"You don't wanna hear it?"

"That bad huh?"

"No, not really, she was just upset."

"Yeah, and she had every right to be, I treated her real bad."

"Why don't you call her sometime, if you ask me that's what she's really mad about."

"That I didn't call?- Yeah, I guess I should have rung, if only just to apologise?

"Well you know what they say, it's never too late."

"Yeah?... Nah. She'd probably just slam the phone down on me."

"Oh boy," Spikey moaned. "And you a big strong detective too! How you gonna make it as a private dick, if can't even make a phone call for fear that someone will hang up on you? Hm?

SHADES OF GREY

Sam Casy, now he's a real P.D. he never takes no for an answer. No wonder your wife....."

Benjamin's eyes widened abruptly, he threw a cold stare though the car windscreen, his lips tightening as if preparing a angry retaliation. But then slowly he began to relaxed, his eyes were blinking an embarrassed admission as he began nodding affirmatively. He looked to be down in the dumps, Spikey had obviously touched a nerve, now she wished she hadn't laid into him so hard.

"I'm sorry daddy, I shouldn't have said that."

"Don't apologise, you're right, you're absolutely right." Spikey gave Benjamin a comforting squeeze of his hand.

"I'll see you tomorrow." She got out of the car and slammed the door shut, she saw her mother lift the corner of the curtain but then quickly let it fall as she realises her daughter had seen. As Spikey opens the gate and begins walking towards her front door she hears the slamming of a car door behind her, she turns to find Benjamin walking through the gate.

"I wanna be like Sam Casy," he said. Spikey smiled.

"Then don't take no for an answer."

Spikey turned the key in the lock and pushed open the door. Benjamin crept in behind her, he was nervous. his heart was beating like the bass drummer in a marching band, and although he told himself she was only a woman, the worst she could do was scream or something, he felt like he had been sent in to disarm a time bomb with only a minute on the clock. Benjamin followed Spikey into the living room where Jeraldine sat eyes down, doing her embroidery.

"Evening mum."

"Goodnight Catherine, I've left your dinner in the..."

"Mum, there's someone here to see you."

"Good evening Jeraldine," Benjamin said. The sound of Benjamin's voice makes Jeraldine freeze in mid stitch, but only for a moment, after which she resumes her embroidery as if nothing had happened.

"Good evening Mr Benjamin," she said without looking at him. 'Boy this is gonna be tough' Benjamin thought, 'she doesn't even wanna look at me. Well, here goes, Sam Casey eat your

SHADES OF GREY

heart out.'

"Jeraldine, I want to apologise for the way I spoke to you the other night, it was un un-forgivable. But I'm going to ask you to try and find it in you're heart to do just that. And if you do feel that you're able to give me another chance I want to invite you out for another date, and this time I'll make sure it's on my night off.

"Well I don't know Mr Benjamin..."

"Please, call me Winston."

"Well, I don't know... Winston, you did say some horrible things to me...."

"Don't say no, just don't say no, because I'm not taking no for an answer....."

"I don't like being told to shut up."

"I know, I know, but I've been having a tough time with this murder case and it must be getting to me or something, you know they think I had something to do with it."

"What!? No, I don't believe it," Jeraldine said.

"Yeah, they accuse me of drug dealing, robbery, assault and now even murder!"

"But how long have you been with the police force?"

"Twenty five years. Twenty five years of dedication, and an unblemished record, but now this. They even tell me I could lose my pension."

"That's disgraceful."

"Not only that, but recently the kids have been playing up and... I think they're missing their mother.- One of these days I'm gonna have to tell them the truth, that... that she's not coming back... It'll break them up... I don't know how I'm gonna do it... I.."

"You poor man," Jeraldine said on the verge of tears.

"Oh it not so bad, if I don't lose my pension well struggle on... somehow." Benjamin wiped his dry eyes. "I'm sorry, I shouldn't come here and burden you with my problems, I'd better go and pick the kids up and get on home. Goodbye Jeraldine, I don't expect we'll be seeing each other again, but I'll be thinking about you. I only hope that if you ever think of me you'll regard me as a friend."

SHADES OF GREY

Benjamin turned and took a step towards the door. His fingers were crossed and he said a little prayer to cupid. The room was silent. He took another step, one more and he would be out, yet still she hadn't said a word, hadn't called him back. He was sure he'd laid it on thick enough to twang the heart strings of a bull elephant. If she didn't respond, either she had no heart or he wasn't as good an actor as he thought he was. He stretched his arm out and gripped the door knob, he wondered what Sam Casy would have done in the same situation. It didn't matter though because he wasn't Sam Casy, private detective of the silver screen who always got his man and the pretty girl at the end of the movie. He was Winston Benjamin policeman of Stratford east London, who didn't have a clue where his man was, and looked to have missed out on the girl too. Yeah, this was how it was in real life. He began to turn the knob, just then he hears a sniffle, at first he wasn't sure if it was Jeraldine fighting back the tears or whether the door knob needed some grease. But then he heard the sniffle again followed by a double. Confidently he turned the knob and pulled open the door.

"Winston."

Benjamin turned to see Jeraldine drying her eyes with a handkerchief, he wanted to scream and jump for joy but managed to hold on to his wretched downtrodden and dejected look.

"Yes Jeraldine."

"Please, call me Jerry."

"Yes Jerry," He said fighting to keep the corners of his mouth from turning up into a broad grin.

"Why don't you bring the kids around for some dinner tomorrow."

"What time?"

"Well, I get home from school about four."

"I get off tomorrow about the same time," he said tentatively, trying to play it cool.

"Give me a couple of hours to prepare something...."

"Shall we say about six then?" he cut in.

"Alright, six tomorrow."

When he got the other side of the door he found Spikey had

182

SHADES OF GREY

been there listening. He jubilantly punched the air, did an Ali shuffle and made a triumphant but silent yelp for joy.

"You crafty old codger!" Spikey whispered. "Sam Casy would never have resorted to such a cheap and corny low down trick. I can't believe she fell for it."

Benjamin ignored her and continued jiving all the way down the path to his Cortina. Jeraldine caught sight of him through the window and almost immediately caught on, but it didn't make her angry, in fact she found herself wanting to laugh.

CHAPTER 33.

Friday.

Toby had been excited all morning, singing and horsing around. Jess was having a hard time containing his exuberance. That evening he was to exchange the jewels for money, after that,

"We outta here!" he said with plenty of attitude. With their last few remaining pennies Jess had managed to scrape enough together for a bottle of Pink lady. They toasted their way through a lunch of diced raw vegetables, cheese, cream crackers and mini sausages against a back ground of dance music from a funky pirate radio station. It had a Sunday afternoon party atmosphere about it. Toby was in a clowning mood for sure, he chased Jess around the room with one of an army of spiders he claimed had infested the bath. Actually there was no such invasion, but it was enough for him to just cup his hands to instil a hysteria in Jess, such was her fear of insects. When he began having a fit Jess thought him to be clowning again until he tumbled heavily to the floor. She looked on helplessly as Toby jerked agonisingly at her feet. He coughed and spluttered, rocking and jittering in random flurries of severe agitation. Jess managed to get him onto the mattress, she knelt down, steadied his shoulders then cradled his head in her arms. She stroked his forehead soothingly as she whispered repeatedly to him that 'it was alright, she was there, it was alright.' Gradually he quietened

183

SHADES OF GREY

down and eventually stopped. Within minutes he was sleeping like a baby.

*

When Toby regained consciousness he saw no sign of Jess, his first sensations were of an aching head, a grainy tongue and a dry throat. And he was hungry! It was hunger Like he'd never felt before. He got up and went into the kitchen. At nine foot by twelve it was a small kitchen by any standard. To the left a blue cupboard unit hung on the wall directly above a matching floor unit. A white enamelled sink, chipped and stained was plumbed on the right, it's chromed taps were dulled and discoloured by limescale, green moss and corrosion. Just above was a four pane window dressed with dirty white net curtains. The wall tiles were a matching dirty off white effect, which all gave the kitchen a distinctly un-hygienic look. The remaining wall was papered. The paper had softened over the years from the steam of heavy cooking, impregnated with dirt and grease, it was now obviously very much darker than when it was first hung. He took from the fridge a six pack of eggs, cheese, ham, a pack of sesame seed bread rolls, mayonnaise, tomatoes and a bottle of milk. He hurriedly cut open a roll, spread on mayonnaise and filled with enough ham and cheese for three. Pressing the jaws of the roll together he bit down into the sandwich, he cut two more rolls open and began spreading mayonnaise on them also. Suddenly he began to throw up, angrily, repeatedly. Within just a few moments a series of violent convulsions had coated the entire kitchen work top in a porridge of slimy vomit. A sickly ache in the pit of his stomach began to spread up through his body, pumping against the bone of his skull. At the same time it sank down through his loins to weaken the muscles of his legs. He rummaged through the cupboards for aspirin, or something, he didn't know what.

"Jess!" he cried out. But there was no reply. His vision became blurred and confused. He ran out of the squat and into the street. A single bird tweeted then stopped. He looked up, the skies began to darken. The strange silence was broken by a sinister howling. He had to squint to shield his eyes as the wind blew up dust and other debris to pepper his face. He walked

184

SHADES OF GREY

down the road towards the public house now barely visible. The old asian lady he'd seen outside the wine bar approached, but this time she walked a vicious looking black doberman. At the sight of Toby the muscle bound hound drew back it's lips revealing a row of horned teeth set in pink fleshy gums, a thick saliva mucus framed it's lower jaw. Its eyes, a deep glazed shiny blackness of deadly intent, were fixed on Toby's, poised to attack. The old lady wrestled with the dog lead stretched taut as the animal pulled her towards the confrontation. Toby felt his arms reach out, saw his hand clasped around the dogs neck and lift it snapping and snarling to his face, tasted the fibres of it's closely matted hair on his tongue, heard the dogs pleading whimper as he sucked the warm sweet blood from it's throat until it's body fell limp an lifeless. He let it fall to the ground. He looked bewildered at the blood on his palms, then at the retreating old lady hysterically screaming. He felt cold. Something in his head began pounding, and the muscles of his body began to ache, he was again in pain. He had to get away. His mind returned to Jess, he had to find her. The howl grew louder the wind more fierce the pain more intense. He buried his face in his hands, he wanted to run, to scream.

Gradually the sound of the howling wind began to fade, the birds again began to sing. Daylight seeped through his fingers onto his eyelids. He took his hands away from his face. He saw the old lady walking peacefully down the road with a little black dog. His palms were clean again.

Toby walked carefully across Water lanes zebra crossing into the saloon bar of the Manly arms, hugging his shivering body as if he were afraid it might fall apart were he to let it go. Blue arteries plotted tracks at his temples and the hollow cheeks of his lifeless powdery yellowed brown skin had a deadness of grey about it. His eyes, veined bloodshot and framed in circles of black, were so deep set they looked as if they were about to cave into his face. A cold sweat exuded from his temples. As his eyes searched about the faces of the beer guzzling patrons, his vision distorted and exaggerated their features to caricature. Their mush of laughing and talking merged to an intense dinning.

Where was Jess? He needed her. He needed help. He had

SHADES OF GREY

had wild trips before, but somehow this was different, it was more than just an illusion. His mind was purged of sanity and rational thought, and his body was twisted in pain, real pain. Inside he fought a compulsion to scream. Something inside wanted to rant and rave, to smash and destroy, but something else held him back. Some of the regulars who knew Toby by sight noted his look and manner of desperation. A few of them commented briefly, some casually, incorporating it in into their conversation, then either dismissing it or letting it pass as a banal futility. Toby's eyes scrutinized face after face alas despairingly in search of Jess. Finally they fall on the an 'Exit' sign above a doors reversed 'Saloon Bar' inscription. He wanted to run, to this desire there was no restraint.

Toby ran and ran. People gave him a wide berth, held protectively onto their children and valuables expecting to see a policeman or someone in hot pursuit. By the time Toby had gotten to the Romford road he felt like he wanted to die, yet he managed to walk the few hundred yards into Stratford broadway. Suddenly it was night time. As he came up by the town hall, he saw a young couple, a black girl and a white guy standing in the yellow light of a street lamppost. For some reason his attention was being drawn towards the girl. As he drew closer he found that she began to look more and more like Jess. The closer he got the more he became convinced that it was her. They were arguing about something but stopped when they saw Toby and started walking.

"Jess!" He called out and ran towards her. He took hold of her shoulder and tried to turn her around. The white guy pushed his hand away.

"Leave off mate!" he cried. Toby saw the 45 in his hand, he pointed the barrel at the guy.

"No please don't shoot," the guy pleaded.

"I don't want to!... I don't want to!" Toby cried, but his finger fondled nervously with the trigger. "Don't fuck with me! Don't fuck with me!!"

Toby hit him across the brow with the butt of the 45. The white guys eye exploded spitting blood like a water fountain. The girl started screaming. Toby threw her a bewildered look. The

186

SHADES OF GREY

white guy was bent over double, his face in his hands. Toby channelled his frustration and his pent up rage into a blow that hit the white guy across the back of his head sending him to the ground. The girl screeched, in Toby's face.

"Leave him alone you bastard, leave him alone. Just because he's white! He's better than you!" she screamed venomously. "He's better than you!"

Toby by this time of course realised that this screaming face was not Jess at all. He backed away, his senses in a state of turmoil. He didn't know what was real anymore. He knew he shouldn't be on the streets, shouldn't be alone, but he needed a fix bad. He was being driven by a hunger that had to be fed. A hunger fuelled by a compulsion that had possessed his mind and body and was now beginning diminish his powers of reason. Where was Jess. He needed her, he didn't want to hurt any more innocent people, but he was afraid of what he might do in his present state.

*

Jess had only left Toby alone for a few minutes while she ran to the store for some medication. When she'd returned he was gone. For a muddle of different reasons Jess felt mildly panicked at his disappearance. Even if he'd recovered, he'd been reluctant to leave the house in day light before, so why should he just take off now? She began to imagine all kinds of nasty things happening to him. It was doing her no good to worry, she knew that, so in the end she convinced herself he'd got up feeling fine and decided to get some air, that made her feel better.

As she looked around the derelict house she started to feel sad and sentimental.

"Not long to go now and I'll be long gone. I wish I'd been able to say goodbye to mum and dad. I'll have to write them.-I'll have to writ to Ziggy too... and Dexter... Oh God, what am I going to say?- I'll send the girls a post card from wherever. They'll probably never forgive me. Ros, Sharon, Max and Beverly. I'm going to miss them badly."

Jess wipes her dampened eyes, she looks around the room then up to the ceiling.

"I'm going to miss you too house. You've been a good home

SHADES OF GREY

for me, I've felt really good being here. Thankyou for having me. I hope the next people who come to live in you take good care of you, fix you up good and make you look nice."

She began tidying up, partly as a gesture to the house for having her stay, and partly because of a kind of 'leave this place as you would like to find it pride' she'd been brought up with. She began by just straightening a few things, picking twigs of fire wood from off the floor and packing their cloths away. Before long her tidying led to dusting, her dusting led to sweeping, next it was wiping down the paint work with soapy water. By the time Toby had got back she had given the house a spring clean from top to bottom.

Toby charged into the house like a bat out of hell being chased by the devil. He crashed to his knees at Jess's feet clutching desperately at her as his eyes darted in terror about the room. He had begun hallucinating again, this time beating off armies of imaginary creatures from his person. It took Jess more than an hour to get Toby just to lie down. She didn't know what they were going to do, the exchange time was less than two hours away but there seemed no way that Toby would be in a fit state for anything that night. There was only one thing for it she would have to make the deal herself. She put on one of Toby's jackets and packed one of the guns in it's pocket. She picked up the bag of jewels and left.

CHAPTER 34.

Jess loitered by the agreed place for the exchange, outside the Mile End tube station. She looked around anxiously for the contact. He was already almost twenty minutes late and she was now debating whether or not to go. Cold and windy it had just begun to rain again. Jess had no overcoat. As she lifted the collar of Toby's jacket the rain changed to an icy sleet and she began to shiver. Her right hand deep in her coat pocket fingered nervously the 38, it's barrel clanged among three coins amounting to only 75p. All the money she had in the world.

She saw a man huddled in the shadows of a hardware store entrance across the street, she knew he had been watching her but she was carrying a loaded gun in her pocket, she wasn't worried. She was tired and hungry yet she remained at all times vigilante. No passerby escaped her scrutiny. Her cold toes continually stamped the pavement stone beneath her feet.

Jess watched an old down and out tramp clothed in rags approaching from a distance. He was dirty and broken, carrying a limp in his right leg. His toes protruded through the front of his shoes. Jess reflected briefly on her own footwear and wondered how far away she and her boots were from this down and out status. The tramp crossed the road and walked towards her. He stared into her eyes. Jess was wary of him though his look was weak and pitiful.

"Spare 10p for a cuppa tea? I only wanna cuppa tea."

Jess fingered a fifty pence piece, fished it from her pocket and offered it to the down and out. The tramp takes the fifty pence then suddenly grabs a hold of Jess, pushing her up against the wall. He presses his damp smelly body up against her's, his dirty hands fondle a sexual assault on her intimates, he breathed a thick and foul stinking stench that smelt like the cooking of rotten fish in piss on her face. She cries out as he ravages about her neck like a starving wolf on it's dead prey. Then a hand slowly lifted his head from hers. Toby looked at the

SHADES OF GREY

tramp with disgust, holding his rancidity at arms length from himself. Jess picked up a piece of metal pipe about two foot in length, and hits the tramp across the face in a vengeful rage, cutting his eye open. The fifty pence piece spins from the tramps hand and rolls down the grove. Oceans of blood gushed out from the gaping wound. Jess allows the piece of pipe to fall carelessly to the ground. Just then a grey XJ6 screeched up. As it skids round into Eric street it sprays a thunderous machine gun fire. Screaming bullets chisel craters from the wall behind them, the tramp is cut down. The XJ6 turns and is heading back to finish the job. Toby draws his 45 and fires just two rounds before he is empty.

"Give me your gun!?" he says to Jess with a deadly coolness. Jess callously pulls the 38 slowly from her pocket, her focus split between the injured tramp squirming like a decapitated worm on the ground, and the returning XJ6. Jess fires four rounds into the windscreen. The car swerves and crashes into the wall. Toby takes the gun from Jess, he runs to the car pulling open the door. The torso of a semiconscious 'Harry' falls out. Toby's right hand tightens it's grip on the revolver. He grips the blood stained shirt collar of the injured man.

"You owe me money. We had a deal."

"That's right." he replied cheerfully, as if he were grateful to Toby for reminding him. He took out a wad and peeled off four fifty pound notes, and placed them on Toby's expectant open palm with a smile. Toby returned the smile, snatched all the money, forces the barrel of his gun into the mans mouth and pulled the trigger. The Harry's head explode, splattering the car interior in blooded brain matter. Toby drops the bag of jewel by the mutilated body. He walks stiff and upright away from the car towards Jess. She takes the gun from him. Toby looks to Jess's dead pan expression following the gaze of her glazed eyes to the tramp, still on his knees, his hands covering his eyes, blood seeping like a thick sticky treacle through the gaps between his fingers. Jess begins to weep, then screams a long and painful cry, but her voice seemed to disappear into nothingness only to return a hollow echo from the empty streets. She fires. The tramp

SHADES OF GREY

recoils, his hands fall slowly from his face revealing a bullet hole between his eyes.

In spite of the gun fire (or maybe because of it) no one came out into the streets, though the upturned curtains of several widows meant an abundance of witness, and that meant the police would soon be there. Toby and Jess ran down into the tube station, luckily they caught a train that was just about to pull out. They got off after only one stop. Toby figured they had a better chance out in the open rather than being trapped on the very predictable destination of an under ground train. When they emerged from Bow road it was still raining.

Toby and Jess huddled together in a dark and shaded shop front. Toby arms were around Jess's shoulders, she held him around the waist.

"You're soaking," she said as she felt the dampness from his shirt. "Let me get a taxi." As she raised her hand to hail the cab she saw that her whole arm was drenched in blood.

"Oh my God, you've been shot!"

Toby leant heavily on the shop window. Jess was trying to stay calm urging herself not to panic, she needed to think clearly she knew that. With his arm still draped across her shoulders she gently took his weight.

"Lean on me I've got to get you to a doctor."

"No!" Toby gasped. "No doctors and no taxis."

"If I don't get you some medical treatment you're going to bleed to death!"

"Get... a car," he urged. They struggled to a deserted side street, Toby took out a bunch of keys. They tried several cars until finally an old Ford let them in. Jess took the car a couple of streets away from the squat. She and Toby walked the rest. She knew the car would eventually bring the police within a couple of blocks of their hide out but she was afraid Toby wouldn't make it had she left him any further to walk.

Inside Toby collapsed to the mattress, Jess tore off his shirt revealing a deep gun shot wound in the left side of his stomach. She bathed it the best she could and bound it tightly in the cleanest garment she could find, one of Toby's shirts. Within seconds a red patch appeared and was growing larger as she

SHADES OF GREY

watched. It was no good, he needed proper help. She began to get this strong feeling that she was losing someone close to her, like a lover or a brother. She decided that she would call Dexter, he was crazy enough about her to do what she wanted without asking questions, and maybe among his professional friends there was a doctor.

"I'm going to get someone who can help you."

Toby did not respond, Jess wasn't sure if it was because he didn't understand her or whether he no longer had the strength to speak. His eyes started to roam deliriously about their sockets. She was scared. Scared because she didn't know if he would still be alive when she got back.

*

The phone rang four time before Dexter picked it up. His voice sounded distant and strangely un-familiar.

"Dexter. It's me Jess."

"Jess! Are you alright? Where are you?..."

"I'm alright," she interrupted, "but I need help, I need a doctor..."

"A doctor?! Why, what's happened?"

"Toby's been shot, I think he's going to die, please hurry!" There was a slight pause as Dexter's registered her apparent concern.

"Is he there with you now? Can he hear us?"

"No he's at the house, he's unconscious, he needs a doctor, please!"

Dexter was puzzled. He then spoke with an over calm rationale, normally reserved for negotiating with armed terrorist, or for talking a suicidal someone down from a window ledge.

"Jess get away from him, now, while you can. Let the police deal with this."

"No Dexter I can't. I want you to help me please. Please Dexter, if you don't he'll die!" There was a long pause.

"Please Dexter, I beg you please."

"Okay. Tell me where you are."

"First you've got to promise me, no police okay?"

Dexter promised. Jess gave him the address, hung up the phone and ran back to the squat.

192

SHADES OF GREY

Toby was as she left him, sprawled across the mattress. He looked like some Saturday night drunk but for the now blood red shirt wrapped around his abdomen. Jess held her breath as she felt for his pulse, it was still there thankfully. Jess renewed the blood soaked dressing and covered Toby in the quilt even though he was burning up a fever and sweating like a horse. She filled an old pot with cold water, took a vest from Toby's laundry and submerged it. She applied the cold dampened cloth to Toby's forehead.

"Hold on Toby please. I can't lose you now, you're the only truthful thing I have."

Jess then realised something strange, she had been doing everything with one hand, her left. She had filled the pot, soaked the cloth and squeezed out the water all with her left hand, even thought she was right handed. She looked at her right, her arm stood vertical and rigidly pointing upwards from her elbow, her fingers clasped tightly the 38 calibre revolver. It was as if her arm had become independent of her, with a mind and will of it's own. It's own objective, even it's own personality. It had been standing guard while she cared for Toby. Maybe she wasn't alone she thought. But if we all have our guardian angels why had hers allowed her uncle to abuse her, her parents to reject her, why hadn't it warned her about marrying Ziggy? Where was Toby's guardian angel when he was taking his first fix? She put the gun down on the mattress and gently caressed Toby's cheek while still dabbing the cold cloth to his face.

"But 'Why' is a question to which there is no answer. We just come and go in ignorance. We are each left to justify our own perception of right and wrong the best we can. If we dare ask the reason, the point to everything, we may then conclude that ultimately there is no point... then all is lost."

Toby opened his eyes and smiled, he just wanted her to know that he had been listening to her every word, that he was with her. He wanted to tell her that he hadn't given up, and so neither should she. But he only had the strength to smile.

SHADES OF GREY

CHAPTER 35.

The surveillance unit, an unmarked van parked in the next street recorded Dexter's every conversation. Even before Dexter had replaced the reciever one of the officers had already written down the address and was now calling the station to inform Benjamin. Franklin took the call and wrote down the message on a page of the memo pad. After several unsucessful attempt at trying to get in contact with the off duty Benjamin, Franklin tore the page from the memo pad and went to the captains office. He knocked on the door.

"Yes," the captain answered. Franklin entered.

"Captain we've got a lead on the Benjamin case, the surveillance unit has...."

"Surveillance unit? What surveillance unit?"

"Eh, Benjamin set up a unit in keogh road sir to..."

"Unauthorized expenditure. Okay, we'll deduct it from his wages that's all. What have you got?"

"The girl has called in, we have an address in Stratford, the thing is though sir, we can't find Benjamin. We've tried his home and radioed his car but nothing."

"Is anyone else availiable?"

"Just Nash sir but he's..."

"Give it to Nash," the captain said.

"But sir, Nash....."

"Give it to Nash!" the captain ordered forcefully.

"Yes sir," Franklin said.

As he exited the captains office a drunk Nash waited. Drink had reddened his broken nose and Franklin noticed for the first time that two of his front teeth were missing also. Nash snatched the memo page from Franklin's hand.

"Is this for me?" he said sarcastically. This was the opportunity Nash had been waiting for. If he could muscle in on Benjamin's case and get a result, it would look good for him upstairs, and bad for Benjamin. While he was at it he aimed to

SHADES OF GREY

incriminate Benjamin the best he could. Water lane, he knew the area of the squat well. Before he'd become the bitter, twisted, womanless drunk he now was, he had trodden the beat along it's paving's many times, it had once been his patch.

"Water lane, hey that's right up my street." Nash said.

He could be there in a matter of minutes he knew it that well. He figured he had an hours head start on Benjamin at least. Maybe he could have this thing sown up before Benjamin had a chance to show. He fully intended to try.

*

Benjamin, his two daughters Natasha and Louise, Jeraldine and Spikey were all sitting at the dinning table. The girls were dressed up pretty in their sunday best. Spikey, at her mothers request had donned a skirt and blouse especially for the occasion, Jeraldine was looking as sharp as ever and even Benjamin looked smart. The table was set with silver cutlery and candles on a pink embroidered table cloth. The light was soft and the music came from a cool Luther Vandross CD. There was fruit juice for the kids, beer wine and champagne. They had a prawn cocktail starter followed by beef, rice, sweet potatoes, sweet corn, mixed vegetables and salad. As ever Spikey managed to get by twice as much as anyone else. Natasha and Louise were debating on whether to have chocolate gateau or home made trifle for dessert.

"Daddy why don't you learn to cook trifle?" Natasha said.

Benjamin caught sight of a dish washer from the corner of his eye.

"Why don't you let me wash the dishes before dessert?" The girls looked astounded at one another.

"Daddy never does the washing up at home you know, he can't cook either."

"Thankyou," Jeraldine said but it's okay, I have a dish washer."

"Well then at least let me help you clear them away." Benjamin and Jeraldine began clearing away the dishes.

"I want to thank you for a wonderful evening, the kids have really enjoyed it."

"It was my pleasure, they're great kids. Maybe we should do

SHADES OF GREY

this again some time," Jeraldine said.

"Maybe we should do this all the time," Benjamin countered cheekily. Jeraldine chuckled.

"Why Mr Benjamin is that a proposal?"

"Shhh! Keep your voice down," Benjamin said embarrassed.

"Are you a detective like my dad," Louise asked Spikey.

"I'm a detective, but not like your dad," Spikey answered cryptically.

Jeraldine approaches the table, she looks at Natasha and then to Louise.

"Right, decision time, Gateau or trifle or.... both."

"Both they cry ecstatically. The phone rings, Jeraldine answered, it was Franklin. Jeraldine hands the receiver to Benjamin.

"It's for you, Franklin?" Benjamin takes the recieiver.

"Benjamin."

"I've been trying to get you, the girl called, I have an address, it's 147 Water lane."

"Got it," Benjamin said, "I'm on my way."

"Wait. Look, when I couldn't find you I went to the captain, he made me give it to Nash."

"What!? Damn! How long ago?" Benjamin asked.

"He's got about a ten minute start." Benjamin hangs up.

"I'm sorry, I've got to go."

"It's okay, like you said, a policeman's never off duty."

*

Dexter pulled up outside the squat with a white doctor friend he knew he could trust. The doctor was a nervous looking man in his mid fifties, thin and frail. He looked like he ought not to be out at this time of night but tucked up in bed somewhere.

All the lights were out at the squat, and the front door was locked. It didn't look to Dexter like a place where anyone would stay, but he was sure he'd taken down the address correctly, 147 Water lane. He shone the beam of his torch on the number just to make sure.

"Are you sure this is the place?" the doctor asked.

"I'm sure, number 147. I guess it must be a squat. Come on let's check around the back."

SHADES OF GREY

They climbed over a wall to the side of the house, and found themselves in the back garden. The garden was thickly over grown and in the pitch blackness proved to be something of an obstacles course. From the torch light he could just make out the broken window pane of the back door. He and the doctor made towards it stepping over huge piles of discarded junk and rubbish. With the back door open there was still no sign of life. Dexter's calls for Jess brought no reply. He followed his instincts to the front of the house and into the living room. Inside the temperature was appreciably higher than it had been else where in the building due to the ferocious flames that blazed from the fireplace. Jess sat on the mattress supporting Toby's head as before. In the darkness Dexter could barely make out Jess's silhouette against the shadowy conglomerate mass of the room. He turned to the doctor, the glint of the wood fire danced in the fear of his eyes.

"You're too late," a sleepy voice said, "he's dead."

Dexter shone the torch that revealed Jess's semi-conscious face. Dexter hastily searched the walls with the beam for the light switch. He clicked it on. The doctor knelt down and began attending to Toby. Dexter pulled Jess out from under Toby's head, an empty bottle of pills rolled from her hands.

"She's taken an overdose!" Dexter fretted.

Toby was in a bad way, but he wasn't dead. The doctor gave Dexter something for Jess to inhale.

"Here, use this to wake her then this to get her to throw up." The doctor turned his attentions back to Toby. Dexter waved the inhaler under Jess nose, he prayed it wasn't too late. Jess began to stir. Just then Nash walked in pointing a gun.

"Police, nobody move!"

Everyone was still. Nash browsed the place with smiling eyes.

"So what do we have here?" he said cockily. "So you've been in on it all along," he accused Dexter. Dexter began to protest his innocents.

"I got a call, I...."

"Shut up!" Nash blasted, pointing his gun threateningly at Dexter's head. Nash held this pose for a moment revelling on a

SHADES OF GREY

power trip, then he switches his attention to the terrified doctor.

"What are you doing here?"

"I'm.... I'm a doctor I...."

"Get out," Nash said.

"But this man needs..."

"Out!" Nash demanded pointing the gun barrel at the doctors head. The doctor gathered his things and left.

"Just let me give her this."

Dexter held up the bottle cautiously. Then he broke it seal and poured the bottles contents into Jess's mouth. Her stomach muscles intermittently knotted in spasms, her whole body pulsated in pain. She wrestled with Dexter's grasp, but he held her firm. Finally she yelped a putrid vomit. As Dexter released her she doubled over gasping for air like a marathon runner, she wiped her mouth with her naked arm. She looked up at Dexter then enquiringly at Nash.

"You're a cop aren't you?"

"You got it in one," Nash quipped. Jess took her look to Dexter where it transform into a venomous attack.

"You Bastard! I asked you to bring a doctor, and no cops..."

"I didn't..." Dexter began to protest.

Nash brought out a set of handcuffs from his coat pocket. He throws them to the floor, just in front of Dexter's feet.

"Here put these on you two. Any tricks I'll kill you. You're murders remember that, so it makes no difference, I can bring you in dead or alive."

Jess fell slowly to her knees in front of Toby, she gently took his hand, he slowly opened his eyes, they looked into hers then slowly they closed again.

Dexter was essentially an innocent man but the sight of the handcuff did something to him. Did Nash really refer to him as a murder?! He had nothing to do with any murders and he wasn't going to spend the rest of his life in jail for something he hadn't done. He had come to help Jess, he cared about her... but not that much, after all, she was Ziggy's wife not his. His composure turned to desperation, where before he protested his innocence now he begged for mercy.

"Look... please.... I don't know what you're talking about...

SHADES OF GREY

I've got nothing to do with any murders.... I...."

Nash butt bashed him across the head with his pistol, Dexter crumbled to the floor weeping. Nash looked on pitilessly, he rolled Dexter on his back with a shove of his foot on Dexter's shoulder. Dexter snivelled like a baby.

"Any mores from you and your dead," Nash blurted, and he meant it. "Whether you had anything to do with it or not, I'm gonna get your ass. Why? 'cause I can, and 'cause you're black."

His ego ignited, he strutted about like the 007 of his dreams. He dragged the whisky bottle from his pocket, unscrewed the lid with his teeth and took a long swing.

No one had heard Benjamin enter. Toby was unconscious and Jess was distraught. Dexter may have done had he not been cowering for his life, so might Nash had his senses not been so numbed by alcohol.

Benjamin stood at the door behind Nash, silently watching the drunken ravings of a madman with a badge and a gun. 'This guy relished in harassing innocent people in the name of the law. It was legalised terrorism and he was messing with my pension' Benjamin thought.

"Okay that enough," Benjamin said. "Give me your gun Nash."

Nash spun round to greet Benjamin with outstretched arms and a huge smile.

"Bengy old boy!- I did it see? I've solved your case for you. See that?"

"Give me the gun," Benjamin repeated walking slowly towards Nash. Benjamin was as scared as hell, he'd never seen Nash acting this crazy before. He had no elaborate strategy worked out, he was just walking forward like he'd seen them do in the movies. He wondered what he would have told Spikey to do in a similar situation, but somehow police academy training didn't seem worth a shit now. If he could just get close enough, Benjamin was sure he could take him. Nash was in poor shape, a fat chain smoking junk food eating alcoholic who took no exercise. A physical wreck even at the best of times, drunk he'd be a pushover. But maybe that was the wrong move Benjamin

SHADES OF GREY

thought, in a struggle the gun could go off and maybe kill somebody, like him for instance. He decided to try and talk him out of it. Maybe just keeping him talking was best for now.

"You thought I couldn't do it huh? Nash boasted. Bet you thought I couldn't do it. I know what you guys been thinking, you've all been thinking that ol' Nash is just a wast of time, but I showed ya!"

"I Knew you could do it," Benjamin said trying to humour him. Nash was instantly suspicious. He stood wobbling unsteadily on his feet with a laughing madness in his eyes, Benjamin got the feeling he was about to do something drastic. But Nash's momentary elation was almost instantly replaced by a heavy sullenness as he through Benjamin an icy stare. Benjamin was stopped in his tracks, he swallowed hard watching Nash's every move astutely, as if he were a crazy pit bull terrier. Nash squinted at Benjamin through his hazy vision, like a tiger about to attack, but then hunched his back and allowed his chin to drop woefully to his chest in a wallow of self pity. The gun slowly fell down by his side.

"Next I'm gonna go get the bastard who stole my wife." Benjamin thought this was his opportunity. He began encroaching as he spoke.

"I know just how you feel believe me I do, and I'm going to help you nail the son-of-a-bitch...."

"Get back!" Nash cried out, he held the gun at Benjamin, "get back, you come any closer I shoot ya!"

Suddenly there was a 'blam!' Benjamin looked astonishingly at Nash with the shocked expression of a man who'd just been shot. He thought he had, and for a moment Nash did too. He peered down at the gun in his hand, at his fingers on the trigger. He hadn't fired, he was sure. Then Benjamin heard a muffled thud in his left ear that made him turn quickly towards the mattress where Toby lay. There was Jess, slumped over Toby's dead body with a gun in her lifeless hand, smoke still smouldering from it's barrel.

THE END.